THE MAN WAS EXASPERATING!

"You seem to make a habit out of being late for your appointments, sergeant," Alexandra said, bristling.

Nick grinned as he took a seat in front of her desk. "If I'd known you were so anxious to see me again, I'd have made a special effort to be here sooner."

"Well...yes." Color rose in Alex's cheeks, and she felt a tingling all the way down to her toes. "Just be on time next time, please."

The devilish gleam in Nick's dark eyes dissipated as he studied Alexandra. His previous assessment kept swirling in his head—soft as baby powder, yet cool as ice water. Her silky blond hair was unbound, and he pictured tangling his fingers in it while he slowly made love to her. It was a crazy thought, he knew. If she could read his mind she'd probably certify him insane....

ABOUT THE AUTHOR

Ruth Alana Smith achieved the near impossible when she first began writing—she sold the first manuscript she'd ever submitted! Now, some six years later, she's the author of eleven novels published under her own name and the pseudonym Eileen Bryan. Ruth looks forward to sitting down at her word processor each day, bringing her characters to life. She lays claim to no unusual hobbies, insists she's "very ordinary," though she does confess to making great chili!

Books by Ruth Alana Smith

HARLEQUIN SUPERROMANCE
158–THE WILD ROSE
208–FOR RICHER OR POORER

Ruth Alana Smith

AFTER MIDNIGHT

Harlequin Books

TORONTO • NEW YORK • LONDON
AMSTERDAM • PARIS • SYDNEY • HAMBURG
STOCKHOLM • ATHENS • TOKYO • MILAN

Published June 1987

First printing April 1987

ISBN 0-373-70265-5

Printed in Canada

CHAPTER ONE

NICHOLAS STAVOS ceased his dogged tracking and stood motionless. A few hundred yards in the distance, a graceful doe pricked her ears and listened. She could sense, but not yet detect, the source of danger. Daybreak trickled through the Colorado aspens and a dense blanket of fog clung low to the frosted ground, making everything appear as Nicholas had imagined James Hilton's Shangri-la to be. They were high up in the thin air of the Rocky Mountains—the hiker and the doe. They were two loners, almost at the timberline and far from the noisy world and their own kind.

Nicholas took advantage of the animal's indecisiveness to admire it for a few moments. Like him, the creature was quick, agile, independent and instinctively wary. Yet, unlike him, it was *truly* free—free to roam wherever it pleased, free to climb as high as its ability allowed, free to disregard every rule and regulation except one—survival. He had no intention of harming the doe; he merely wished to inspect it from close range.

At the sudden rustle of autumn leaves, the skittish doe tensed, poising for flight. Simultaneous with the animal's leap into the air, a deafening blast cannonaded, startling Nicholas and felling the majestic doe.

As if in slow motion he watched in horror as the wounded deer dropped to the earth with a sickening thud, and then lay convulsing in a gully grave of brown and brittle leaves.

"Nooooooo!" His anguished scream reverberated through the mountain stillness as he blindly tore across the brambled space between him and the dying doe. The damage inflicted by the high-powered rifle was massive—a gaping chest wound from which crimson blood gushed. Still, Nick tried in vain to arrest the bleeding...to save the doe. But she lay inert, her brown eyes staring lifelessly ahead. The gentle and fleet deer would never again climb the mountain and, although Nick was not responsible for the doe's death, her blood was on his hands.

"Nooooo," HE GROANED, thrashing about in his bed and tangling the sheet as he tried to escape the recurring nightmare. At the point in the dream when the sensation of warm blood upon his hands became so vivid that it nauseated him, Nicholas lurched awake, bolting upright and breathing hard. He was soaked in sweat—a weak, panicked sweat that came from within and had nothing to do with the muggy New Orleans climate.

A ceiling fan whirled overhead. The illuminated clock on the nightstand read midnight. Outside the open window, a prowling tomcat harmonized with the muffled blues wail rising from the nearby French Quarter. And Nicholas Stavos, of pure Greek origin, Spartan stature, and a veteran of six danger-filled years working undercover for the New Orleans Police Department, was shivering with unassignable dread.

He sat with his elbows braced upon his knees, his forehead cupped in his palms, and his fingers webbed within his jet-black hair, awaiting the pounding of his heart to slow to a reasonable rhythm. Squeezing tight his eyes, he willed the haunting dream from his tormented mind. Three nights out of seven, he relived the killing of the doe. Three nights out of seven he awoke in this disgusting condition and was unable to cope until dawn. The remaining four nights he avoided a reoccurrence by undergoing a grueling workout at the precinct gym, followed by several large shots of Stolichnaya, which left him in a state of benevolent numbness. Only then was sleep a blessing; only then did he escape the phantom guilt that plagued him.

Even so, Nick was careful to moderate his drinking habit. Throughout his years on the force, he'd seen too many good cops become dependent on booze and incautious about their job performance. Therefore Nick Stavos only drank on certain nights, never consecutively, and then only in the excuse of inducing a sound sleep. He was okay. He was definitely in a lot better mental and physical condition than some of his co-workers. He was still a top-notch cop, still the "stud" of Central Precinct, and barely thirty. Everyone would agree that Nick Stavos, except for a few bad nights, was in his prime.

Finally his fingers relaxed their grip on his hair and he dared to open his dark brown eyes. He forsook the rumpled bed, hauling his nude body upright and slipping on a pair of Adidas jogging shorts over his muscular limbs. The cramped room felt stifling. The cloying sweet smell of magnolias blooming in the courtyard below reminded him of the latest woman he'd picked up in a buzzing singles' bar and brought home on a whim. Yet another bad choice, another distasteful experience. Maybe his mother was right. Maybe he ought to be more selective. Obviously the disappointing encounters had to be the fault of the pretty featherheaded types he preferred. Next time he'd choose a bed partner who possessed a little more substance.

He staggered to the tiny kitchen, retrieved a half-empty carton of milk from the fridge, then slouched into one of the two mismatched kitchen chairs and gulped straight from the cardboard spout. The milk was not as effective as the Stolichnaya but it was definitely more satisfying than impassive sex. He propped his legs on the cluttered table and stared blankly at a Playboy calendar tacked to the pantry door. He wasn't focusing on Miss June. Instead he was concentrating on a particular date. Friday the thirteenth. Until last September, it had always been his lucky day.

He used to brag to the guys about how windfalls always seemed to come his way on the thirteenth, like the time three years ago when a local radio station had been conducting one of those giveaway promos and he just happened to be the hundredth caller thereby winning a brand new Camaro. On the same date the following year two incredibly sexy twins had invited him to spend a lost weekend aboard their plush sailboat and he'd had to phone in the following Monday to request a day's comp time in order to recuperate. If the guys weren't impressed at first, they were downright awed after the second incident, and even the most cynical had to admit that there might actually be something to Sergeant Stavos's spooky good fortune.

But last September, Nick's luck suddenly soured. Friday the thirteenth became a nightmare that still haunted him nine months later. Not even the rookies dared to mention the date in his presence. He had confided in no one about the miserable nights he spent trying to escape the unconscious effects of the guilt he carried like a cross, the nights he spent sweating and shaking and pacing. He offered no explanation or made no apologies for the times he was impatient and mean-tempered the day following another hellish battle with the covers and the blues. To be Greek was to possess an excessive amount of pride. To be an effective vice cop one worked mainly alone and had to be as tough as gristle. Nick Stavos was both, which made it more difficult for him than most to admit, let alone share, his private grief.

He finished off the milk, tilted the chair back on its hind legs, took aim and neatly tossed the carton into a trash can. "So, what now, Stavos?" he muttered, swinging his feet to the floor, standing and beginning the ritual of his invariable pacing. "By what ingenious method will you pass this night?" he asked himself.

In the pale cast of moonlight, Sergeant Stavos roamed the 900-square-foot territory of his apartment like a caged and agitated soul, fighting an impulse to indulge in a woman or a shot of Stolichnaya so that he might quell the blues that emerged after midnight and vanished at dawn. Instead he elected to take a tepid shower—a means by which to wash away the remnants of glistening sweat from his olive skin, ease his frustration and cleanse his guilty conscience. The purifying act accomplished two of the three objectives. The third, his misplaced guilt, lingered.

IN A POSH St. Charles Street penthouse overlooking manicured gardens and a tinkling fountain, Alexandra Vaughn wadded the pillow under her blond head and moved restlessly in the poster bed.

"Catch me, Mama. Catch me, if you can," a laughing voice called out from her dream.

She smiled in her sleep, releasing her tight clutch of the pillow and rolling over onto her back. She was once again in Connecticut. It was spring. The flowers were in full bloom and she was playing a child's game among the sculptured hedges and vibrant roses on an estate that had once been her home. Through the maze of greenery and a rainbow of petals, she glimpsed the telltale bob of the pink grogram bow that bound her daughter's flaxen hair. Then, in a giggle and a flash the six-year-old vanished.

"Where is Jenny?" she called, playing out the game and searching for the illusive imp.

There was no response.

"You can't hide from me. I'm going to find you and when I do..." The threat was left dangling, meant to entice another giggle and a clue to her rascal daughter's whereabouts.

Not a sound was forthcoming. There was not a sign of Jenny.

At this stage of the dream, Alexandra Vaughn's slim body grew rigid in the bed. Maybe because unconsciously she knew the outcome; maybe because she yearned for it to be different—just this once.

"Jenny! I give up. Come out. The game is over and I don't want to play anymore." She combed every nook, every cranny, every hiding place a child might choose. It was getting late and Jenny was nowhere to be seen. Snagged on a thorny rosebush was the pink ribbon, yet her daughter did not answer the summons.

Unfounded hysteria coursed through the seeking mother. The pond... Dear God! Surely Jenny wouldn't have sought concealment near the pond. Not after all the stern warnings to the contrary. Not after she'd witnessed the dragging of it for a toddler who'd been missing since Easter.

Alexandra's lithe frame curled into a shrinking ball. Again she buried her pale face in the pillow. She wasn't in a silk-sheeted bed on St. Charles Street in New Orleans; she was breathlessly running toward the pond, the drum of a panicked heartbeat pounding in her head.

"Jenny!" The desperate cry echoed in the stillness. "I'm frightened. Please, answer Mama. It's getting dark. Jenny?...Jenneeee!" she pleaded, scouring the bank of the pond, scattering the ducks and wading out into the mossy water.

In her dream, Alexandra was slinging off her shoes and diving under the murky surface... gasping...crying...cursing. In reality, Alexandra was slinging off the covers and writhing with indefinable pain...moaning...thrashing...cussing incoherently.

Half drowned, half mad, the mother could not find her daughter among the willows and amid the pond.

Half asleep, half crazy, Alexandra Vaughn rolled over and over, then spilled onto the Persian-carpeted floor, the jarring impact awakening her. She was disoriented, her filmy gown a mass of wrinkles hiked about her hips and clinging to her perspiring body. Sheer instinct was all that prompted her to clutch the lavender comforter and haul herself back onto the bed. She sat drained and shaking uncontrollably from her polished toes to the damp ringlets framing her forehead. When she finally switched on the ginger jar lamp, her blue-green eyes darted to the clock, deciphering the position of the hands—straight up midnight.

Alexandra glanced about the tastefully decorated bedroom, regaining her bearings and herself. Connecticut was miles and miles away, the lucrative practice she'd once enjoyed a thing of the past. But Jenny was not a case she had transferred or closed. Her missing daughter was the reason for her relocation to Louisiana—the reason a successful psychologist had relinquished private practice and applied for a civil position with the New Orleans Police Department.

She laced her fingers through her long, blond mane and drew a composing breath before opening the nightstand drawer and removing the hidden pack of cigarettes and matches she hoarded. *The surgeon general's warning—smoking is hazardous to your health.* Smiling ruefully, she slung the pack aside, and lit up. She didn't smoke in public and she didn't display her grief in public. To be the ex-wife of a controversial federal judge was to be discreet. To be a trained professional who dealt with anxiety daily meant one had to be immune and in control. Alexandra Vaughn was both, which made it doubly hard for her to deal with the emotional side of herself that surfaced after midnight.

"You're going to be in sorry shape tomorrow," she mumbled, taking several drags on the cigarette before butting it out and falling listlessly back upon the disarrayed sheets.

Tomorrow represented a new beginning, a fresh start for her. The last thing she wanted to do was show up for her first day on the job suffering from a case of nerves and sporting dark circles under her eyes. Since the newly acquired resident psychologist had accepted a probationary arrangement, it would hardly instill a healthy respect for her tenuous position. And from what she could gather from her dear friend and staunchest supporter, Vivian Deneaux, there had been strong opposition from certain city council members against the motion to hire an "in-house" psychologist for the police department, even though there was a dire demand for the position and in spite of the fact that Alexandra's years of training were expressly suited for such a need. The fact that she was a woman who'd have to relate to primarily male problems and adapt to a predominantly male environment only added fuel to her critics' arguments.

Her hand slipped between the pillow and the embroidered slip, extracting a faded pink grogram ribbon. She closed her eyes and pressed the scant remembrance to her cheek, murmuring, "If only I knew, my darling Jenny...if only I could be assured that you are well and safe."

Catch me, Mama. Catch me if you can, came the singsong chant from the past.

Tears gathered in the corners of her eyes and trickled into the natural curly tangle of her ash-blond hair. "I'm trying, sweetheart...I'm not giving up," she whispered, wiping away the telltale traces of her grief, slowly rising, and lovingly replacing the ribbon inside the pillow slip. Not a night had gone by since Jenny's disappearance that Alexandra did not pray for her safe return or sleep without the pink ribbon beneath her head. She returned the pack of cigarettes and matches to the nightstand drawer, then pulled out a manila file folder containing over a year's worth of negative reports from the private detective she had retained shortly after Jenny's disappearance. Quincy Lucas was supposed to be the best, and yet not even he had been able to come up with a clue as to her daughter's fate. His last letter had been the most discouraging.

...since my investigation has produced no new evidence or concrete leads, I think it only fair to advise you that to continue this search may be a futile waste of my time and your funds...

Her reply had been swift and firm. *I refuse to accept that our search is futile. The expense is of no consequence. Continue, Mr. Lucas. Go over the same ground if you must, but continue to look for my missing daughter.*

An urge to pour over the stack of reports in the hopes of discovering some crucial bit of information that might've been overlooked seized her. It wasn't an unfamiliar impulse. Countless times after midnight, she had lain awake scanning the details of Quincy Lucas's investigation until she was bleary-eyed and dawn had broken. But she resisted the impulse this night, knowing the probable antagonism she'd encounter in a few hours and realizing she must be one hundred percent in order to deal with it.

Shutting and setting aside the folder, Alexandra switched off the lamp, eased under the sheet and stared blankly at the bisque-colored ceiling. Had she made a mistake by relocating and taking on an entirely different sort of practice? Perhaps the challenge of it might not be the blessed neutralizer she had thought. A change of surroundings and an absorbing commitment couldn't hurt, she supposed. Yet it was the memories of Jenny that filled her heart and held her prisoner after midnight. And it was the love of Jenny and the belief that she would find her missing daughter one day that gave her purpose. Though a new phase of her life would begin tomorrow, it was also merely one more day that she marked time, vigilantly waiting and fervently praying for news about Jenny.

CHAPTER TWO

AT 7:00 A.M. the first floor of the Central Precinct was a milieu of utter chaos. Remnants of the graveyard shift's arrests were still awaiting booking while the day shift officers were already filing out of the briefing room, griping, joking and threading their way to the garage downstairs. The seasoned sergeant manning the front desk had his hands full as frenzied citizens pushed and shoved, each arguing that the complaint they'd come to register was the more urgent. At the same time several rouged and skimpily clad prostitutes squabbled over who'd get to call her pimp first. To add to the chaos, three or four cantankerous lawyers were demanding immediate consultations with their clients. The harassed sergeant's voice rose above the crowd. "One at a time, folks. I told you, we don't have a Leroy Krebs in the hold. Try Southside Station.... Sure, sure, honey—you weren't solicitin', just socializin'.... I don't care who you represent, counselor, you're gonna have to wait your turn like everybody else."

Looking bewildered and totally out of place in her tailored summer suit and pearls, Alexandra caught a firmer grip on her attaché case and ventured into the jungle. After being pushed, shoved and pinched on the tush by some phantom pervert, she managed to reach the front desk, a bit wilted but still basically composed. "Excuse me. I have a seven o'clock appointment with Chief Oliver. Do you suppose you could direct me to his office?" Her entreaty was followed by a wince when one of the prostitute's spiked heels caught her ankle and snagged the expensive swiss-dotted nylon stockings she wore.

"Sorry, toots," the gum-smacking redhead apologized, the smell of her cheap perfume mingling with the various body odors that offended Alexandra's senses.

"That's all right," she lied, upset no end that a skunk-sized stripe was probably already working its way up the back of her leg.

"The chief's office is on the top floor at the end of the hall. Take the elevators over by the drinking fountain," came the curt directive from the testy desk sergeant.

She nodded her thanks, placing the attaché case protectively in front of her as she once again weaved her way through the swarm of people. By the time she reached the designated elevators, she looked as though she'd braved a cyclone: she was missing several hairpins, her upswept coif was beginning to droop, and the sleeve of her jacket bore the stains of some klutz's carelessly sloshed coffee.

Terrific. I'll really impress the hell out of them now, she silently groaned as she pressed the call button. Glancing over her shoulder, she frowned at the long run inching its way from her heel to her hemline, then attempted to mend the irreparable damage done to her hair. She was too distraught about her disheveled appearance to notice the man behind her assessing her every move.

Nick chewed on his after-breakfast toothpick and studied the svelte blonde in the ivory suit. Unlike her, it was his habit to take into account every minute detail of his surroundings—a curse of the trade, so to speak. An unobservant vice cop could very well be a dead one. One small, seemingly unimportant deviation from the ordinary could mean a blown cover, so a cop learned to pay attention to new faces and trust intuition. The lady sporting the fancy attaché case and a doozie of a run was definitely a new face. She was a bit too slim hipped and much too uptight, but pretty in an understated way. He couldn't help but be amused by the way she kept checking her watch, then her bronze-glossed nails. Obviously she hadn't any prior experience with the antiquated elevator system. Taking stairs would be faster.

At last the call light extinguished with a ding and the elevator doors opened. Alexandra entered the dimly lit conveyance and hit the appropriate button for the top floor. As more riders boarded, she retreated, then moved back farther still, until once again she was feeling claustrophobic and rather like a squashed sardine in a packed tin.

Always an opportunist, Nick maneuvered himself so that he was stationed directly behind the lady. She smelled nice—rather a curious blend of sweet baby powder and a hint of sexy musk. Because he stood a head taller than her, it was easy enough for such a connoisseur of women as he to determine that she was a natural blonde. At the bare nape of her neck, the clasp on the strand of pearls she wore was coming unlatched. Though he'd had vast experience at rezipping, rebuttoning and refastening ladies' apparel, that sixth sense he relied on so much warned him not to touch those beads. As skittish as this woman was, she'd probably react like a high-strung cat and scratch his eyes out for the courtesy. Instead he shifted the toothpick from one corner of his lips to the other, relaxed against the back of the elevator, and admired the well-defined outline of the lady's tush.

"Out, please," several voices chimed as the elevator arrived at the second floor. Alexandra tried to reposition herself in order to allow the "get offs" to pass. In the awkward process, she fell against a rock-hard body in the rear. "Sorry," she offered, too embarrassed to meet the eyes that belonged to the white canvas deck shoes she had just tromped.

"No problem, sugar," was the amused response.

She cast a quick glance over her shoulder, engaging the dark brown eyes of Nick Stavos and telegraphing her disapproval of his demeaning familiarity.

He flashed her a cocky smile, at which her blond head abruptly pivoted. Availing herself of the additional space, Alexandra stiffly sidestepped to an empty corner and stared straight ahead, thereby evading the sensation of warmth she'd felt on her neck moments before.

Nick took the rebuke in good humor. His first instincts about the lady had been right on the money. Miss Baby Powder was a narrow-hipped, narrow-minded prude. The sexy hint of musk was an illusion.

He'd bet she hadn't been with a man in years, if ever. He, too, focused on the blinking panel, in a hurry to reach his floor and dismiss the lady as an unfortunate encounter.

Alexandra felt the cool slip of the beads from about her neck into the divide between her breasts. Discreetly she tried to retrieve them. Mortified, she blushed as the strand of pearls slid between her breasts, slithered down her midriff and spilled from beneath her jacket onto the floor. An abundance of cleavage she did not possess. Her breasts were small, wide-set and firm—a fact that Nick surmised when bending to pick up the necklace from off the floor and handing it back to her.

Simultaneous with his exchange of the strand of pearls into her outstretched palm, the elevator arrived at the third floor and his destination. "Cultured, I'll bet," he speculated with a devilish grin as all but the two of them exited the elevator.

"Yes," she confirmed, affected by his stark handsomeness, even though she disliked his bold manner. She surveyed his casual attire—loose-fitting pleated slacks, a tight-fitting T-shirt, suspenders, no socks and canvas shoes.

He jammed the door with a foot to keep it from closing. "It figures," he said, slanting her an ambiguous look that could best be interpreted as half-admiring and half-mocking.

He stepped out into the bustling corridor, leaving her flattered yet irked by his brazenness. Between the third and fourth floor, Alexandra attempted to gather herself. Whoever the olive-skinned stranger was, he had certainly contributed to her first day jitters. And quite intentionally, too. She fastened the strand of pearls around her neck, securely this time, and mentally prepared herself for the interview with Chief Oliver. *Forget the damn run and the coffee stains,* she told herself, stepping off the elevator. *Ignore the butterflies in your stomach and bluff your way through this,* she silently coached, proceeding into the chief's offices.

"May I help you?" A pinch-faced secretary inspected her from behind bottle-thick lenses.

"I have a seven o'clock appointment. I'm Alexandra Vaughn. The new psychologist," she explained.

"You're fifteen minutes late." The reprimand was given without so much as a flicker of compassion for the new kid on the block.

Alexandra stiffened. "I know. I had a problem with—"

"Follow me, please," the sourpuss instructed, leading the way into Chief Oliver's office. "Your seven o'clock is *finally* here, sir. Shall I reschedule your eight-thirty interview with the press?" She addressed herself to the back of a chair and a bald spot at the back of Chief Oliver's head.

"Absolutely not. Those headhunters will think I'm deliberately trying to avoid their questions about the alleged payoffs in the Narcotics Division. The shrink and I won't be long. Get us some coffee, will ya?" Chief Oliver still did not swivel about in his chair, nor greet the newest recruit. Instead the bald spot disappeared from view as he bent lower to examine closer the purple toes of his bare right foot. "Swear to God, at least two of 'em are broken," he cussed beneath his breath. "Hurts like a son-of-a-biscuit every time I try to wear shoes. Too bad you're not an orthopedist 'stead of a shrink." He rubbed the swollen appendages, instructing, "Sit down. I'm supposed to give you the welcome spiel."

Apprehensively, Alexandra sank into a chair before his desk. The orientation session was worse than she'd imagined. She felt like an intrusion—a nondescript inconvenience whose presence was barely tolerated. She hadn't expected open-armed acceptance but neither had she anticipated the indifference she'd thus far encountered.

Chief Oliver swung around in his chair, hoisting his sharply creased, blue-trousered leg and propping his throbbing tootsies atop the desk. He peered at her between bruised toes as if she were an alien, then flipped through his appointment calendar in the hopes his secretary had made some disastrous mistake. "You're A. L. Vaughn?" he said in an incredulous tone.

She nodded, smiling pleasantly, realizing he was flustered and reveling in it. It was the first time since arriving at the Central Precinct that she felt in charge.

"There must be some mistake. I was expecting...ah, I mean, I was under the impression that—"

"That I was a man," she supplied. "Sorry to disappoint you, but I'm afraid you're stuck with a woman for your new resident psychologist."

Above the brass-trimmed collar of his immaculate uniform, Chief Oliver blanched. "Damn fools could've at least told me," he ranted as the dour sec-

retary served them each the requested coffee, then retreated from the tension-filled office with a submissive
tuck of her chin and a soft click of the door.

He reached into a drawer, popped two tablets from
a bottle of aspirin into his palm, and washed the relief down with a gulp of the stout brew.

Inexplicably, Alexandra grew more calm. She
sipped the coffee and awaited the befuddled chief's
promised welcome speech.

He wriggled his bare toes and winced. "Where are
you from, *Miss* Vaughn?"

"New England. Connecticut to be exact." She analyzed his reaction. It was a curse of the trade, so to
speak.

He leaned back in his chair, a glimmer of confidence stealing over his ruddy face. "Very proper,
Connecticut. I suppose you had a very proper practice. A very lucrative income?" He was baiting her.

"Very," was all she replied.

Chief Oliver seized upon what he perceived to be a
revealing remark. "New Orleans is hardly what you
would call *proper*, Miss Vaughn. Sleazy is more like it.
I don't think you can imagine the problems that my
men are confronted with daily. I suspect that your
most difficult cases have had to do with infidelity
among the rich and the tragic loss of a beloved and
neurotic poodle."

Alexandra's patience was being sorely tested, along
with her ability to not take personally the almost tangible hostility. She resented the chief's immediate and
preconceived conception of her. A trained and dedicated psychologist, she did not intend to be intimi-

dated or unjustly censured because she was of the wrong gender or because she was Yankee. That's why she would never admit to the chief that the accusations he'd leveled at her were founded and the express reason she had wished to make a change. "Regardless of what you may believe, Chief Oliver, I am a capable professional who can and will contribute to the emotional stability of your men, as well as assist on those investigations that warrant the need."

Oliver drained his coffee cup, studying her as he did so. "Believe it or not, Miss Vaughn, my reservations are valid. Can I be blunt?"

Were you being subtle? was her unspoken thought. "Please do," she said aloud, setting aside her trusty attaché case and relaxing within the chair.

"My men are tough...tough as rawhide. Every day they witness and have to deal with the most despicable crimes committed by the scum of the earth. It makes 'em hard...harder than hickory nuts. You ever tried to crack a hickory nut, Miss Vaughn?" He did not give her a chance to rebut. "Have you any notion of the animosity or the danger they encounter every time they go out into the streets? Hell, no! How could you? This isn't sedate Connecticut; this is the sin capital of the world. And you're kidding yourself if you think you can relate to this town or my men. Cops do two things well, Miss Vaughn." Chief Oliver's expression became stoic. "They make cases and women with equal regularity and vigor. The only reason they would get on your couch is not because they wish to confide their innermost anxieties, but in the hopes of persuading an attractive woman, like yourself, to join them. Do I make myself clear, Miss Vaughn?'' He quirked a brow and shoved aside the empty coffee mug.

Though stunned by his crude forecast of the impotent role she would play at the precinct, Alexandra remained poised. "You underestimate me, Chief Oliver. The fact that I am a woman will not have the slightest bearing on my effectiveness as a psychologist. I've been propositioned by the slickest of men and I can assure you that I haven't a fetish for cops. Uniforms and brass do not turn me on. Now, if it's not too much trouble, do you suppose I might request an introduction at every shift's role call tomorrow, an inspection of my office today, and perhaps a refill on the coffee in the next few minutes?''

The debate about her competency was ended as far as Chief Oliver was concerned, but the controversy surrounding a woman psychologist adequately serving the needs of more than a thousand men, many of whom suffered from varying degrees of disillusionment, low-esteem and burnout had only just begun. Theoretically, Alexandra Vaughn had emerged victorious in her first battle with sex discrimination, but it remained to be seen if she would prevail when her idealistic words were put into actual practice—when she was pitted against the hard-shelled, deeply troubled likes of Nick Stavos.

NICK'S STOMACH CHURNED but he did not display the anxiety he felt. This command appearance before Captain Lewis was inevitable. Logically he knew he'd been taxing his superior's patience, had been bending the rules and taking risks only a madman would dare. There were regulations to which Captain Lewis had to adhere. Of course, there were also extenuating circumstances to which Captain Lewis could no longer relate. It'd been years since he had worked the streets. It had been eons since he'd had to live by his wits and improvise the facts in order to make a bust. He had grown soft. He preferred a gentlemanly round of golf to an exciting game of danger. That's what happened when a good cop lost sight of the battles waged in the real world and channeled his energies toward climbing through the ranks—and in the process became subservient to red tape, penal codes and squeamish district attorneys.

"Effective tomorrow, you're being transferred to Detectives, Stavos." Captain Lewis watered his precious ivy plants, pretending not to notice the decaying leaves or the reflexive snap of Nick's body as he sat erect in the chair.

"You can't be serious." The insubordinate remark burst from Nick's lips before he could check himself.

"Do I look like I'm kidding?" Lewis set aside the watering can and took a seat behind the desk, reviewing his ace vice cop and regretting very much the confrontation ahead. He'd known this discussion would not be a pleasant one and had purposely postponed it for as long as possible. Nick Stavos was a clever, resourceful and tough individual, who'd given him plenty of headaches while making more busts than any other narc in the history of the department. But he was also a nonconformist and a hothead, who constantly bent the rules and had come to believe he was invincible.

"I'm the best you've got." Though the immodest assessment was accurate, Nick's cocky attitude was a contributing factor in the decision to transfer him.

Lewis rearranged various objects atop his desk in an attempt to avoid meeting the scathing look leveled at him. "That's why I haven't rotated you before this. You know as well as I do that it's risky to remain undercover for as long as you have. Risky and totally against procedure." He stood and adjusted the venetian blinds so that the angle of sunlight directly struck his ivy plants.

The bright glare also hit Nick square in the eyes. He was sure Lewis was covertly trying to make him as uncomfortable as possible. Impudently, Nick flipped on his aviator shades and slouched back in the chair. "To hell with procedure. What counts is that I'm still effective out there on the streets. I can smell a drug deal or spot a numbers racket a mile away. Polyester suits, silk ties and gumshoeing, isn't my style, Captain."

Lewis expelled a sigh. He would've preferred not to have to delve deeper into the issue, especially knowing that the subject was a sore one. "Look, Nick . . ." His tone changed to one of entreaty. "This transfer is for your own protection. You been out there much too long. You've begun to believe that you're the great imposter and superman all rolled into one. You forget that Vice isn't the only division within the department. Detectives may not be as exciting as you'd like, but I think the change into plain clothes is in your own interest." He hesitated, not wanting to mention the real reason behind the transfer. "Dixon is the third partner of yours who has requested a change and not without good cause. In the past nine months you've been involved in three shooting incidents. You're becoming a jinx and a pain in the butt for the Internal Affairs boys."

"Dixon's a pansy and every one of those *incidents* was justified." A muscle twitched in Nick's cheek.

"And damn lucky for you. Ever since..." Lewis floundered. "Well, ah, that bust at the wharf, it's like you've been on some sort of personal vendetta."

Nick's blood turned to ice at the mere reference to the unmentionable bust. He fidgeted in the chair.

"I know an experience of that sort can make the best of cops edgy, but you're too quick to draw your gun on a suspect, and you're making things rough on your backup."

"I'm not going to let a bust I've been knocking myself out for months to nail take a hike with the front money because my *backup* is tied up in traffic or answering a call of nature. When you're out there alone, you have to make snap judgments. What do you want from me? I made the cases, didn't I? I gave you statistics that impressed the hell out of the brass."

Lewis frowned. "The truth is, you're causing me heat, so you're going to cool your heels in Detectives for a while," he countered firmly. "What's more, you will report to the new resident psychologist this coming Friday afternoon for counseling." There, he'd said it at last. It went against his grain. Since time immortal, cops had been privately dealing with their secret traumas and it broke the code to make personal matters public.

"I'll what?" Nick vaulted to his feet. This was too much—a transfer to Detectives along with a degrading mandate to consult with a shrink.

"You heard me." It was all Captain Lewis could do not to cringe in the face of the Greek's wrath, but he held his ground. "You've got a personal problem and it's affecting not only your performance, but the general morale of your co-workers. We want you to avail yourself of the help and get it together."

Nick's fist pounded the captain's desk, sending all his neatly arranged paraphernalia scattering. "For two cents I'd turn in my resignation. I don't need this garbage—"

"Neither do I," Lewis snapped back. He'd had his fill of Stavos's foul humor and mouth. "You're a good cop, Nick. Nobody can deny it. But lately you've been a thorn in my side. I should've pulled you off Vice right after..." Again the captain stumbled over his choice of words. "...after the Espanosa case. I didn't, and now it's out of my hands. I have to follow orders, too. Either you agree to a stint in Detectives and some therapy sessions or I'll have no choice but to suspend you indefinitely. Take the transfer, see the shrink and don't make waves, will ya, please?"

Nick wanted to tell him to go to hell—wanted to throw his badge on the captain's desk, turn his back on six years and head for the mountains. Instead he swallowed hard, raised the sunglasses up into his raven hairline, and stared unflinchingly into Lewis's apologetic eyes. "I might be a little battle fatigued but

I'm a far cry from crazy, Captain. Okay, you win," he gave in. "I'll hibernate in Detectives for a while. I don't like it much, but I'll do it. As for spilling my guts to some shrink, you can forget that idea."

"It's part of the package, Stavos. I don't care whether you talk about the weather or how you've always hated your mother's chicken soup. Just put in an appearance. That's all I ask."

Nick flipped the sunshades back upon his somewhat large Greek nose and smirked. "Maybe it'd be a great opportunity to unload about my degenerate sex life. I mean, what the hell, maybe the doc can figure out why I've got this masochistic need to be all things to all women."

Nick's hollow laugh as he exited the captain's office caused a shiver to run down Lewis's spine. The new psychologist had his work cut out for him. No matter how flip Stavos might be or how much he pretended that the Espanosa case still didn't haunt him, it was a coverup. Stavos was not going to be cooperative. In fact he would probably go out of his way to be totally obnoxious.

CHAPTER THREE

TRUE TO FORM, during his first few days in Detectives, Nick did not make things easy on anybody, especially himself. He blended in with the routine about as much as a festering splinter and was twice as exacerbating. By Thursday, his immediate supervisor, Lieutenant Troutman, had taken all the guff from Stavos he intended to and had decided that a medicinal chat between them was definitely in order. Nick was twenty minutes late reporting for duty and Troutman posted himself like a sentinel outside the men's room across the hall from the Detective Division, awaiting the truant sergeant.

"I want a word with you, Stavos." The lieutenant shoved open the door and gestured with a file folder he was carrying for Nick to step inside the tiled confines.

Nick thought his choice of a meeting place a bit peculiar, but then Troutman had never been exactly what he considered orthodox. "Gee, Lieutenant, I appreciate the personal interest, but couldn't we postpone this little tête-à-tête until after—"

"Shut up, Stavos," Troutman snarled, checking the stalls to be sure they were alone. "I thought it best if the other men didn't know of this talk. You're unpopular enough as it is.''

Instantly Nick's sarcastic smile dissolved. ''What's this all about?''

Satisfied that the two of them could speak frankly and confidentially, the lieutenant leaned against the washbasin. The only sound breaking the strained silence was the whoosh of the file folder as he tapped it against his thigh. ''It's about your attitude,'' he said at last. ''I don't like it. Truth is, there isn't very much I do like about you. You're a hot dog who thinks because you made a few sensational busts and headlines that you're exempt from the mundane garbage the rest of us have to swallow. Well, I got a flash for you, boy. Like it or not, you've been transferred and you're not the Lone Ranger anymore.''

Nick withstood the insult well, giving the impression that the lieutenant's opinion of him, or for that matter the whole of the Detective squad's, bothered him little. Actually it bothered him a great deal. He knew he was resented. It was natural for those who seldom received any praise or recognition for their long hours and methodical efforts to be bitter about others whose achievements were glorified like a popular and exaggerated television series.

Lieutenant Troutman did not know how to interpret Nick's moody silence. The tap of the folder against his thigh increased. ''In Detectives there are no prima donnas. You're just one of a team. I expect you to pull your weight, Stavos. I expect you to show up on time, to work your share of cases, and wear a tie like everybody else.'' Pointedly he focused on Nick's opened collar and bare neck. "So far, you've been freeloading and deliberately causing friction by setting yourself apart. I like harmony in my department, Stavos. Sour notes, like you, grate on me."

"I'm fond of you, too, Lieutenant." Nick's temper got the better of him.

Troutman leered at him. "Don't give me a hard time, hot dog. Shape up or you'll find yourself buried in the catacombs of I.D. and Records." He slapped the folder against Nick's chest. "Here. Let's see if you're as good at solving problems as you are at creating 'em. The kid's been missing for two days, but his *busy* mother just got around to reporting it last night."

"Real motherly concern, huh?" Nick cast a quick glance at the contents of the file.

"Yeah. The kid's probably a runaway, but check it out." The lieutenant made a move to leave, then turned back to Nick, a bemused expression upon his sallow face. "Remember this. When I catch flack from up above, you can count on the fallout eventually raining down on you. Give us both a break, Stavos. Do your part and conform. I'll be happier and your co-workers won't feel so threatened. And I can practically guarantee that you'll have a much easier time of it in Detectives than if you continue to buck the system."

After issuing the sage advice, Troutman vacated the men's room, leaving Nick with his conflicting thoughts and one of a hundred missing-person reports. On one hand, he'd like to take a hike into the sunset, the same as this runaway kid. At the moment he understood what it was like to feel as if you were up against it, the frustration of having no alternatives. Nick had given his all to working undercover and because of one lousy mishap he was doing penance in Detectives and seeing a shrink tomorrow afternoon. Sighing, he flipped over the folder and scanned the top statistic sheet.

Vinnie Stevens.
Male, Caucasian. Age: 12.
Address: 22 Market St. #3-C.
Parents: Divorced.
Habitual truancy. No prior arrests but questioned by Juvenile regarding a shoplifting complaint, December 1985. Last seen in the vicinity of Brechtel Park at approximately 11:00 p.m. on June 10, 1987.

Nick shut and set aside the folder, reached into his pocket and withdrew a crumpled tie. Buttoning his shirt, he slipped the despised object under the collar and made a stab at tying a Windsor knot while rehashing the statistics in his head. The West Bank, Vinnie Stevens's neighborhood, was his old turf as a narc—a rough and dangerous part of town. He almost hoped the kid had taken off in search of something better than what existed on those hard, hard streets. Yet the possibility that Vinnie might have met some dire fate nagged at Nick. The worst of all vermin roamed that area at night. Many times while posing as a vagrant or vendor, he'd been tempted to risk his cover in order to alert the street urchins and get them out of the line of fire.

Nick swore at his ineptness in managing a simple Windsor knot. Subconsciously it wasn't the obstinate tie that flustered him; it was only an excuse by which to vent the frustration smoldering inside of him. His inability to help the disadvantaged Vinnie Stevenses of this world to escape the stigma and the danger that lurked upon those streets ate at Nick. Even tough narcs had their soft spots—strong and seemingly indomitable Greeks their weakness. Nick's Achilles' heel was abused kids.

"GOOD GOD! YOU LOOK TERRIBLE," was the shocked greeting that spilled from Vivian Deneaux's lips as Alexandra joined her at the table for lunch.

Normally Alexandra would not have taken the remark to heart. Today, however, she was extremely sensitive to criticism. "Could we dispense with the compliments, please?" she retorted, easing into a chair and making much ado over looping her shoulder bag on a rung and discreetly arranging the high front slit of her skirt.

"Of course," Vivian said calmly, handing her rattled friend a menu. "Shall we have a glass or a bottle of Chablis to accompany our lunch?"

Alexandra peeked over the top of the menu, smiling in spite of herself. "A bottle and let's skip lunch."

"My, but we are in a mood. Perhaps as an appetizer, you'd like some iron nails to munch on."

Alexandra could feel the tension ebbing within her. Vivian's dry wit always had a positive effect. "The wine and something sinfully fattening will do."

As Vivian placed their order with the waiter, Alexandra sat back and viewed the pleasant surroundings. Meeting for lunch in the cobblestoned courtyard of the quaint café had been Vivian's suggestion. Even in their bygone Ivy League years, she'd had an uncanny knack for timeliness. The sun shone warm and bright; the gulf breeze was balmy; the staff and cuisine Creole; and the mood infinitely more affable than that which she had just escaped.

"So, dare I ask how it's been going over at Central?" Vivian extracted a cigarette from a sterling-silver case and offered it across the table.

Alexandra declined with a shake of her blond head.

Vivian clicked shut the case and lit up. "This closet habit of yours is absurd. I'll bet if we analyzed it, we'd discover something Freudian. You used to drive me crazy, sneaking smokes in the dorm. Our bathroom smelled like an ashtray."

"It probably has something to do with my staid New England upbringing." Alexandra caught herself fiddling with the water glass and immediately ceased the uptight motion.

"Probably," Vivian said with a lazy exhale as the waiter served two generous goblets of golden Chablis. She waited until he had departed to repeat the crucial question. "Why do I suspect that you're deliberately avoiding the subject? Are things so awful on the new job, Alex, that you'd prefer not to discuss it?"

Alexandra shrugged and sampled the wine. "Honestly?" Her hedge was as transparent as the excellent vintage.

"When have we ever been anything but brutally honest with each other? I feel instrumental in your decision to accept this post, and now it appears that the transition into public service is not going as smoothly as we'd both hoped." Genuine concern glimmered in the sultry brunette's hazel eyes. Though the contrasts between she and Alex were stark, both in appearance and personality, their friendship was a long and steadfast one.

"I am really resented, Vivian, from the chief down to the rookies. They view me as a threat, not a source of assistance. In their minds I'm not even an equal; I'm an inside joke." She hadn't meant her sigh to be an audible one. Fortifying herself with another sip of Chablis, she continued to enlighten her trusted confidante as to the united resistance she'd encountered. "I insisted that I be introduced at every roll call in the hopes that a few of these troubled men would come forth and avail themselves of my help. Well, if ever I've had a more noble but utterly impotent notion, I can't recall. The get-acquainted session was a fiasco from start to finish. I've never been so humiliated. The men wolf-whistled, made rude remarks, and generally turned the entire affair into a burlesque. The duty sergeant had to assert himself in order to restore some semblance of order. It was the most degrading experience of my life."

Vivian smiled patiently. "I tried to prepare you for exactly such a disastrous reception, my dear. If you'll recall, we discussed the ostracism you would encounter. These men aren't gallant blue knights; they're walking, talking time bombs about to explode. Of course, you pose a threat. You represent all those volatile feelings they refuse to acknowledge.''

"It's worse than we anticipated. You should see the office they've graciously supplied. It was previously used as a property room for forgotten confiscations. If they attempted to ready the dismal quarters, I can assure you that it was a sorry and probably an intentionally sloppy endeavor. The place is musty and oppressive, hardly the sort of atmosphere that lends itself to relaxation."

Alexandra's seething indignation surfaced in the form of a chronic pattern of red blotches materializing on her chest and neck. Ever since she was a child, whenever she became unduly agitated the telltale rash appeared. Vivian had come to know the symptomatic splotches well.

"Oh, I'm sure their indifference and discourtesies are quite deliberate," Vivian agreed. "They're testing you, Alex—an initiation rite, if you will. You'd be hard pressed to find a more cliquish fraternity than cops, and believe me, the clannish code does not preclude the few members of our own gender on the force as well."

The two women lapsed into silence as the waiter served their lunch. As they consumed the endive salad and tasty shrimp creole and fresh-baked bread, Vivian tried to circumvent the touchy subject and Alex made a supreme effort to appear interested in her inconsequential banter.

Finally deciding it was useless to distract Alex, Vivian gave up her diversionary tactic and launched into a full-scale assault. "Obviously you've only one thing on your mind and I'm wasting my breath trying to discuss anything else." She shoved aside her plate, signaled the waiter and requested two café au laits. "All right, let's get down to it," she said matter-of-factly. "What is it you want to do? Give up in less than a week? Resign and return to the security of dull Connecticut?"

"Of course not." Alex, too, dismissed the meal, longing for a smoke to abate the tension coiling within the pit of her stomach. "But I have to ask, Vivian. Why did you suggest to Charles that he put forth my name for the position?" Charles was Vivian's husband and a longtime member of the city council. "Surely you knew the controversy and ill will my presence would incite?"

As the coffee was being served, Vivian pondered her good friend's inquiry while again indulging in another cigarette. *When have we ever been anything but brutally honest with each other?* Her earlier statement pricked her troubled conscience. Involuntarily she met Alex's searching blue-green eyes. "I'm not a fool. Yes, I realized the problems, but I sincerely believed that you were the best candidate for the position. You're an outstanding psychologist, Alex, and this city's police department was in great need of someone with your credentials. So when the hiring of a resident psychologist came up before council, I thought it a fine idea for Charles to recommend you. After all, he's not without influence." She glanced away, seemingly preoccupied with a speck of lint on her navy suit.

Alexandra hadn't spent years in close company with Vivian without gaining a great deal of insight into her character. She was concealing something. Though she was basically a candid person, she could, on occasion, be subtle. "There's another reason, isn't there, Vivian?" she pressed. "Ever since you first approached me with Charles's offer, I've suspected that there was more to it than merely a professional interest. I think you owe it to me to be completely truthful."

Vivian sighed and extinguished her cigarette in the ashtray. "Oh, all right," she relented. "Yes, I had an ulterior motive for dabbling in politics and maneuvering your appointment." Her hazel eyes softened, a hint of strain seeping into her voice. "Do you realize, Alex, that this is the first time in over a year that we've carried on a conversation that lasted longer than fifteen minutes in which Jenny's name was not interjected? And that was my intention all along—to offer you something new and encompassing that might divert your attention from the search that claims nearly your whole life. I know that sounds cold and calculating. I don't mean it to." She reached across the table, squeezing Alexandra's hand. "I know how much you love the child and how hard her disappearance has been on you. But, as your friend, I couldn't bear to see you go on the way you've been—existing only for a monthly private detective's report or a phone call that never comes. It's masochistic."

"It's natural," was all Alex could say. At the mere mention of Jenny's name, the indescribable ache that sometimes lessened but never entirely released her, intensified. "I'll never give up the search, Vivian...never give up hope that she is alive and lost and needing me."

"I know that. Of course, you should believe that you'll be reunited with her one day...at least until there is concrete evidence to the contrary. My only point is that you should be doing something constructive while you wait for word. I hardly think your private practice offered the opportunity to engross yourself in challenging cases, whereas public service in New Orleans does. Crude as those officers may be, they are in great need of your assistance. And whether you want to admit it or not, so are you in need of a chance to be useful." She sat back in her chair, sipping the coffee and studying Alexandra's reaction over the edge of her cup.

"You make it sound selfish of me not to be grateful for the abuse I've been withstanding these past few days." Alex stared pensively into space.

"Actually, I'm glad it's not going so easy at Central. For the first time in many months, I'm seeing a spark of life in you. I think at this point a healthy challenge is good medicine. You're too vital a woman to wither away in Connecticut. Get disgusted, get fighting mad at these men, but don't give up on them. It's their job to be invincible on duty but they're mortal men who need a safe harbor at a shift's end—a place where they can come and confide their deepest fears and desires. Only you can offer it to them, Alex. Who knows? Maybe in the process you'll also find refuge from your own private nightmares."

Vivian was a wise woman and a good friend. Alexandra yearned to tell her so, but that proper New England conservatism interfered. An impulsive act, such as a public display of affection, was not permissible. "I suppose you realize that you're a better politician than Charles." She grinned, conveying a silent thank-you with a loving look.

"Charles might feel threatened by your observation, my dear. In the interest of marital bliss, let's just keep it our little secret, shall we?" Vivian winked and signaled for the check.

VIVIAN'S PEP TALK HELPED. Despite the initial hostility and cynicism, Alexandra had nearly made it through her first week at Central. Friday morning she busied herself with tidying and brightening her cramped office, using plenty of soap and polish and adding touches of art and greenery. The place looked better—not great, but better.

By late afternoon, a severe summer storm had descended upon the city, its gloom, flashes of lightning and claps of thunder penetrating the refurbished quarters and rattling the light fixture overhead. Alexandra glanced at her watch, noting that her week's one and only scheduled appointment was now five minutes later than when she'd last checked. Shutting out the storm with a flip of the blinds, she snapped on the desk lamp, assumed her chair, once more slipped the tortoiseshell glasses upon the bridge of her nose, and skimmed the personnel record of Sergeant Stavos.

A graduate of Loyola University with a major in Police Administration and Law Enforcement; a minor in Ancient History.

Again she found the man's diversity intriguing.

Distinguished Service Award, 1983. Two commendations for bravery, 1984 & 1985. Four written reprimands and one week's suspension for insubordinate conduct. Three times investigated by Internal Affairs for shooting incidents that were subsequently deemed justified. Many times credited for major narcotics busts in the New Orleans area.

It would seem that Sergeant Stavos's makeup incorporated both dedication and rebelliousness, courage and recklessness. His profile was fascinating—a classic example of someone with a strong sense of honor, a volatile nature periodically clashing with his peers and the system.

At the knock on the door, she set aside the personnel record, smoothed an errant wisp of hair off her neck and into the upswept twist atop her head, and gave the tardy consultee permission to enter her analytic domain.

Nick stepped into the dimly lit interior, a jacket slung over his shoulder, his tie undone and dangling about his neck. Since he had skipped the "support your local shrink" roll call earlier in the week, he was stunned to see Miss Baby Powder poised behind the desk. "Nick Stavos," he announced himself. "Sorry to be late. I got detained." The apology was only half-hearted and half-truthful. He'd been lingering in the hall, making sure the coast was clear before entering the psychologist's office.

She was as shocked as he to discover that her first session would be with the irritating rake from the elevator. Unnerved though she was, she managed to maintain a cool smile and civil tone. "Please, take a seat, Sergeant."

He surveyed his choices, a two-seater couch or a stiff armchair before her desk. He slung his jacket onto the couch and chose the armchair for obvious reasons. Geez! How in the hell did he get so lucky as to have to humble himself before the frigid blonde? Well, he had no intentions of bearing his soul to anyone...especially not to her. "So, what would you like to talk about, Doc?" He assumed a defensive posture. "I think it's only fair to warn you that I failed ink-blot tests in the third grade."

"It's your hour, Sergeant. We can discuss whatever you like." She sounded much more confident than she felt.

The slash of rain against the windows heightened. The immediate area surrounding the Central Precinct was prone to flooding. At the moment Nick's most pressing concern was the unsavory prospect of becoming stranded with Miss Baby Powder until the water receded. "Maybe we should discuss the weather, Doc," he suggested. "In case you haven't noticed, it's getting pretty nasty outside. These streets flood. If it's all the same to you, I'd just as soon get out of here before we need an ark to do it."

Alexandra ignored his request. She leaned back in her chair and cast him a superficial smile. "Are you always so wary of rainstorms, Sergeant? Or is it merely this consultation that poses a threat to you?"

He smirked, his tone condescending when answering. "Gee, you're perceptive, Doc. Okay. I admit it. The thought of being cooped up here alone with a woman who wants to rape my mind scares the living daylights out of me. Be gentle, won't you?"

Beneath the crocheted and loosely draped sweater she wore, the telltale splotches began to form. Yet she maintained her unruffled ambiance. "I'll try not to take advantage. Tell me, Nick... You don't mind if we're informal, do you?" she asked, unconsciously twiddling with the heart-shaped locket dangling from a gold chain and nestled within the soft folds of her sweater.

"Whatever makes you comfortable." Nick slouched deeper into the chair, his grin lazy and his gaze intent as he studied her womanly assets.

Alex was unaware of the sergeant's mental undressing of her. "Then, tell me, Nick," she continued, "why is it that you resent authority so much?"

"Do I?" was his indifferent response, though he was taken off guard by Miss Baby Powder's directness. He'd thought it was the nature of shrinks to tippy-toe around and be abstract.

"According to your personnel record, it would seem so." She still methodically worked the locket to and fro on its chain.

"Is that how you shrinks do it? Research a subject like some alien insect?" He snatched up his personnel record from off the desk, flipped through the sterile pages, then tossed it disgustedly aside.

Alex studied him as he stood and strode to the window. He cracked the blinds, then stared pensively down at the submerged streets below. Intermittent flashes of lightning emblazoned his solemn face. She couldn't help but admire the strong definition of his profile. Though Sergeant Stavos possessed an unmistakably rugged cachet, there was also something intensely melancholy about him...something curiously sensitive and appealing. He tried too hard to be crass. He wore cynicism like armor.

"It'd be real nice if everything was as black and white as those pages, Doc. Yes, sir, it'd be a nice 'n tidy little world, tied up in a pink ribbon."

She all but flinched at his ironic description. A faded pink ribbon represented the only tangible bond left between her and her missing daughter.

"Yeah, it'd be real simple if we could categorize people," he was hypothesizing. "Just put 'em in the proper column under a heading of 'all good' or 'all bad.'" He raked a hand through his black hair, then turned to face her. "But, unfortunately, there're messy and extenuating reasons behind each and every human act. Sort of a chain reaction. You think you can untangle the knots we're all tied into? Get serious, will you? You gotta be as confused and inept as the rest of us, Doc. You don't know one end from the other."

Strangely she did not take offense. As a matter of fact, she took heart in witnessing a tiny crack in the sergeant's impregnable veneer. She believed his questioning of her ability was more out of hope than apathy. "I don't want to categorize you, Nick. I'm sure there are very valid reasons for your resentment. I want to try to unravel the knots you're tied into, but I can't do that without the opportunity of your cooperation."

It suddenly became his turn to study her. The muted lamplight accentuated her cameo face. She was different from most of the women who'd touched his life, he thought. Genteel and softer than perfumed talc...so full of ideas...so cool and controlled. The opposite of the hard and wild world he'd come to accept as the norm. Maybe he was crazy, for oddly enough he found himself wanting to spend some more time in her company. He didn't understand it. In truth he was shaken by the vulnerability he felt in her presence. But he'd never admit it, especially not to her.

"You want another shot at me, huh?" He retrieved his jacket from off the couch. "You want to see what makes Stavos tick?" Without a backward glance he retreated toward the door. "Okay. I'll play your head games, Doc. But don't be surprised if it's you who ends up learning some things about yourself you'd just as soon not know."

"Then I'll schedule you another appointment for next Wednesday at the same time."

Stavos paused at the doorway, turning to grin devilishly at her. "Yeah, I guess that would be okay. Say, sugar, what kind of car do you drive?"

The smug endearment riled her, but the query took precedence. "A blue Mercedes," was her haughty reply.

"Parked across the street and outside of the flower shop?" he asked.

"Yes, that's mine. I haven't been assigned a parking place in the garage yet. Why?"

"Nothing important, except that I just saw two punks hot-wire it and I think you're gonna be here awhile longer, filing a stolen vehicle report. Maybe I should hang around to give you a lift?" he offered.

She wasn't about to be taken in by such a transparent ploy. "I appreciate the concern, Sergeant, but it's not necessary."

"Suit yourself." He bid her adieu with a wink.

Alex rushed to the window to discover that he had not, in his blasé way, been kidding. Her Mercedes was gone—lock, stock and prestigious emblem.

She was hotter than a smoking pistol by the time she marched into Auto Theft to report the heinous deed. How could that insufferable, egotistical lowlife just stand idly by and let two hoods make a clean getaway with her car? He was a poor excuse of a cop. And to think she was actually feeling a twinge of compassion for the louse!

The detective to whom she addressed herself appeared to be more interested in his take-out Chinese supper than her plight. She was out of patience and on the verge of an unprecedented outburst. "This may not seem like a major crisis to you, Officer, but I can assure you that it's traumatic to me. I'd appreciate it if you would quit stuffing your face and make out the necessary paperwork." She snatched the carton from his hand and slammed it atop a stack of completed forms in his Out basket.

"Lady, have a heart, will ya? That's three hours' worth of pencil-pushing you just splattered chop suey all over."

They glowered at each other as he wiped the soggy pages.

"It's a 1986 blue Mercedes. Licence number K-T—"

"K-T-M 995," he completed the number, much to her amazement. "Sergeant Stavos already informed us. He also recognized one of the perpetrators." He riffled through the maze of paperwork on his desk, extracting a nearly completed report. "One J. J. Haag—a user who used to snitch for Stavos now and then."

"A user?" she said dumbly, her mind reeling from Stavos's unexpected efficiency.

The officer shot her an exasperated look, retrieved his carton of chop suey, and once more resumed the devouring of his supper. "A user...a dope fiend...an addict," he explained between bites. "Stavos knows J.J.'s favorite haunts. I expect we'll locate him and your car before it's stripped at some chop shop." He took a swig of Coke.

"Chop shop?" She was having great difficulty distinguishing between chop shop and chop suey, not to mention absorbing the notion of Stavos's gallantry.

"It's where they work your car over, lady. Usually some back street garage. Lucky for you, Stavos saw the whole thing. He can spot trouble like nobody else. He's the best. Weird as hell, but the best."

"Yes, the best," she repeated numbly.

"All you gotta do is make the complaint official. Stavos took care of everything. Sign on the line and we'll notify you when we locate the car." He flipped a standard typewritten form across the desk.

"May I borrow your pen?" she said meekly.

"Lady, you can borrow my fortune cookie, if you'll just put your John Henry on the dotted line and let me finish my supper in peace." He held out a pen, muttering beneath his breath, "Stavos sure gets mixed up with some dingy broads."

She curbed an impulse to slap the insolent officer's chubby cheek. Instead she scribbled her signature in the appropriate place, flung the pen aside, marched back to her office, and called a taxi.

Though she truly appreciated Sergeant Stavos's intercession on her behalf and greatly regretted the unkind, near wicked aspersions she'd secretly cast upon his character, she resented greatly the preposterous classification expressed by the impertinent officer. She *was* not, and would never be, included in the sergeant's stable of "dingy broads."

CHAPTER FOUR

ALEXANDRA'S AND NICK'S PATHS did not cross again during the interim between appointments. The sergeant occupied himself with following up on the Vinnie Stevens case; the psychologist immersed herself in the few and reluctant referrals who sought her counsel only as a last resort.

One such referral was a veteran cop by the name of Arnie Kotter. Nearing retirement age and at a loss as to what life held in store for him after thirty years on the beat, Arnie had developed a severe drinking problem. It was affecting not only his personal life but his professional one as well. His latest blunder had been the last straw for his superiors. Arnie was moonlighting as a guard in a department store that was undergoing remodeling and it was his responsibility to keep a vigil against looting after hours. In Arnie's words, "It was a gravy job. Nothing hard. All I had to do was make periodic swings about the premises to be sure everything was copacetic. The most trouble I had was staying awake. Maybe that's why I bought the wine that one night. You know, just as a way to pass the time. Actually, looking back, I'm not real sure what made me do it. I guess it doesn't matter now. I went sort of nuts. Why else would I have used one of those fancy designer bags to ice down the wine? The damn thing cost a fortune. I had to be whacko to chuck it full of shaved ice and bottles of wine, then proceed to drink myself into a stupor."

"You appear very sensible at the moment, Arnie. Why do you suppose you behaved so incautiously?" she had asked at the onset of their first session.

"Damned if I know. I wanted a cool drink. I was bored. I was sick of walking in circles around that crummy store."

"Do you feel that you do that a lot, Arnie?" At his befuddled look, she elaborated. "Walk in circles?"

His expression changed to one of pensiveness. "Yeah, especially lately." He leaned forward in the chair, braced his elbows on his knees, and focused upon the geometric pattern in the rug. "I suppose you know about my, uh, moving the mannequins that night." His tone was sheepish, his embarrassment evident.

Arnie, during the drunken rampage at the department store, had rearranged nearly every mannequin on the first floor into either a grotesque or lewd pose. It was all in the report filed by the aghast store manager and part of Arnie's confidential file. "Yes, I know the details of the incident," she answered.

"I've been really waxed before, Doc, but I ain't ever done anything as crazy as that." He looked up at her, his bloodshot eyes telegraphing confusion, fear and pain all at once.

"You're not crazy, Arnie. I don't treat crazy people. You're disturbed and together we are going to explore the reason or reasons behind your excessive drinking." And so the rehabilitation of Arnie Kotter began.

As it turned out, the session with the veteran patrolman was enlightening and encouraging. It didn't take Alexandra long to discover the basis for Arnie's chronic depression and défiant acts. He was rebelling against a retirement he dreaded, and somehow he felt the force was deserting him in his autumn years. Twice divorced, he had long ago lost touch with his now grown children, and his only friends were fellow cops. He was going in circles, afraid the nonstop ride on the cop carousel would soon be ending and knowing his ticket was outdated and he was expected to graciously get off. It galled Arnie that some fresh young rookie would take his place on the beat, interact with and intermediate for the same folks he had shielded and befriended, that someone new would occupy his customary stool in his favorite café and receive the respect and freebie lunches that was Arnie's due, that another would fill his shoes and usurp his position at the local haunt where everybody went to unwind after shift. His name would be removed as top scorer above the pinball machine and his fellow officers would quickly forget Arnie Kotter because in him they would perceive their own fragile mortality.

"Your life did not begin the day you became a cop, Arnie," she told him. "Neither will it end the day you cease to be one. Life is a series of changes. When we're young we tend to think of ourselves as a pliable green twig, bending to whatever happens and shaping ourselves to accommodate whatever curve life throws us. When we get older, we suffer from some preconceived notion that we're brittle, inflexible, and will snap in two at the slightest deviation or pressure. That's not true, Arnie. The human spirit is a very resourceful thing and it does not wither with age.''

Alexandra paused for a moment to see how Arnie was taking this. When he said nothing, she continued. ''Let me give you an example. Columbus disproved the concept that the world was flat...he showed us that there is adventure and personal treasure beyond the horizon. You, too, are about to embark on a new adventure. It's natural to be a little apprehensive but I promise you that if you approach it with a positive attitude it will not be overwhelming. You'll now have the time to pursue hobbies and interests that have long been suppressed. If after you retire, your comrades shun you, it's more than likely out of envy. But they'll have nothing to envy and everything to pity if you allow yourself to grow sour on cheap wine and squandered opportunity.''

Silence loomed as she eased back in her chair and studied him. Though she had done her best to penetrate the ''uselessness syndrome'' that made him a prisoner of his own anxiety and alcohol, she found herself second-guessing her approach and formulating another. It was impossible to decipher his thoughts by his impassive expression.

He let out a long sigh, got up from the couch, stuck his thumbs in his cumbersome holster belt, and tugged the sagging waistline of his trousers back over his bloated belly. ''You're a pretty smart cookie for a dame, Doc. It didn't take you long to finger my problem. I appreciate the chat. You've given me a lot to mull over.'' And for the first time old Arnie Kotter actually smiled. Ironically the fine crinkles at the corners of his eyes made him look boyish.

"I only hope I helped, Arnie.'' Her tone was sincere, her smile tentative.

"You have, Doc. For a month of Sundays I've been seeing this ad in the *Times-Picayune* for a small marina in St. Tammany Parish. The price was right and I had a twinge everytime I read the ad, but I told myself I was an old fool . . . that all I had any experience at was making busts and hoisting brews with the guys. Well, to tell you the truth, the smell of bait buckets and a taste of the simple life appeals to me. Instead of pouring two fingers of bourbon into my coffee this coming Sunday morning, I think I'll take a drive over the bridge and investigate it further. What do you think, Doc? Do you suppose a has-been cop can make such a drastic switch at this late stage of his life?''

"I think you'll be successful at whatever you choose to undertake in the future, Arnie. I also think you should see me a time or two more, if for nothing else than to keep me posted.'' She extended her hand.

His felt like a giant, gentle bear paw as it enveloped hers. "You betcha, Doc. I'll be in touch.''

And with that old Arnie Kotter exited her office—a heretofore missing zip in his step and a gleam in his previously dull eyes. Alexandra couldn't help but feel a bit heartened by her first victory in the ongoing battle with Central's rank and file. Unfortunately, near the end of her day and at the tardy arrival of Nick Stavos, the dram of confidence soon faded. Sparks of a conflicting nature ignited between the two of them immediately upon contact.

"You seem to make a habit out of being late for your appointments, Sergeant." Though the censure was spoken mildly, her posture was stiff and her blue-green eyes annoyed.

Wordlessly Nick removed his gray sports coat, tossed it on the couch, loosened his tie, and unbuttoned the top few buttons of his shirt before assuming the chair in front of her desk and tilting it back on its hind legs. "If I'd known you were so anxious to share my company again, I'd have made a special effort to be here sooner."

Inwardly she bristled at his arrogant smirk; outwardly she managed to muster a tolerant smile as she, too, leaned back in her chair, a notepad in her lap and a pencil in hand. "Why do I get the distinct impression that you are convinced most every woman you come into contact with develops a sexual fixation about you? Don't you think that's a bit presumptuous?"

He grinned wider, truly amused by her oh-so-proper hauteur. "Probably, but then again I've had good cause to presume it's true. I could give you a list of the 'fortunate 500' if you like. Would you prefer it done alphabetically or chronologically?" He deliberately tried to rattle her.

"That won't be necessary," was all she replied before averting her gaze and jotting down a pertinent notation.

The devilish gleam in his molasses eyes dissipated and he reviewed her as she analyzed him. His previous assessment kept swirling in his head—soft, like baby powder, yet cool as ice water. He wondered why she pinned her hair up in such a sober style and pictured the silky blond strands unbound, falling wild and free. He'd love to tangle his fingers amidst that hair while making love to her. It was a crazy thought, he knew. If she could read his mind, he was sure she'd believe him to be certifiably insane. The legs of the chair creaked as he shifted his weight. "So now that we've established the fact that I'm a conceited chauvinist, what else did you want to discuss?" His eyes hardened.

"I think it would be beneficial to just chat without anything specific in mind. Perhaps you could tell me a little about yourself," she suggested.

"Sure. Should we begin at the cradle, skip to puberty, or go straight for the bitter narc's hard-core experiences?" His cynicism did not deter her.

"Unless you think some childhood trauma is relevant, I'd like to hear about your day-to-day routine. Do you live alone? Have much contact with your family? What is an average day like for you? What is it that you value the most? Dislike intensely? In other words, just generally tell me what Nick Stavos is all about." She straightened in the chair and solicited his cooperation with a solemn look.

"Tell you what Nick Stavos is all about," he parroted, lacing his fingers behind his head and gazing intently up at the mildewed air-conditioning vent. "You could parallel him with New Orleans, I suppose. He's got a hot nature, a dark side, stamina, a style all his own. Yes, he lives alone, travels alone, eats alone, and occasionally sleeps alone. He relies on no one but himself 'cause when you get right down to it the only one who's got any real stake in his well-being is Nick Stavos himself.''

Alexandra was fascinated by both his description of himself and the impersonal method by which he conveyed private details. She found it very revealing that he chose to explain himself in an estranged third-person voice. As he continued, it became abundantly clear that she was dealing with a complex and contradictory man.

"He has strong family ties. Greeks always do. He used to spend a fair amount of time with them but not so much anymore."

"Why not?" she interjected. A slight twitch of his jaw muscle told her she had treaded upon a sensitive subject.

"I don't know." He shrugged. "Maybe because he isn't the same Nick they love. Because they refused to admit the changes that had taken place in him and it became difficult to fake it. I don't know," he repeated numbly.

It was plainly evident to Alexandra that much had occurred during the course of his stint in Vice to have radically altered Nick's basic character—experiences so ghastly that he wished to spare his family from the truth of the metamorphosis he'd undergone in order to survive on the streets. She skirted the issue for the present and guided the conversation on to a different direction. "I'm interested in hearing about an average day in the life of Sergeant Stavos."

He eased the chair upright, his faraway gaze deserting the mildewed vent and refocusing on her. "It used to be that he couldn't wait for the next assignment. He liked changing characters like a chameleon changes colors. Outsmarting the punks and the pushers was a game. The element of danger was an incredible high. After a bust, sometimes he wanted to get mellow and mingle with the other cops, sometimes he wanted to be with a woman and make believe that life consisted of something better than the injustices he'd witnessed. Then there were times he sat alone and contemplated resigning the next day, getting the hell out before his luck ran dry."

"Why didn't he?" She'd forgotten about making any more notes. So engrossed was she in the man that she temporarily lost her professional distance. She didn't even realize that she was also referring to Nick in the third person.

"Because each and every time he made a bust, removed some small element of the scum from the streets, he felt satisfaction. Maybe there would be one less unsuspecting kid hooked on poison, one less innocent victim who'd escape being written up as a statistic in some homicide report. It was his rationale, his reason to take on another assignment, bend the rules just one more time, go undercover and ferret out the vermin. A smidgeon of satisfaction goes a long, long way."

"And now that he's been transferred to Detectives and it's a team game rather than a one-man vendetta, how has he adjusted?" A rebellious lock of hair wriggled free from the pins and feathered across her brow.

She smoothed it back in place, curious as to the peculiar smile that flitted across his lips.

"Not well," was his honest reply. "It's not his style."

"No," she agreed. "It's much too confining for a rebel." In spite of herself, she grinned.

The impromptu grin made Nick suspect that there could be a hidden facet to the seemingly pragmatic shrink. His gaze drifted down her slim figure, taking in the slight swell beneath the sheer, but prim and proper high-necked blouse.

Alexandra became aware of his flagrant scrutiny and blushed. "You've yet to tell me what Nick Stavos values above all else." She tried to camouflage her susceptibility by reverting back to the role of the detached analyst.

He sensed her retreat and thought it odd that a woman as attractive and poised as she could be so easily shaken by the slightest exchange of sexuality. "Truth," he replied, the answer being both spontaneous and firm. "When a man has spent years making people believe he's what he pretends, telling lie after lie to save his skin and dupe the bad guys, it becomes a hard habit to break. The dishonesty filters into your private life and it becomes difficult to distinguish between truth and fiction anymore. You start thinking that everybody lies to protect their interests. You begin to just naturally distrust and have this urge to stay undercover 'cause it's the only way you know how to play the game."

He met her gaze and Alexandra could plainly perceive the distrust of which he spoke. "Unfortunately, sometimes even the most honorable of people feel it necessary to be less than candid with others. It's not deliberate deception, Nick, it's more a matter of personal preservation. Total honesty makes us vulnerable. So we're guarded and, at times, not completely truthful."

"Yeah, I suppose," he agreed with another shrug, glancing away. "Everybody's playing a game of some sort. Some are more dangerous than others, that's all." Pointedly he glanced at his watch. "Gee, time's almost up, Doc."

"We still have a few minutes. I'd really like to hear an answer to the last question I posed." Her motions were slow and exaggerated as she removed her glasses and rubbed her aching temples.

"Am I giving you a headache?" A lazy grin spread across his swarthy face.

She cast him a faint smile. "No."

He didn't believe her. "We've talked about so much. I forget. What did you ask me last?"

She knew better. Sergeant Stavos most likely had total recall. He overlooked nothing and forgot not one minute detail of any given conversation. "What do you intensely dislike?" She repeated the question, a bit irked to have to play the game by his rules.

"Senseless violence and answering these ridiculous questions," he blurted out, unstrung by her damnable persistence. "Don't you ever get tired of picking people's brains, lady? I'll bet you're real fun on a date."

"We're not having a *date*, Sergeant," she reminded him, flipping open her appointment book. "I think we've made some headway today, though I'm sure you'd disagree.''

Wordlessly he deserted the chair, strode to the couch, and grabbed up his sports coat. ''Not entirely, Doc. Believe it or not, you're not the only one who's gaining some insight. I'm learning a lot about you, too.'' He slung the coat over his shoulder as he turned and assessed her.

''Such as?'' she baited, realizing it was a mistake but daring his reply all the same.

''Such as, in spite of all of your expertise, you're not so together yourself, sugar. You're uptight, especially when a man gives you the once-over. I got a suspicion about why you suffer from headaches and a suggestion about how to alleviate some of your frustration.'' His innuendo was perfectly clear, his smirk positively wicked.

''Do us both a favor and spare me your crude theory,'' she retorted, pretending to be absorbed in scheduling his next appointment and not the least bit ruffled by his words. ''I'm free next Tuesday at three. Is that convenient for you?''

''Sorry, that's my day off. Don't take it personally but I intend to spend it with a more sociable skirt than you.'' Deliberately he goaded her.

''All right,'' she drawled, her agitation mounting as she did her utmost to appear nonchalant. ''Then, how about one o'clock Wednesday?''

He shook his head. ''Gee, that's going to be a conflict. I have a standing appointment with my manicurist on Wednesdays at precisely that time.'' His blatant antagonism tried her patience.

Alexandra closed the appointment book with some force and concluded the absurd volley. "Why don't we make this easy on both of us? You can contact me whenever it's possible for you to fit another appointment into your hectic social life."

For some inexplicable reason her casual acceptance of his inane excuses really frosted him. "Don't save space in that little book of yours on my account. Letting you probe and pick me to pieces isn't exactly a priority of mine. So long, sugar." He shot her a malicious wink, then exited the cramped office with a vicious slam of the door.

It was all Alexandra could do not to follow him out into the hall and bid him as curt an adieu. Instead she vaulted to her feet, slinging files and cursing beneath her breath. "Fine, just fine, Sergeant Stavos. Go crazy! Go to hell for all I care!"

She jammed the confidential files into the cabinet without the slightest regard for order and shoved the drawer closed, locking away the secrets of those she treated, including the obnoxious sergeant's.

It was late. It had been an especially hard day. She wanted to escape the drab precinct, unwind, check the mailbox and her answering machine in the hopes that there might be some word from Quincy Lucas about her daughter's fate.

Twilight and mugginess greeted her as she stepped through the main doors and descended the stone steps to the littered street outside the precinct. Her parking space had yet to be approved by Chief Oliver. Though she strongly suspected that the delay was intentional, she had no choice but to wait his lordly decree while continuing to park a block or so away. Exhaling a weary sigh, Alexandra struck out across the narrow cobblestone avenue, ignoring the unsavory vagrant loitering beneath a streetlight on the corner.

CHAPTER FIVE

SHE DIDN'T HEAR THE FOOTSTEPS until it was too late. The stalking vagrant was poised to snatch her purse from behind at the same instant she looked over her shoulder. From then on everything became a blur— she being knocked off balance and stumbling into a brick wall; the scruffy-looking perpetrator grappling for the bag she still clutched; Nick Stavos appearing from nowhere, arm-locking the thug about the throat and warning, "Drop it, Mackey, or I'll break your thieving neck."

Undoubtedly, Mackey, the snatcher, had had occasion to tangle with Nick before and was a believer. He instantly conceded the contest with a hoarse, "I didn't mean the lady no harm, Nick. I ain't ate in days. I just needed some dough, ya know?"

Dazed, Alexandra blinked and tried to collect herself as Stavos's brawny arm slowly unwound from about the quaking fellow's throat. "Yeah, I know," he muttered, dredging his pocket for a ten-spot and tucking it into the bib of the offender's tattered overalls. "If you enjoy fresh air, put some distance between us, Mackey. I don't want to see your ugly puss around here for a while."

"Color me gone, Nick. I'll be invisible. Sorry about roughing up the lady." And with that, Mackey disappeared into the darkness, grateful that the vigilant sergeant was in a charitable mood.

"Are you okay?" The inquiry was spoken gently and with genuine concern.

Dumbly she nodded an affirmative, though in truth she wasn't quite sure as she leaned against the building for support.

"You're shaking like a leaf." He claimed her arm and pried her from the bricks. "Come here. Your hair is a mess." Ever so easily, Nick smoothed the sides of her hair back and secured the loosened pins.

His touch was nearly as unnerving as the encounter with the snatcher. "Lucky for me you happened by," she babbled.

His massive palm lingered, cupping her flushed cheek for a second. "Luck had nothing to do with it, sugar. I keep a watch on you. These streets are too damn dangerous for a good-looking woman to be roaming alone."

She was utterly dumbfounded. Gallantry was not an attribute she had assigned to Nick Stavos. "I don't know whether to be flattered or wary. I'm not sure I like the idea of being kept under surveillance."

He squared his broad shoulders and grinned rakishly. "You look like you could use a drink. Every newcomer to New Orleans owes it to themselves to experience one visit to Moran's. I'm buying," he offered.

"I appreciate your assistance, Sergeant, but I'm all right now." As she made a move to leave, her purse spilled from her grasp, cosmetics and other assorted essentials scattering on the sidewalk.

He retrieved each item and crammed them inside her purse, then retained the leather clutch bag as insurance against her declining his invitation once more. "I'll behave. No snide remarks. No fast moves. Just some company and a drink or two."

Something about the entreating way he looked at her was too appealing to resist. Though her better judgment argued that a personal association with the sergeant was detrimental to their professional one, she accepted. "You're a very peculiar man, Nick Stavos. You make it hard to refuse."

"I know, sugar. I'm like one of those challenging jigsaw puzzles—you're sure the pieces go together but you can't quite figure out how they fit." He gave the purse back to her, placed his hand on the small of her back and steered her in the direction of a sleek Mercedes. "I'll buy, but you drive. I'd kind of like to see if a classy chassis like yours is as great in action as it looks."

Her eyes flashed at the subtle potshot. He picked up the pace and changed the subject.

MORAN'S WAS ALL that he had promised—a breathtaking view of New Orleans and the river at night and smooth Irish coffees that warmed even a prim New Englander down to her dainty toes.

"Why did you give that creep who tried to snatch my purse money? First you choke him and then you reward him. I don't understand you." It took until midway into the first drink for Alexandra to work up the courage to ask Nick about the incident.

He was intent on the dab of whipped cream clinging to her full bottom lip. "Old Mackey and I go way back. He saved my life once. When you've been around Central and can relate, you'll realize that there are degrees of bad, just like there are degrees of good. He's down on his luck and hungry, sugar. All he wanted was your money, nothing else."

"So why did you come to my rescue?" It was a valid question. The answer, however, stunned her.

"Maybe because I wanted to get back into your good graces…apologize for the asinine way I acted in your office this afternoon. I can be an SOB at times. Ask anybody at Central. They'll confirm it." He swigged from the mug, avoiding her eyes.

"And you like the image," she ventured.

"Yeah, it suits me, don't you think?" He cast her a sideways glance.

"Perhaps," was her noncommittal reply.

They lapsed into silence—he enchanted by the soft planes of her cameo face, she intrigued by the primitiveness she beheld.

"You feel threatened by me, don't you, Nick?" The man on the next bar stool lit up a cigarette, and Alexandra found herself craving a smoke.

Nick ordered another round and was astounded when she requested a pack of menthol cigarettes from the bartender.

"That's a nasty habit, sugar. It doesn't go with *your* image." It wasn't a criticism, merely an observation.

"I know," was all she answered, carefully shearing the cellophane, extracting a cigarette, and awaiting him to strike a match and ignite it. "I go to great lengths to conceal my weaknesses." She inhaled deeply, letting the smoke fill her lungs. "I suspect you do the same."

He blew out the match, studying her. "Yeah, occasionally. And, yeah, I'm threatened by you."

"Why, Nick? What is it that you conceal? How do you explain a remark like 'senseless violence'? When does violence ever make sense?"

He visibly stiffened and reached for the fresh drink the bartender placed before them. The whiskey mellowed his response. "Outside of the gray streets, maybe it's a black-and-white world, sugar. Maybe it's easy to see the difference. The territory I used to cover had no distinct color, no certain lines, no exact code of honor, except to be slicker and smarter than the rest. You smoke a cigarette; I smoke a big-time operator who wants to waste me first. What's the difference?"

What's the difference? The calloused sentiment hung in the air. For the first time Alexandra fully comprehended the apathy she was up against. "There is a difference, Nick. You spoke of your family and the man you once were before the job and the 'senseless violence' became synonymous. It bothers you. You're still a man with a conscience who knows his colors."

She gave him an out and he seized it. "Yes, ma'am, I still know my colors. I know that your hair is the color of wheat, your skin the color of cream, your eyes the color of the Caribbean." He continued to gaze at her, his hand brushing hers as she extinguished the cigarette.

The sensation of his flesh was too electric, too disarming. She extricated her fingertips in the excuse of sipping the Irish coffee. "I'm sorry. This is hardly the time or place to continue your analysis. I have a tendency to practice after hours."

"Apology accepted." He, too, felt awkward.

They turned their attention to the river as a gaily lit paddle wheeler churned upstream.

"Why don't we talk about you for a change?" he suggested, trying to fill the noticeable lag in the conversation. "What did your life consist of before New Orleans and Central?" Observant, he caught the hint of sadness that flickered across her face before an imperturbable mask fell over her features.

"My life consisted of a private practice in a plush office with scores of wealthy patients who thought it was in vogue to be in therapy." Guilefully she focused only on her professional life.

"You must've done well for yourself," he conjectured.

"Yes, I had an impressive bank account," she admitted.

"So why did you exchange such a swank setup for this headache? You'll never get rich treating flaky cops."

Alexandra had no intention of revealing the primary reason for her defection from Connecticut. "I needed a change. There came a time when I realized I had sacrificed my ideals for a Mercedes and mink. I had originally majored in psychology because I had a burning desire to help people cope with the hardships and heartaches we all encounter. Somehow I lost sight of that along the way. It was rather a gradual acknowledgment but eventually I was forced to admit that I didn't care very much for the person I'd become."

He sensed her explanation was not a full disclosure of the facts, but let it pass. "Central had to be a real shock. Have you had regrets?"

"A few." She glanced in his direction, a spark of amusement in her eyes.

"At least daily, I'll bet." His smile was warm and sympathetic. "And what about your personal life, sugar? Did you leave anyone special behind in Connecticut?"

The mug shook in her hand as she lifted it to her lips. For her sake, Nick pretended not to notice.

"An ex-husband," she murmured between sips.

"A louse, huh?"

"A federal judge, too."

He let out a low whistle, then drained his mug. "You were really in the big leagues, sugar."

"I suppose that depends on one's definition. A host of people admired my ex but there were many who despised him."

"Which category do you fall into?"

"I'm neutral. Our marriage became intolerable to each of us for different reasons. It was a mutual decision to end it," she explained.

"How very civilized. Want another?" he asked, signaling the bartender.

"Marriage or a drink?"

He grinned at her wry humor. "I meant a drink, smarty."

She declined with a shake of her head, checking her watch out of habit.

"Am I keeping you from something important?" He wondered about a male interest.

She appeared duly embarrassed. "Not really. I just like to pick up my messages in case a patient might need me after hours."

He didn't completely believe her. "That's a relief. I thought perhaps there was a man in your life . . . some jealous black belter who'd gladly rearrange my nose for trespassing on his turf."

For the first time she laughed aloud and the melodious sound traveled all over Nick. "Hardly. I haven't had anything even closely resembling a date since my divorce."

"And how long has that been?" He sampled the fresh Irish coffee and nodded his approval to the bartender.

"Nearly two years."

He nearly choked on his drink and quickly reached for a napkin. "You've got to be kidding." The idea of a two-year celibacy was incredulous to him. "Are you frigid or what?"

At the tactless remark, she drew another cigarette from the pack, slanting him an exasperated look as he lit it. She exhaled appreciatively. "I assure you that I'm not sexually repressed, merely selective."

"It's unnatural for a warm-blooded woman to do without for—"

"My sex life is really none of your concern, Sergeant," she interrupted, drawing a deep drag.

"You're absolutely right," he conceded. "But it does prove my theory about your headaches."

Fuming at his smugness and upset with herself for having unintentionally revealed something so very private to the likes of Stavos, she forcefully ground out her cigarette in the ashtray. "Actually, your first assumption about my headache was correct. Sometimes you do give me one, Stavos. If you don't want to have to beg a ride back to Central you had better drink up." With a haughty lift of her chin, she deserted the bar stool and him.

"Don't worry about me, sugar," he called after her as she weaved through the jubilant patrons. "And you're welcome for the drink."

Alexandra didn't deign to glance back. She felt justified in leaving him stranded at Moran's. Every time she let her guard down with Nick Stavos, began to think he wasn't a total degenerate, he struck a raw nerve. The man was beyond a doubt the most crass, most conceited, most infuriating male she had ever had the misfortune of meeting.

THERE WAS NO MESSAGE, no letter from Quincy Lucas awaiting her at the penthouse. Every day she anticipated some thin thread of a lead that might give her a reason to go on hoping that Jenny would be found. Every night her faith was tested and the fear she denied in the light of day seized a firmer grip on her heart.

Bathed and donned in teal-blue baby-doll pajamas, she sat with her legs curled beneath her and a photo album in her lap. The leather-bound journal chronicled Jenny's existence from her birth until her disappearance a month before her sixth birthday—Jenny bundled in a pink bunting and cradled in Alexandra's arms as an infant; Jenny clad in only a diaper and bow, kissing a frog at age two in the backyard; Jenny proudly displaying her cowgirl outfit and riding her daddy's back as a substitute pony on her third birthday; Jenny posing with the calico kitten Santa had left under the Christmas tree at age four; Jenny on her first day of kindergarten, smiling bravely but hesitating at the schoolyard gate; Jenny beaming for the photo that immortalized her missing two front teeth. Jenny...Jenny...Jenny! Page after plastic-protected page.

Lovingly Alexandra traced her daughter's image with a fingertip while torturing herself with the notion of getting out the projector and watching the home movies of Jenny at play, at sleep, at mischief and sweetness. Tears blurred her vision and anger—unchanneled and unassignable—exploded within her. She slammed the album to the coffee table and vaulted to her feet, sobbing, "Why...why...why?" While pacing in ceaseless circles. "I wanted her so much...loved her so much. I'm a good person...a good mother. I don't deserve this. Please, God, I don't deserve this." The same as sweet olive vines foundered over the courtyard walls, Alexandra wilted to the carpeted floor, burying her face in her arms and moaning incoherently. "Just let her be alive. I couldn't

bear it if anyone was mistreating her. A sign...
something, anything that will give me peace about my
darling Jenny.''

Exhausted and weak from crying, she lay for hours
on the living room rug, clutching the album to her
bosom and staring forlornly into space.

Nick Stavos was not on her mind. Only Jenny.

NICK HAD STAYED until closing time and then hitched
a ride back to Central with the bartender. Amazingly,
he was sober and feeling acutely contrite about his
behavior toward Alexandra earlier. He'd sensed her
wariness, her reluctance to disclose anything personal
about her life before arriving in New Orleans. And
he'd been really interested to know more about Miss
Baby Powder. Yet, insensitive jerk that he was, he'd
pushed her too hard and mocked her. He knew better. After all the years he'd spent interrogating suspects, he knew how to wean the information he sought
without making a subject hostile. But he'd blown it
tonight. Bungled it badly. Handled it all wrong. Why?
he wondered. What was it about the lady that made
him lose his composure and act like a fool every time
they encountered each other?

He contemplated his reaction to her while sitting in
the squad room alone, going over the precious bit of
information he'd managed to piece together on the
activities of Vinnie Stevens a few days prior to his disappearance. The kid hadn't done anything out of the
ordinary—shot baskets in the schoolyard; hung out
with his friends in the park pavilion after dark; fought
with his mother about a missing twenty-dollar bill that

evaporated from her wallet; bought a Springsteen tape from a local record outlet; ate twice at a greasy hamburger shack nearby. There was nothing, no lead, not a damn clue as to what had become of Vinnie. The only significant fact Nick had culled from interviewing Vinnie's pals was that he'd lingered in the park that last night after the rest of them had split. It sure as hell wasn't much, except a place to concentrate the investigation.

He tossed the slim file atop the desk, stretched and yawned. Unwittingly his mind traveled back to Alexandra. Women usually only occupied his thoughts if they had recently been or might possibly be a conquest. She was different. He didn't really consider her a serious possibility. It was obvious that they were incompatible in every sense. They mixed about as well as oil and water. Yet he couldn't dismiss her from his mind. Neither could he dismiss the odd twinge he'd experienced when sleeking back her hair or touching her soft skin. There was an essence about her that was unlike any other woman he'd ever known—fragile, breakable, unmistakably cultured and costly, the same as fine china or rare porcelain. Her dedication was admirable but not quite believable. Why did he have this nagging suspicion that she was using Central as a substitute for something sorely missing in her life? And why would an attractive woman deprive herself of healthy sex in the excuse of being *selective* for two damn years? It was abnormal. Even more weird was the fact that he was moping around the squad room at two in the morning analyzing his shrink. Between bouts with Miss Baby Powder and the dead ends he kept running into on the Vinnie Stevens case, he really was getting a complex. Seldom did Nick Stavos not come up with a crucial clue or perceptive angle that eventually unraveled the riddles he pondered.

He rubbed his palm over his stubbled cheek. It both amazed and perturbed him that the lady had gotten under his skin and made him sweat worse than the 19th-century cholera mortalities entombed in Lafayette Cemetery.

No woman was gonna get the best of him, he vowed, snatching a pen and pad from the desk drawer and improvising an excuse to meet with her again tomorrow.

Okay. You had me pegged. Maybe I'm not as tough as I think. I want another meeting to discuss a nightmare I keep having, but I'd prefer to talk someplace less formal. Noon tomorrow. A ride on the St. Charles streetcar. The Canal Street stop.

Nick

He slipped the request into a manila envelope, licked and sealed it, then slid it under her office door as he vacated the precinct.

CHAPTER SIX

UPON DISCOVERING NICK'S NOTE the next morning, Alexandra's first inclination was to ignore the summons. She'd had a rough night and the idea of another set-to with the opinionated sergeant was not a prospect she relished. Yet, ethically, she knew she could not refuse a petition from a patient on the flimsy excuse of a personal aversion.

She arrived on time at the Canal Street stop. Typically, Nick was five minutes late.

"I swear it's not deliberate," he explained, a bit breathless from sprinting the two-block distance between the only available parking space and the streetcar stop.

She slanted him a skeptical look, then shrugged the padded shoulders of her geometric print shirtwaist dress.

The army-green streetcar approached, the overhead electrical cable spitting sparks as the trolley slowed to pick up the two passengers. Nick could not resist a quick canvass of her sleek legs as she climbed aboard. Preoccupied, he had to be reminded by the motorman to deposit the sixty-cent fares before following Alexandra to the rear of the trolley and settling beside her on the wooden-benched, open-windowed conveyance.

"We used to have two streetcars...." He tried to make small talk. She focused on the statue of Robert E. Lee, while covertly cataloging every slight body movement the sergeant made. "The other became much more famous before the tracks were retired. It was the namesake for Tennessee Williams's play, *A Streetcar Named Desire*."

"I've heard of it." She hadn't meant her reply to sound so condescending.

"Yeah, well, I thought he captured the mood of the Vieux Carré better than any other writer to date, except maybe Ellen Gilchrist. 'When I get lonesome for New Orleans I just go down to the grocery and get a box of powdered sugar and pour it on my hands and lick it off,'" he quoted.

He succeeded in capturing her undivided attention. "I'm impressed. Somehow you didn't strike me as a connoisseur of good literature."

"Don't give me too much credit. I'm a collector of Dick Tracy comic books, too. It's just that a few certain descriptions of this town are authentic to me, such as what Walker Percy said in *The Moviegoer*, '...in New Orleans, I have noticed that people are happiest when they are going to funerals, making money, taking care of the dead, or putting on masks at Mardi Gras so nobody knows who they are.'"

Alexandra truly was astounded and wished to pursue the intriguing conversation further. "I always thought Percy's view of the city was cynical and his hero rather bitter, especially when he describes the ca-

thedral in Vieux Carré as being located in the midst of
the greatest single concentration of decadence in the
hemisphere. I thought his line, 'but isn't that where
cathedrals are supposed to be?' was pretty disparaging.''

"It struck me as realistic," he replied, pointing out
Audobon Place, a palm-treed retreat of the wealthy,
sequestered from the rest of the world by wrought-iron
gates and guards.

She deferred to him and allowed the comment to
pass as the streetcar continued on its way. The smell of
jasmine mingled with the distinct scent of the sergeant's spicy cologne. Both essences permeated her
senses and vied to be the stronger stimulant.

"You wanted to speak to me about a dream that's
been troubling you," she reminded him at length,
forcing her mind to the real reason for the trolley
jaunt.

His amiable disposition evaporated like an afternoon's sweat cooled by a sudden breeze. His moment
of truth had arrived. He could either string her along
with a wild fabrication or confide the vivid nightmare
that imprisoned him after the stroke of midnight,
month in and month out. He stared at a discarded
gum wrapper beneath the bench in front of him, his
mind aimlessly focused on litter rather than truth.

"Nick?" she prompted, sensing he was losing his
courage.

He inhaled a deep lungful of humid New Orleans
air, then reluctantly revealed the nightmare. "I'm in
the Rocky Mountains. Dawn has just broken down
and it's eerie quiet. I feel free . . . really free. The air is

clean and cool. I'm high on it...high above the stench of this crummy world. It's Shangri-la in autumn and at eight thousand feet, ya know?''

She nodded, afraid to venture a comment. For once he was actually allowing himself to open up and she was not about to interrupt. "Go on, Nick."

"I'm not alone. There's this doe I spot. I trail her. I don't want to harm her, you understand, I just want to admire her."

"What does she represent to you?" Instinctively Alexandra realized the doe was symbolic.

A muscle in Nick's cheek twitched. He wished to God he had chosen not to disclose the scene that played itself over and over again in his head, but it was too late to switch to an outrageous cover-up now. "A lot of things," he admitted. "Independence, intelligence, grace..."

"You're some distance away and admiring her. Then what happens?" Alexandra paid no attention to the world beyond the streetcar. She was focused intently on the man beside her.

"A shotgun blast shatters the air and the doe falls to the ground in slow motion. She's hurt bad, writhing and bleeding." The doe's pain seemed to transfer itself to Nick. He grew pale and sullen.

"Did you shoot her, Nick?" She had to ask.

"Lord, no," he groaned. "What do you think I am? Some psychotic sniper?" His dark eyes flashed. She could read the veracity and experienced a chill.

"Who did?"

"I don't know. It's not clear. I go to her. I try my damnedest to stop the bleeding. It's a chest wound.

The worst. Her blood is all over me. But I'm not to blame.... I'm not," he insisted, his knuckles turning white as his fingers clamped the armrest.

Reflexively her hand eased over his, soothing his anguish. "I believe you, Nick. It's only a dream. One we have to explore," she murmured.

He shuddered in spite of the heat, then said not another word until the trolley reached South Claiborne Street and came to a halt.

"End of the line, folks," the motorman announced, strolling down the rows of brass-trimmed benches and pushing the wooden backrests from one position to another. "A five-minute layover and the St. Charles streetcar will be making a return trip. Please exit to the rear," he requested.

"We have to get off, Nick." Strangely this time it was she who took charge, prying him from the seat, then leading the way to the shaded platform.

Not only was Nick shaken, but furious with himself for having displayed a weakness he'd kept under wraps for months. He avoided looking in her direction, although he could feel her eyes on him. "Do me a favor and let's discuss something else." He walked to the edge of the platform and stared blankly down the length of track.

"Whatever you like," she agreed, realizing that Nick was retreating within his hard shell but unwilling to push him any further.

He appeared relieved and stood for a moment, hands thrust in his pockets and squinting into a scalding Louisiana sun. "Your lunch hour won't be a total waste. On the ride back we pass Sweickhardt's. It's an institution to native Awleenians," he explained, reverting to local lingo.

"And what exactly is Sweickhardt's?" She yearned for a cooling breeze as she wiped a tissue along her neck and discreetly dabbed at the perspiration beading between her breasts.

Nick caught a glimpse of her lacy white bra but never let on. "It's a genuine 1940's drugstore—full of clutter and nostalgia with the best fountain sodas this side of the Mississippi."

"Cream sodas?" Her smile was half teasing, half serious.

"They're a specialty of the place. Do you want to stop off before heading back to Central?" He strolled closer, removing a roll of breath mints from his pocket and offering her one.

She declined the mint but accepted his invitation. "Something wet and cool would be refreshing."

He sucked the peppermint disk, deciding to keep to himself the alternate suggestion by which she might alleviate the Delta heat that had filtered into his head. Somehow he figured she wouldn't be nearly so receptive to a "nooner" shower at his place. He entertained himself with the erotic notion—visualizing the two of them naked in a tiled shower stall, the water pulsating over olive and ivory flesh, her arms entwined about his neck, her slick body molded to his, her head languishing backward, her hair cascading in wet ringlets down her slim shoulders, her mouth upturned and hungry, his manhood aroused and—

"Are you back in your dream, Nick?"

He blinked and shook his head as he attempted to loosen the tie that was suddenly choking him. "I'm not really thinking about anything in particular." As if on cue, the trolley's bell pealed an "all aboard."

LATER THAT DAY, Alexandra recalled the dreamy look she had glimpsed in the Greek's eyes before reboarding the streetcar. It hadn't lasted but a split second and was quickly extinguished yet it had been compelling. She wondered what had he been thinking about at that moment, and why she suspected there lurked a soft core beneath his ossified layers. More importantly, what significance did his nightmare about the killing of the doe hold?

Her pondering was interrupted by the arrival of a new patient by the name of Martin Emanuel Martin. Upon first glance at his personnel record, Alexandra had decided the redundancy was a clerical error. However, after a brusque shake of her hand, patrolman Martin affirmed the duplicate name.

"It was my mother's idea. She figured it was catchy. And it was. I've been catching nothing but flack over it since kindergarten. Around here everybody calls me Marty. You can, too, if you like." The ruddy-faced officer had an infectious smile and personable manner.

Alexandra returned the smile as she stood and pulled the ceiling fan cord, in an attempt to get the air circulating in the small office. "In reviewing your file, Marty, I was unable to ascertain an express reason for our appointment. Suppose you enlighten me." She reseated herself, modestly adjusting the hemline of her dress over her knees.

He cracked his knuckles and laughed nervously. "Actually, now that I'm here 'n all, I feel a little dumb about requesting an appointment. I don't have a major hang-up or anything heavy going down in my life. Nothing like that," he reassured her with an uneasy look.

"So then should I assume this is merely a social call? Are you selling tickets to the annual policemen's benefit or what?" Normally Alexandra would have let Marty come to the point in his own good time but it was obvious to her that he could filibuster away the afternoon if she allowed him the opportunity.

"No, ma'am. I do have a personal reason for coming. It's no biggie. Just one little quirk that's been causing me a lot of grief."

She arched a brow, prompting him to elaborate.

He drew the starched sleeve of his shirt across his upper lip before rapid firing a reply. "Every time I get assigned a female partner, I get heavy-duty involved with 'em."

"How many have you had?" It was a poor choice of words on Alexandra's part.

"Three," he said, twiddling with the decorative brass band on his hat.

"Could you be a bit more explicit, Marty? What exactly do you mean by the term 'heavy-duty involved'?"

"It's not what you think. I don't just get intimate with 'em. It's more complicated than that. Hell I marry 'em." He slung the hat aside and expelled a disgusted sigh. "It's a joke around the station—pair Marty up with a skirt and he'll propose within a month."

Alexandra maintained a placid expression, though it took some doing. This was the most extraordinary complaint she'd heard to date. "Have you ever been paired with male partners?"

"Yeah, I've had two. But don't get nervous. I only propose to the females. Mind if I smoke?" He pulled a pack of cigarettes from his shirt pocket when she nodded.

"I got two ex-compatriots who are also ex-wives and I'm engaged to my current partner. The marriages never last long. Fidelity isn't a strong character trait of mine," he admitted, his eyes searching for an ashtray.

She handed him one from off the desk, asking, "Why do you think you develop such a strong attachment to these women? I find it curious that you feel it necessary to marry them. You certainly don't suffer any such extreme bonding toward the male partners with whom you've ridden."

"Pretty strange, isn't it?" he said wryly. "I can't figure it out. After two weeks of being partnered with a woman, I start getting the itch. It just isn't the same as riding with a guy. I start noticing their perfume and each and every time they wear a new shade of lipstick. I can't concentrate on much of anything, except the wiggle of their fannies beneath the blue uniform. I begin to feel protective, like it's my responsibility to make sure they don't get that cute fanny in a jam. Before you know it, I'm picking up the check whenever we take a coffee or supper break. You probably can't relate, but take my word that it can get pretty tense being cooped up in a patrol car for eight- and ten-hour stretches. It's natural to kid around as a way to break the monotony. First it's about general stuff, then it gets more personal. One thing leads to another—a compliment, a friendly pat or hug. Next thing I know, I can't back off. I'm hugging for real and telling 'em I'm serious about making our partnership into an off-duty commitment. And once I share their bed I got this sense of honor that makes me propose. Is any of this making sense?" He stubbed out his cigarette and studied her face for a reaction.

"Some." She struggled to sound convincing. "I think you've confused commitment on both a personal and professional level, Marty. Though this sense of honor you speak of would ordinarily be commendable, in your instance it is adolescentlike and ultimately injurious to everyone, including yourself. I can't help wondering why these women have succumbed to your amorous nature. From what I gather most female officers go to great lengths to avoid any intimate exchanges with their male counterparts. Why would not one of these women be immune, especially since you have acquired a reputation for having little willpower against sexual complications?"

Though his reply was meant to be humorous, an unmistakable note of machismo crept into his voice. "I suppose they just can't resist me, Doc. I love women and have no problem expressing it at the slightest encouragement."

She ignored the endorsement. "Physically, perhaps not; emotionally, I'm inclined to believe your expressions are shallow. Secure men do not fall in love with every woman with whom they come into close contact, Marty. For some reason, which will probably only come to light after further therapy, you have a tendency to want to exert ownership over these women, the same as some men initial their cuff links. Mrs. Martin Emanuel Martin. The solution to your *quirk* is far simpler than the underlying cause."

He snatched up his hat from off the couch and snapped it atop his head in a dismissing fashion. "Is that a fact, Doc? Well, would you like to share your easy answer with this insecure and shallow layman?"

"The first thing you do is uncommit to the current fiancée. Then you go to the duty sergeant, explain your susceptibility to female partners, and request reassignment with a male. Remove the temptation to become 'heavy-duty involved,' Marty, and in the meantime we will work together to discover why the pattern developed."

His pleasant manner had slowly but surely waned throughout the last few minutes of the session. He cast her a derisive grin as he stood and replaced the ashtray atop her desk. "You got it wrong, Doc. I don't plan to be one of your regulars. Like I told you, it's not a major hang-up. Not in my books, anyway. It's been interesting hearing a second opinion, but I think I can manage my own love life. Who knows? Maybe the third time's the charm. True love 'n all that garbage. I might even break the cycle and reform." He squared his cap at a perfect angle over his nose, mumbled an insincere "Thanks for sparing the time," then marched out of her office with a curt slam of the door.

Once again she had encountered mulish resistance to her solicited expertise. What on earth was wrong with these guardians of the peace? Day after day they filed into her office, confiding anxieties—some serious, some petty—expecting her to empathize and provide instantaneous solutions to advanced neurosis. She swooped up the ashtray and dumped the smelly residue into the trash, mumbling to herself, "They're like a bunch of damned clones programmed to deny any human shortcomings or emotions. And pity the analyst who suggests that they are anything less than infallible."

Disgustedly she gathered up Marty's file and jammed it amidst the unalphabetized section of the inactive drawer. "Why do they bother to come?" she demanded aloud as she closed the drawer with a resounding bang. "They don't want assistance or the truth. They want a commiserating echo. I could just as well be a mindless recording. At the sound of the beep tell Dr. Vaughn your problem, then press the response button for a quick cure."

In a spurt of rashness she practiced the absurd notion, speaking into the Dictaphone machine and recording a sarcastic message. "You're just fine. These alien feelings you are experiencing and abnormal behavior patterns are merely a healthy vent for the unimaginable stress. Be assured that in the context of what is the norm for Central's finest, you are no more disturbed than your fellow officers. Feel free to contact me in person if you require further—''

She started at the appreciative clap and wry, "Witty, real witty,'' interjected by Stavos. A crimson flush suffused her cheeks as she pivoted about to discover him lounging in the doorway. Shirt-sleeves rolled up to his elbows, mauve tie dangling around his neck, he stood with his arms folded across his chest, smirk on his face.

"I would appreciate it if you would knock before eavesdropping, Sergeant.'' She faked a sufficient show of indignation.

"What? And louse up a chance to witness a first-class temper fit by our well-adjusted and always cool, calm and collected shrink? Perish the thought.''

She seethed beneath the surface. "Contrary to what you may believe, I was not having a temper fit. I was merely...''

"Yes, you were,'' he insisted, amusement glinting within his dark eyes.

Visions of using the dangling tie as a garrote by which to choke him danced in her head. "Choose to believe whatever you like.'' She looked away.

"I usually do,'' was his smug comeback.

"Is there some reason in particular that you are hovering about? Or do you make a habit out of invading a person's privacy without probable cause?'' She switched off the ceiling fan, hoping to make him as miserably uncomfortable as she.

"Maybe this isn't the best time to bear my soul without an appointment.'' His expression changed to one of uneasiness.

She relented slightly. "Has it to do with your dream?"

His entire body went rigid. "It's always business with you, isn't it, sugar?"

"What else should it be?" she retorted. "And would you please stop referring to me as 'sugar.' It's not appropriate."

"By all means let's be appropriate," he mocked.

They glared at each other for an endless moment. Oddly, it was he who finally made a conciliatory gesture. "Look, I know it makes no sense, but I had this crazy impulse to ask if you'd like to cruise up the Mississippi on one of those steamboat excursions tomorrow night. It's a relaxing outing. Moonlight and some jazz. Nothing serious," he hurried to add. "Just supper and small talk."

She continued to stare at him as though he'd suggested something amoral or ludicrous. Finally she managed to utter a stiff, "Though your invitation is most flattering, Sergeant, I don't think it's a good idea for us to socialize."

"Why?" he asked, somewhat surprised by her refusal.

"In order to treat you properly it's necessary for me to maintain my professional objectivity. That would become difficult if we were to see each other socially." Rattled, she rummaged through her purse for her car keys, hoping he'd take the hint and realize she wanted to make a quick getaway.

"I'm willing to risk it." He did not budge from his sentinel-like post at her doorway or give an inch on the issue.

"I'm not. You don't fraternize with the people you arrest," she put forth. "It's the same principle, Nick."

"No, it's not and I have on occasion," he responded with a disarming grin. "I *fraternized* with one certain lady of evening and it didn't affect my professional objectivity in the least. As a matter of fact, it made things a whole lot more congenial the next time I escorted her into Central."

"You're not serious." She knew by his frank expression that he most certainly was.

"Try me," he challenged. "I can separate the woman from the analyst. One date and if it's a bust we'll go strictly by the rules—yours, of course."

Alexandra's better sense told her to refuse. Yet something—something reckless and totally alien to her conservative nature—overrode her better judgment. "You are persistent. I'll give you that." Unwittingly her gaze lifted to his. Charismatic and smoldering, his eyes willed her to accept. "Oh, all right," she agreed. "Just this once I'm going to make an exception, Nick. I only hope this isn't a disastrous mistake."

"Relax, sugar. I'm not proposing anything other than a leisurely cruise. Pick you up at seven." He made a move to leave.

"You don't know my address," she called after him.

"Wrong, sweetheart. I staked you out weeks ago." He winked, then left the door ajar and her mouth agape as he disappeared down the corridor.

CHAPTER SEVEN

STAVOS FIDGETED IN HIS CHAIR and rat-a-tat-tatted his pencil against a brass paperweight. He'd never been a clock watcher, yet today he'd noted every fifteen-minute interval the white-faced squad-room clock had ticked away. Only one more tedious hour remained before the shift's end and thereafter sixty short minutes before his date with the shrink. And he was getting more antsy by the second.

"Hey, Stavos, do you think you could knock off the Buddy Rich imitation? It's beginning to grate on me." The surly request came from a fellow detective who was futilely trying to hear the ball game score on a pocket transistor radio. "What's with you anyway? I've never seen you so jumpy."

The tapping instantly ceased. "I'm just bored, that's all. What's the score?" Nick really wasn't interested in the pennant race but he knew very well that Hugo was a baseball addict. He preferred for him to concentrate on the game instead of making astute observations.

"Tied up, four-four, bottom of the fifth."

Nick nodded. Hugo pressed the transistor to his ear and lapsed into a welcomed silence. Though the static from the radio was irritating, Nick didn't dare complain. He glanced up at the clock once more. The countdown was proceeding with excruciating slowness. Fifty-five more minutes and still yet another hour to go until the launching of the riverboat. He vacated his chair and made a return trip to the water cooler, not that he was thirsty but his mouth was dry.

Hugo let out a whoop and rotated his chair one revolution. "Brett hit a double and the Royals got the lead."

"Great." Nick tried to sound enthusiastic. Actually he could care less which team cinched a spot in the World Series. All he had on his mind was the upcoming date with Alexandra. For the first time ever, Nick Stavos was tied up in knots over spending time with a woman. Throughout the day he'd vacillated between an impulse to buy her a bunch of posies from the flower vendor's cart stationed on the corner or standing her up without so much as a lame excuse. Never had he suffered from such indecision, such a lack of confidence. It wasn't his style. Not since he was fifteen and self-conscious about a severe case of acne, had Nick Stavos been intimidated by a skirt. Yet, today, his palms were sweating and his stomach was churning in anticipation of the upcoming evening.

"Damn! I wish I was in Kansas City watching the game from the bleachers," Hugo bellyached.

Nick slanted him an annoyed look before reassuming his chair and once again trying to focus his attention on the burglary report spread upon his desk. Right about now he wished *he* was in Tahiti, drinking cuba libras by the liter and admiring bikini clad bodies by the score. Instead he was mildewing in New Orleans and enduring Hugo's periodic belches and instant replays of the game. This was turning out to be one of the longest days of his life.

At the recognizable creak of Lieutenant Troutman's office door opening, Hugo snapped straight in his chair and attempted to shove the transistor inside a drawer.

Fortunately for the goldbricking detective, the lieutenant's hawk eyes had zeroed in on Nick. "I just received another M.P. report from downstairs, Stavos. I think you should have a look at it. There's some similarity to the Stevens case." He motioned for Nick to join him in his office.

As he sauntered through the frosted-glass door, Nick couldn't help but resent the lousy timing. He knew perfectly well that Troutman wouldn't want to waste time following up on any fresh leads and, just as certainly, he knew his night would be spent tracking more dead ends instead of cruising up the lazy Mississippi with Miss Baby Powder.

Troutman's expression was even more grim than usual as he thrust the report into Nick's chest. "This is all we need—another ragamuffin gone missing from Brechtel Park. Boy, oh, boy, you can just imagine the heat we're gonna get from the press if this isn't kept under wraps."

Nick deferred a response until he'd skimmed the latest data Troutman had so graciously bestowed upon him.

Lacey Graham.
Female, black. Age: 10.

Guardian: Lucille Clover—aunt.
Father: Unknown. Mother: Sarah Graham—
serving 2 to 4 in Arcadia State Prison for drug
trafficking.
Last seen August 2nd at approximately 8:00 p.m.
skateboarding in Brechtel Park.

"I want you to talk with the aunt personally. The
officer who took the preliminary report felt that the
woman was holding back on us. See if you can find
out what she's hiding. Perhaps we'll get lucky on this
one and there won't be any link to the Vinnie Stevens
case. Maybe the fact that both kids disappeared from
the same park is purely coincidental." Troutman was
grasping for straws and knew it.

"You don't believe that and neither do I." Nick
flatly rejected the theory. He reached for the door-
knob, then hesitated. "I don't suppose someone else
could have this little chat with Lucille Clover? I sorta
had plans for tonight," he explained, knowing his
chances for a reprieve were slim to nothing. At Troutman's steely glare, he shrugged and muttered, "Yeah,
that's what I figured. I'll take care of it...*personally.*"

Upon exiting the lieutenant's office, he found Hugo
primed to share with Nick every run, hit, error and
strikeout of the game.

"Tell it to someone who gives a damn," was his
foul-humored reply as he slung the folder aside and
picked up the phone to cancel his date with Alexandra. A busy signal buzzed in his ear. He slammed
down the receiver with another curse.

"Maybe super Greek's striking out, too?" Hugo smirked, increasing the volume on the transistor. "Oh, well, Stavos, you can always do what I do—tune out dames and tune into the games." He slurped down more Coke and belched aloud.

"You're pathetic, you know that?" Nick dialed again, only to find Alexandra's extension still busy. "Listen, Hugo, I've got to follow up on a case. Troutman insists. Do me a favor and if a lady should call asking for me, tell her something unexpected came up and I'll be in touch as soon as I can."

"Hustling during duty? You're pathetic, you know that?" Hugo couldn't resist giving Stavos a dose of his own sarcasm. "Okay, I'll give her the message," he agreed, chugging down the last of his Coke.

Nick had no choice but to leave his excuses in Hugo's incapable care.

ALEXANDRA SAT with the buzzing receiver in her lap, staring numbly into space. Her entire body quivered from the aftershock of Quincy Lucas's call. Though she told herself it was all right—that the unfortunate child Lucas spoke of was not Jenny—the gruesome picture he had depicted was too vivid, too terrifying to dismiss.

"I received a call from a local sheriff in Litchfield County. He'd contacted me in regard to the leaflets I'd circulated about Jenny's disappearance," Lucas had begun. "The general area is mostly a haunt for campers and backpackers, kind of remote and rough terrain."

Topography was not on Alexandra's mind. "Did this sheriff have any information to share? Had he recognized her?" she'd asked, her heart pounding at the possibility that someone might have recently seen her daughter alive and well.

"Not exactly," he'd hedged.

"Please, Mr. Lucas, just tell me whatever it is you've found out." Dread—cold and paralyzing—began to trickle down her spine.

"Well, Mrs. Vaughn, he said that a body had been discovered by a pair of backpackers along a trail in a densely wooded area and though it was badly decomposed, the sex, approximate age and vague physical description matched that of your daughter."

"Oh, my God," she'd groaned, feeling the room spin and the receiver slip from her grip.

"I made a trip up there to make a positive ID," he'd continued, "and after a thorough comparison of dental records it turned out that the child was not Jenny."

"You're absolutely sure?" she'd choked.

"I'm positive. It isn't her, Mrs. Vaughn," he'd assured her. "I'm afraid it was just another wild-goose chase."

Every muscle in her body went slack. "This other poor child...do the authorities have any idea what..."

"You don't want to know," had been his curt reply. "Just be grateful you were spared the details her parents must withstand. I was undecided whether or not to tell you of this latest development, but I figured you'd want to be kept apprised of all the facts my investigation discloses."

"Yes, of course. I appreciate your keeping me informed, Mr. Lucas. Stay in touch." The words had been delivered succinctly and mechanically.

"I have to be honest, ma'am. The longer this drags on, the dimmer our chances of finding Jenny."

"I know that," was her disheartened response.

"I'll do my best. Have courage, Mrs. Vaughn." Lucas had hung up, leaving her ashen and on the verge of hysteria.

Alexandra hadn't the vaguest notion how long she sat pinned to her chair, the buzzing receiver cradled in her lap. Time had no meaning. Daylight had been replaced by dusk and dread by depression. Dazedly she hung up the phone, stood and walked to the window. At this time of evening New Orleans appeared haggard—like a woman past her prime, powdered too heavily and looking pasty in an unbecoming light. Not that it mattered. It was just an inane thought. A way to avoid the terror that claimed her mind.

Where was Jenny at this moment? Was it sunny and warm where she roamed? Or cold or dark? Was she hungry? Afraid?

Alexandra leaned her forehead against the walnut window frame, trying to erase the abhorrent vision of a small child's body left to decay in a wooded lot. Nauseous, she bolted from her office to the bathroom across the hall, sequestering herself within one of the stalls and retching until she was limp.

Several times the phone in her office jangled but the resident psychologist was in no condition to assist anyone. At the moment it was all she could do to hold herself together.

NICK RETURNED to the interrogation room and made yet another inept apology to Lucille Clover. It was the third time he'd left the black woman to sit and sweat while he made a phone call from the outer office.

"I've answered all these questions for the first officer. I got babies at home. I can't be leaving 'em too long," she complained.

"We can send someone from Juvenile out to the house to stay with the children if you're truly concerned, ma'am," he offered.

"No, uh, I mean, I suppose they can manage for a while longer. I want to cooperate but I don't know nothin' more." The hankie with which she'd been mopping her plump face was twisted and knotted between her fingers. "Lacey, she just left to go to the park about four yesterday and that's the last we seen of her."

"You are her legal guardian?"

"Yes, sir."

"You mentioned children at home. I assume you have some of your own?"

Lucille avoided any eye contact whatsoever with the seasoned sergeant. Though on the surface his manner was blasé and the questions he asked routine enough, she sensed it was a ruse and that he was hoping to extract some crucial and contradictory remark from her. "I have four others that be mine," she answered truthfully.

He reviewed the statement she had previously given, searching for a defect, some minor discrepancy that would make her a prime suspect in her niece's disappearance. "You're divorced," he quoted from the statistics before him. "It must be quite a burden raising five children alone. I suppose you receive subsistence from the state?"

"I get welfare, if that's what you mean." She didn't like the twist the interview was taking. "It ain't much. Sure not enough to feed and clothe a litter of kids. I'm no sponger. I work in a laundry ten hard hours a day to keep a roof over our head and shoes on our feet. It's an honest job. I ain't ashamed." She recrossed her chubby legs and dared an indignant glance.

"I'm not insinuating otherwise, Lucille." His shrewd eyes studied her. She was too defensive, too quick to deny the slightest impropriety. Instinct told him she definitely felt responsible in some way about the little girl's as yet undetermined fate. "But it does get wearisome, I'm sure...constantly having to provide for these kids...the endless worrying over how you're going to make ends meet." His sympathetic mien wasn't totally an act.

"Sometimes," was her wary reply.

"Yeah, I'll bet sometimes you wish you'd win the lottery or hit it big at the track. No more scrimpin' and scrapin' and strugglin'." He was lulling her into a false sense of security by feigning a common denominator—the yearning for a miracle that would change unalterable circumstances.

A trace of wistfulness flitted across her haggard face. "I think on it now and then," she admitted, momentarily forgetting that he represented a threat—that it was his job to prove intent, or at the very least, neglect.

"Sure, you have. It's only natural. Everybody wants a fairer shake...a better life. Time and again I hear folks fantasize about stumbling upon a sack full of unclaimed money or some long lost relation dying and leaving them a fortune. Believe it or not, I've had a few abused wives who prayed on a daily basis that their boozed-up old men would stagger into the Mississippi and they'd collect on a double indemnity clause. Yeah, I hear it all. You ever daydream about being the sole beneficiary on a sizable insurance policy, Lucille?"

Her eyes hardened and she mopped her brow with the hankie. She might not be educated but she was savvy. She knew the sergeant was doing his level best to wheedle an incriminating admission from her. "I ain't no fool, sergeant. I know what you're after. I wouldn't harm Lacey for no amount of money. You think folks like us can afford to pay insurance premiums?" she sneered. "I did the best I could by her most all the time. Only thing I might be guilty of is not paying her enough attention. I feel bad 'bout that.... I do," she confessed, her bosom heaving as she breathed an inaudible sigh. "So many kids...going different directions all at once. I can't keep track of 'em always. Most the time I do try, but every once in a while a person's gotta have a little time out. Get away 'n unwind, ya know?" Lucille wanted to relieve herself of the guilt. She was practically begging for Nick to accuse her of neglect.

"You lied about the last time you actually saw Lacey, didn't you, Lucille?"

She nodded and wiped her nose with the hankie.

"How long has it been since you can personally account for her whereabouts?"

She hung her head, admitting, "I ain't been home in two days. The kids told me she'd been gone the same. I was afraid to tell the truth. Them social workers are tough. They might decide I'm unfit and take my own kids away from me." She began to sob, rocking to and fro miserably within the chair. "I swear I ain't never left 'em before. I met this Lafayette man and he sweet-talked me into visitin' him. Two days...just two lousy days of no troubles, no sass...two days of feelin' special...that's all I wanted. How was I to know this would happen?" she moaned.

Nick had heard such confessions more times than he cared to remember. Lucille Clover's admission did little for his attitude and even less for his particular case. Lacey's trail was two days colder than originally reported, and Nick was obligated to file an amendment to the Clover woman's statement that could possibly result in abandonment charges against her.

"Has Lacey ever before taken advantage of an opportunity to venture off while you're away?" Since at the moment the aunt was remorseful and vulnerable, he seized an opportunity to press an advantage himself.

"I told you—" she quickly collected herself "—I never done nothin' like that before. I know what you're thinkin' and it ain't true. I don't let those kids run wild like rabbits. They got a curfew. Lacey ain't never missed one."

For some absurd reason he believed her. What's more, he felt a queer empathy with her. He understood how the pressure could get to a person—how in a flash of desperation a grievous, but unintentional error in judgment could result in tragedy. "Okay, Lucille. I think we've exhausted the facts tonight. Go home to your kids. Get some rest." Though his dismissal was spoken lightly, in truth her predicament had touched him deeply.

Through red-rimmed eyes, she looked at him for some shred of assurance. "You think there's a chance those social folks will understand? Maybe have a little mercy on a fool?"

"I think it's possible that you could be put on probation." His eyes mellowed as he observed the defeatism she projected.

"Lacey ain't gone missing of her own free will. I feel it in my bones. She's a good chile, Sergeant. Worth searching for. You find her, if you can." Her voice quivered as she slung a worn tapestry tote bag over a slumped shoulder and wearily made her way down the dimly lit corridor.

You find her, if you can. The simple plea beat in Nick's brain as he switched off the light and sauntered back to the squad room for his jacket. There was a connection between the Lacey Graham and Vinnie Stevens cases. He could feel it in his bones. And it was an ominous sensation.

As he collected his jacket from off the back of his chair, a note Hugo had left upon his desk caught his eye.

No calls. Looks like the lady wasn't real upset by your "no show." The Royals pulled it out in the last of the ninth. They're scoring better than you.

Nick was not amused. It truly bothered him that a woman would not even wonder why he had failed to keep a date. He crushed the slip of paper tightly within his fist, his pride telling him to let the haughty shrink think the worst. But by the time he'd strutted out of the station and reached his Camaro, an equally compelling notion seized him—to deliver an apology in person to Miss Baby Powder and satisfy his curiosity about her nunlike existence outside of Central.

ALEXANDRA SAT IN THE DARKENED ROOM, a stream of light from the movie projector silhouetting her somber face. Her eyes were misty, her body tense as she watched the images of Jenny flicker across the screen. Though reliving the precious moments was pure torture, somehow she could not shut off the projector—could not relinquish the celluloid memories. A faint smile broke her lips at the point in the reel where she had filmed Jenny's first solo bicycle ride. She could almost hear her gleeful shouts. "I'm doing it! Watch me, Mama!"

"Yes, love. You're a regular Amelia Earhart without training wheels," she whispered, recalling the encouragement she had given Jenny that long-ago day.

At the chime of the doorbell Alexandra blinked back to the present, reached behind her and snapped off the projector. The last thing she wanted was company. She looked a sight—no makeup, puffy eyes and clad only in a black silk caftan. Her guess was that Vivian had decided to pay an impromptu visit. Her fear was that her perceptive friend would instantly know how she had been passing the evening and scold her royally. The door bell chimed a second time as she hurried to switch on a lamp and smooth her unbound hair before answering the summons.

"Nick?" The greeting was not exactly friendly— more like utter bewilderment.

"Am I interrupting something?" His black eyes skimmed her from head to toe, taking in the clinging caftan, dreamy look and mussed hair. A jab of jealousy pierced his chest.

"No, I, uh . . ." *How did she explain? Yes, he was interrupting something very private but not what his expression so overtly implied.* "Why are you here?" she asked, clasping together the lapels of the plunging neckline.

"I wanted to apologize for not making the cruise this evening. If I'm going to have to humble myself, I'd prefer not to have to do it publicly. Do you suppose that I could come in for a minute?" He was banking on her proper New England upbringing. It would be inhospitable of her not to extend him an invitation to enter her ritzy apartment.

She eased open the door and allowed him to step inside. The cruise! She'd completely forgotten all about their date. But her biggest problem right now was explaining away the movie equipment in the living room.

Once his eyes became accustomed to the muted light, he surveyed the spacious and expensively furnished quarters with critical interest. "This is real cozy, Alexandra. Original oils and authentic Persian rugs. I'll bet one month's lease on this fancy pad is more than a year's worth of my rent receipts."

"Would you like something to drink?" she offered, thankful he had not yet mentioned the projector or screen.

"A Scotch neat would be good." He continued to inspect the room, pacing the hardwood length and breadth.

Going over to the bar, Alexandra poured an ample portion of Scotch into two crystal tumblers. Handing him his drink, she suggested he take a seat.

He settled on the jade brocade couch, sampled his Scotch, then turned his attention on her. "Are you into educational or porno flicks?" The projector had not escaped his notice.

A sip of Scotch, a tight smile, and she bluffed her way through the tricky question. "Which do you think?"

A sip of Scotch, a crooked grin, and he sidestepped the loaded response. "I'm not sure." His slow up-and-down assessment of her left no doubt in either of their minds that he was sure of one thing—that she wore not a stitch beneath the seductive silk wrap.

His once-over was penetrating, steamy and penetrating. For an added moment she could not look away from his kinetic eyes. And in that split second, her body betrayed itself—her nipples hardening, her breathing growing shallow, her heart stilling.

"Excellent Scotch," he remarked.

"It's imported." Forgetting herself, she leaned over the coffee table between them to extract a cigarette from a small bronze box.

He caught a glimpse of her taut breasts as she reached for a smoke. "You shouldn't mix habits. It's bad for your health."

"Are you trying to reform me, Stavos?" Her smile was tentative as she attempted to garner some willpower.

He eased back against the cushions and studied her genteel face. "No, but I do wonder about you, sugar."

"In what way?" Purposely she placed herself at the opposite end of the couch and safely out of his immediate reach.

"Most women would've been hot about being stood up tonight. But it doesn't bother you, does it? I have a sneaking suspicion that you never gave me a second thought until I showed up on your doorstep to apologize. My ego wants to believe that something really heavy occupies your mind—" he took a swig of the Scotch, then set aside the glass "—but instead I think you don't really give a damn about men or moonlight or..."

"Why is it that whenever you feel your masculinity is threatened you find it necessary to attack my femininity?" Alexandra's tone was sharp, her remarks patronizing.

"Could we for once drop the Ph.D. from your repertoire?" Strangely, the request sounded more resigned than surly.

"You're really upset about this, aren't you?" His wounded reaction came as a surprise. She found it difficult to believe that a man who was accustomed to women being at his beck and call, would care about one inconsequential lady's passiveness. "Would it offend you if I admitted that I did, in fact, forget about our outing?''

"Hell, no. I thrive on rejection," was his caustic reply.

"Look, Nick." She sighed and scooted closer. "Something happened today that erased everything else from my mind. You'll just have to accept that it's a personal matter and has nothing to do with you."

"Do you want to talk about whatever it is that's troubling you?" His tone implied concern and discretion.

"No." She polished off the remainder of Scotch and refused to look in his direction. "I'm not in therapy. You are." Immediately she wished she could retract her words.

"Excuse me. No disrespect intended." He sprang to his feet, his Greek temper flashing and his entire body rigid with repressed anger.

She lifted her gaze to his and caught his hand. His palm was rough and strong and warm. Regret shimmered within her expressive eyes. "Please, forgive me, Nick. I'm not myself tonight."

The softly spoken apology was as irresistible as the lady herself. For the life of him, Nick did not understand the chemistry at work between them. They were all wrong—a stuffy New Englander, a brassy Awleenian. They mixed about as well as fine champagne and salty pretzels. Nonetheless she aroused him. She had the ability to both irritate and excite him. At this precise moment the latter was the stronger stimulus.

Gently his fingers laced with hers. "I like your hair without all those damn pins. Wild and loose becomes you. Humor me and wear it the same way tomorrow night. 'Cause lady I'm taking you aboard that river-boat. Personal problems and unsolved cases aren't interfering again.''

His confident smile left no doubt that Sergeant Stavos fully intended to pursue the unlikely prospect to the bitter conclusion.

CHAPTER EIGHT

A MISTY RAIN FELL as the giant paddle wheel churned the muddy waters and the *Creole Queen* slowly made its way upriver.

Protected under a canopy, Nick and Alexandra stood at the promenade deck rail, watching the glimmering lights of New Orleans fade into the distance. The overcast skies obscured the stars, the same as the ebony darkness cloaked the shoreline, making it impossible to distinguish heaven from earth and instilling a feeling of infinitesimal limbo.

They exchanged not a word for the longest time, yet their private thoughts were quite similar: *how in the midst of such serenity could there exist such chaos?*

"This is very pleasant." Alexandra tilted back her head and savored the purging coolness of the river's breeze.

Nick nodded. "Mark Twain knew of what he wrote. There's a mood about the Mississippi—busy levees and lazy paddle wheelers, murky agelessness and polluted nostalgia."

She found herself slightly awed by his eloquence. "What a profound description."

He smiled and slanted her a sideways look. "Occasionally I can be a sensitive person, Alexandra. I'm not a hard bastard every waking minute."

"I'm beginning to realize that, Nick," was all she replied.

Silence enveloped them again. The only sound breaking the stillness was the wash of the Mississippi against the *Creole Queen*'s paddle wheel and the toe-tapping Dixieland music coming from the Victorian-decorated bar a level below.

"It's stopped sprinkling. Would you like to stroll the promenade before we eat?" His arm slid possessively about her waist.

"If you'd like." She synchronized her steps with his leisurely pace, but averted her gaze to a passing barge.

"When I first became a cop I thought I was going to right every wrong in the world," he remarked at length. "I had this idealistic notion that life had quality and people had integrity. Then I got a taste of what it's all about . . . saw firsthand the brutality that exists on the streets . . . realized the potential of people to abuse, maim and even kill one another for greed, jealousy, spite and sometimes just for the thrill of it. It doesn't take long to become disillusioned . . . to become a hard bastard. 'Cause that's the only way you can deal with it."

"But life does have quality and people integrity, Nick. It's a hazard of the occupation that you are frequently exposed to the seamier side. Sure, injustices and cruelty exist. But so do reasonableness and compassion. People have a great potential for good also."

They debated as they strolled. She couldn't help but notice that his embrace about her waist grew firmer—more intimate.

"Yeah, I know I've seen too much. It's made me cynical. But for the most part I can handle it . . . put it in perspective. But every now and then a case comes along that eats at me. I'm in the midst of one now that—" He stopped in midstride, released her, then turned to the rail, braced his arms upon it and stared into the darkness. "I shouldn't lay this on you. I don't usually talk shop when I'm with a pretty woman."

She joined him at the rail. "I'm glad you finally feel comfortable enough to share your thoughts with me, Nick. Tell me about this particular case."

"Are you asking in a professional or personal sense?"

"Both," she answered truthfully.

He couldn't help but grin. "You don't give a man much encouragement, do you, sugar?"

"I do take a personal interest in you, Nick." She committed herself without fully considering the repercussions.

His expression held both a quizzical quality and a trace of expectation as he turned and faced her. "Yeah, well, I take a personal interest in you, too."

A faint smile settled on her lips. "Why does this case bother you so much?" Deliberately she shifted the emphasis.

"I got two kids missing and a bad feeling. It's too coincidental that they were both last seen hanging out in the same park. What's more, if I'm right and there is a connection, the chances that another kid will soon disappear are almost certain. We could have an epidemic of child snatchings that will throw this city into a full-scale panic.''

Alexandra paled at the mention of missing children. She was grateful for the moonless night that partially veiled her features.

''I got a soft spot for kids, especially underprivileged ones. They get few breaks in this hard world. What chance do they have existing in a cesspool of vice and prey for every variety of pervert? My guess is that these two kids have met with foul play and I haven't a clue, no leads, just cold trails and dead ends. It's frustrating, ya know? The search becomes futile at the edge of the park. There's a thousand different directions to go and not enough hours in a day to pursue it.'' Nick shook his head defeatedly. ''Worse yet, the brass tie your hands. They want it played down...don't want the media to get wind of it. They're afraid that if the facts become public all hell will break loose. Well, maybe it should. If there's a chance that a deluge of media attention would bring about one lousy lead, it's worth any bad press the department might get. I'm about ready to risk suspension and leak the story myself.''

''I know how you feel, Nick, but you can't lose your objectivity. Your being brought up before a review board won't help those children. Because you care so much, their best chance to be found is having you on the case and following up on every insignificant bit of information. It's discouraging but I believe that temporarily missing does not necessarily mean permanently lost. You have to believe that, too, Nick. It's important to keep a positive attitude." She, better than anyone, knew how hard a task it was to keep faith without a glimmer of hope.

Nick noted the conviction in her voice. Yet he also perceived the pain in her blue-green eyes. "You're fond of kids, too," he observed.

"Who isn't?" She prayed he would not pursue it.

Mistakenly he thought that her marriage had been childless and thus a source of unfulfillment. It became his turn to try to change the subject. "I'm catching a whiff of the buffet they're serving. Are you hungry?"

Relief flooded her face. "Ravenous."

"Is there a chance you could be seduced with seafood gumbo, round of roast beef and pudding with rum sauce?"

Alexandra misinterpreted the gleam in his dark eyes. She believed he was teasing. Whereas Nick had never been more serious in his life. Taking her arm, he led her down the narrow steps to the lower deck and inside the ruby, velvet-draped, gold-gilded dining room. They followed the maître d' as he weaved through the maze of damask-covered tables to the rear of the room.

"Will this be satisfactory?" the maître d' inquired, pulling out Alexandra's chair.

"Perfect," Nick concurred, thankful that they were well away from the jazz band. He preferred not to have to compete with a trumpet and trombone while trying to converse with Alexandra throughout the remainder of the evening.

"I love the decor. It really does put you in mind of riverboat belles and dapper gamblers." She glanced around, thoroughly enchanted by the nostalgic setting.

Nick placed their drink order with the waiter, humoring her whimsical mood by ordering mint juleps, a specialty of the bar. "Wide-brimmed hats and ruffled petticoats would've suited you, Alexandra. Yeah, it isn't difficult to picture you in the role of a riverboat belle." He cast her a rakish grin.

"And it wouldn't be difficult at all imagining you as a wily faro dealer with an eye for the ladies. Of course, heaven only knows how many duels of honor you would have fought because of deflowering some giddy Southern magnolia." She enjoyed the make-believe.

He allowed the comment to pass as the waiter served their drinks. "Geez, Alexandra. Give me a break, will ya? Why do you always think of me as a shady character? I could just as easily have been a cotton baron rather than a no-account gambler," he put forth.

She shook her head, then sampled the mint julep. "No, the image doesn't suit you somehow. I find it far more believable to visualize you as a blockade runner. Swarthy and daring and enterprising."

"Why is that?" He was truly curious as to how she arrived at the deduction.

"Because you'd never have been satisfied living a gentleman's life. Too dull. No," she mused, "danger and derringers would've been more your style."

"Yeah, well, I suppose you have a point. I'm more inclined toward adventure than complacency," he admitted.

"And more disposed toward earthy women than society ladies," she ventured.

"Usually," was his candid reply. He set aside the silver-etched tumbler and leaned back in his chair. "Most of the women I've known have fallen into two categories—wild and/or not too bright. I liked 'em that way. Superficial was fine by me. I wasn't looking for any complications or a commitment, just a temporary diversion." He shrugged his broad shoulders and glanced across the table at her. "There was a time when I changed partners like I did my socks and with about the same amount of interest. But that's a habit I've since broken."

The conversation had taken an unexpected blunt turn. Alexandra didn't know quite how to respond. "So, if you're no longer interested in shallow types, what sort of woman do you fathom yourself becoming involved with in the future, Nick?"

A slow smile tugged at his lips. "In my line of work you don't make any long-range plans, sugar. You live day to day and act only on the spur of the moment. Any pre-arrangements about your future can be hazardous to your health because then you start giving a damn...start playing it too cautious. Before you know it you're ineffective. The bad guys sense your wariness and take advantage. It's a sure way to take a short trip to the cemetery. Relying on instinct has saved my hide more than once. I think I'll continue to play it that way. When the woman and the timing is right, I'll know it."

"How will you know?" She pressed the issue, not really certain as to why his options and opinions mattered.

His expression suddenly sobered and his eyes slowly traveled over her face. "Chemistry," he explained. "When that special woman comes along, she'll make me want to linger. I've had my share of sizzling sex, but I've never had a yen to hang around for the after-the-lovin' pillow talk or breakfast. The day this cop would rather snuggle than hit the road is the day he's ready for a forever kind of commitment."

She could not only feel his sincerity but the heat of his unflinching gaze as well. "And you'd base such a serious commitment on such a simple act as tarrying for breakfast?" She found the notion incredulous. "That's the craziest thing I've ever heard," she scoffed.

He shrugged again, retrieved the tumbler from off the table, and raised it in a mock salute. "Maybe..." was his ambiguous reply as leaned closer to the table and cast her a rueful smile. "Have I told you how sensational you look tonight?" The compliment came out of the blue.

She lowered her gaze with a demure, "Thank you, Nick, but it's not necessary to ply me with flattery. I'm only your doctor, not a candidate for a bed and breakfast partner," she reminded him.

He reached out a hand to still the nervous drumming of her long nails upon the linen tablecloth. Though the gesture was meant to be reassuring, his slight touch had a completely opposite effect. "You can't fault me for trying to light a fire. It doesn't mean I'm out to burn you. Just for tonight, let's drop the professional courtesies. I'm not a cop. You're not a shrink. We're just a man and a woman sharing a pleasant summer evening. Nothing is going to occur between us that you don't want to happen. We're two grown adults and seasoned enough not to wind up in bed for all the wrong reasons." He squeezed her fingers, then tactfully withdrew his hand.

She smiled unsteadily. Though he sounded earnest, she could plainly read the unmistakable desire in his eyes. Even more disturbing was the fact that the bastion of resistance Alexandra had erected against him was crumbling.

As it turned out, it wasn't the fine food or exotic drinks that compromised Alexandra's professional ethics. Nor was it Nick's smooth dancing or flattering remarks. It wasn't even the romantic setting or the torchy blues tunes the jazz combo played. Her submission to his good-night kiss at the penthouse door was much simpler and terribly more complex than such conducive influences.

She was lonely; so was he. When he slipped his arms around her and drew her tight against him, she had sufficient curiosity about his legendary prowess to dare a test. And somewhere deep in her subconscious lurked a reckless desire to disclaim the icy New Englander image. Her initial receptiveness to his embrace was quite guileless indeed.

It was when his lips made contact with hers, igniting an unanticipated warmth within her that spread like wildfire that things became complicated. Nick moved to deepen the kiss, his tongue probing the intimate recesses beyond her trembling lips. One hand played idly in her hair, the other pulled her even closer against the evidence of his arousal.

Excitement and apprehension left her breathless. "Please, Nick," she groaned, staggering backward a step as she broke free from his spell.

"Please, what, Alexandra? Please do. Please don't. Please go. Please stay. You want me to. Admit it." His tone was husky.

"I don't. I can't." Her hands shook so badly that inserting the key into the lock became an insurmountable task.

He moved behind her, reaching around and taking the key from her trembling grasp. He was damnably steady when unlocking the door. And he was damnably sure of himself when following her within the posh penthouse and cornering her with truths.

"You can, if it's what you want. The world isn't going to know or care if we spend one night together. There is a life outside of Central for both of us." He approached her, slowly, cautiously. She was as skittish as the deer in his haunting dream—poised to bolt at the slightest inkling of danger. Gently he grazed his palm along her bare arm, then weaved his fingers through the side of her hair.

She stood motionless, her eyes closing at his sensuous touch. How could she deny the passion he had awakened in her? It would be wonderful to have someone hold her, if only for those few miserable hours that came after midnight and lasted till dawn.

To for once not think of Jenny exclusively and just for a solitary night be able to feel something other than numbness.

"Tomorrow we can pretend this never happened, if you like," he murmured. "But tonight I think you need me as much as I do you."

She shuddered, then ever so slowly opened her eyes to his and admitted her yearning with a reluctant nod.

Nick couldn't exactly define what emotion he read in her eyes, but it really didn't matter. All he knew was that he wanted to share himself with this woman, this night, more than with any other he had known. Wordlessly he swung her up into his arms and strode toward the hallway.

"My bedroom is the last room at the end." She rested her head on his broad shoulder, her mind reeling with abandoned logic and rash desire.

"Silk sheets and scented pillowcases, I'll bet." He kissed her temple and crossed the threshold.

"Satin sheets and monogrammed cases," she corrected as he eased her down upon the poster bed.

Eyes downcast, she reached to unfasten the front buttons of her dress, only to find her fingertips stayed by a firm clasp of his hand.

"Let me. I want to kiss and memorize every inch of you, Alexandra." Expertly he stripped away garment after garment and, as each article of clothing drifted to the floor, he then explored the unsheathed, alabaster portion of flesh with his lips and fingertips. By the time he had completely undressed her, Alexandra writhed feverishly beneath him and repeated his name deliriously.

Nick's own desire was as intense even as he considered the fact that such a wondrous night might never occur between them again. By tomorrow Alexandra would want to deny the intimacy. In a week she'd want to blame him entirely for taking advantage and compromising her objectivity. So tonight had to be so special as to nullify any forthcoming rejection. Because for him it was different—for him there had never been a woman quite as beautiful or nearly so satisfying.

"Easy, sugar," he coaxed, stroking the curve of her slim hip and sleek thigh and stringing kisses along her throat.

"I can't be patient, Nick. Make love to me now. Make me forget everything else but you." She clasped the back of his neck and brought his mouth to hers, expressing a need so great that even the cynical Stavos was left shaken.

Nick was no stranger to the pain of invisible wounds. He recognized a plea for release when he heard it. Gathering her to him tightly, he attempted to reassure her. "I'd like nothing better than to be your sole desire. Whatever ache is inside, let go of it, sugar, at least for a few short hours." His palm caressed her cheek and his lips brushed softly back and forth over hers. He felt the intensity ebb from her shapely body. "Cling to me, Alexandra," he urged.

He made it so easy—so incredibly easy—to relinquish the pain and forget the impropriety of an impulsive act, Alexandra thought dazedly. He made it so natural—so effortlessly natural—to make love for hours. His words were perfect. His touch was electric. He possessed the skill to please a woman but, even more, his every caress, every kiss, every thrust was a sensitive expression of respect and caring. He was not what Alexandra had expected. No, not at all. She was unprepared to deal with this gentle and sensuous Adonis. For once in her life, Alexandra was taking more than she gave. And though she felt a due amount of shame, she could not stop, for Nick—unselfish and sexy Nick—brought back to life the woman she had sacrificed in the name of motherhood. It was fantastic to feel sinewy muscle beneath her palms. It was extraordinary to inhale a musky male scent. It was heaven to gradually build to a climax while hearing sincere groans and endearments from a man who did not utter them lightly.

"I'm not as experienced as you, Nick," she confessed later, pressing his hand to her midriff and snuggling next to his reassuringly hard body spoon fashion. It was not difficult to admit one's faults with your back turned. Never look in another's eyes. Never expose one's vulnerability.

"One man, one marriage and no fooling around," he assessed. "I admire your innocence, sugar. Experience doesn't necessarily mean satisfaction. There's only one trade-off that's worth exposure—unconditional love. And I'm not sure such an idealistic arrangement exists. Maybe when you're willing to give more than you take. Maybe when you're seeking more than is smart. Maybe when you've nothing else to lose. Then, it begins to have meaning." He stroked her smooth back and nestled his cheek in her silky hair.

"This should have never happened." He felt her resigned sigh. He also believed her regrets would eventually overshadow the memory of this night.

"Yeah, well, I took advantage. It's my nature. I've no scruples. Blame me, not yourself, sugar." Again he made it so easy to deny the need that precipitated the act.

"You know me better than I do you, Nick. Tomorrow I'll wish I had not succumbed. How are we going to go back? I'm supposed to be the lady with all the answers. Now you know I have times when I can't cope, either. Nights when I long for a warm body beside me...someone who gives a damn whether I make it through or not."

He kissed her shoulder. "Close your eyes. Sleep, Alexandra. Know that I give a damn."

He sounded so sincere. It was very comforting to lie in his protective arms, to escape into a temporary peace. Exhausted and content, in minutes she fell fast asleep.

Nick held her close throughout the remainder of the night. Hardly did he move a muscle as he studied her fragile features and wondered about the source of her agony. Alexandra was not what he had bargained for, either. Quite the contrary. She was an extraordinarily passionate woman. What she lacked in experience she made up for with enthusiasm. Though he'd been with a variety of women in his prime, Alexandra was beyond a doubt the most naturally sensuous. Yet a part of her had remained detached tonight—a part of her past. Miss Baby Powder kept secrets. But who did they concern and why was she so guarded? The questions tormented Nick. He was unaccustomed to coming in second to a memory. He prided himself on his ability to make a lady forget everything but the moment.

His arm beneath her head tingled from the lack of circulation. Carefully he eased it free and rolled over onto his back, slipping his hands beneath the pillow to prop up his stiff neck. It was then that his fingertips accidentally became entangled in a wisp of grogram ribbon. He withdrew the frayed and faded object, examining it in the first faint light of dawn that seeped into the room. What significance could a soiled pink ribbon hold for Alexandra? He glanced at her, assuring himself that she had not awakened, then replaced the ribbon and eased from the bed.

Soundlessly he dressed, all except for the tie that he purposely left draped over the end post of the bed. It was insurance—insurance that Alexandra would not attempt to deny the intimacy they had shared. No, he did not intend to let her explain him away as a vivid dream or a major mistake.

Slinging his jacket over his shoulder, he turned for one last look before he slipped out of her bedroom. He had to be crazy, he thought, watching her stretch sexily beneath the satin sheet and desiring her once more. Were she any other woman, he'd crawl back under the covers for an encore roll between the sheets. Suddenly it was he who wasn't sure that a repeat performance was wise—he who wanted something more serious than a purely physical relationship. Lord! He should've never insisted on staying the night. He needed a shower, a shave, some coffee. But most of all he needed to get out of here before he got any deeper involved.

Only the street cleaners noticed the tall Greek as he climbed into the candy-apple red Camaro and peeled up St. Charles Street. And they really didn't pay a lot of attention. Tomcats on the prowl and hollow-eyed lovers making indiscreet exits at dawn were a common sight in New Orleans.

CHAPTER NINE

A RELENTLESS CHIMING reverberating in her skull roused Alexandra. Reluctantly she squirmed from beneath the covers and sat upright on the edge of the bed. She was disoriented and unable to comprehend the bright sunlight streaming into the room.

She glanced at the clock on the nightstand, then noted the rumpled space beside her where Stavos had lain. She hadn't time to wonder about his premature departure. In her confusion the night before, she'd forgotten to set the alarm. It was nearly midday and the doorbell's chiming wouldn't cease.

"Okay, okay," she muttered, fumbling for the chenille robe at the foot of the bed and haphazardly clinching it as she stumbled into the foyer to answer the persistent summons.

"Well, it's about time. I was about to call security to let me in." Vivian breezed past her—dressed to the nines and looking more than a little flustered. "I've been worried sick. First I call your office and receive no answer. Then I check with the front desk and they tell me you haven't shown up for work. Next, I ring you here and keep getting a busy signal. So I have the operator check the line and she informs me that either your phone is out of order or the receiver's off the

hook. Well, that puts me in a real tizzy. I start thinking that you're ill or have been mugged or worse.
Then, after driving like a madwoman to your doorstep, I can't get you to answer the bell. Would you
please tell me what is going on?'' She paused to take
a deep breath, then wilted onto the couch.

"I assure you I'm perfectly all right. I just overslept, that's all." Alexandra hoped she looked as
nonchalant as she sounded.

Vivian peered at her skeptically. "Overslept, huh,"
she grunted. "That's out of character. In all the time
we've known each other and dormed together you've
been fastidiously punctual—never late for a class, an
appointment, a date, a wedding or a funeral. Tell me
the truth, Alex. Has this something to do with Jenny?
Have you received some news?''

"I wish, Vivian, but no. I simply forgot to set my
alarm. I'm sorry to have worried you, but I'm
fine... really," she insisted at Vivian's disbelieving
pout.

"Well, I suppose it's understandable. Do you realize that you've been so wrapped up in saving souls at
Central that you haven't as much as called me to have
lunch? My feelings are hurt. After all, I am your
dearest friend and the one who pushed for your appointment. I should think you would at least find the
time to call and inquire about my health." Vivian
could be a bit overly dramatic, not to mention over-
bearing at times.

"How is your health?" Alexandra humored her
while discreetly trying to replace the phone's receiver.

Obviously the wily sergeant had taken it off the hook the night before.

"I'm in the pink, thanks." Vivian withdrew her sterling-silver case from her purse, extracted a cigarette and lit up. "Why was your phone off the hook?"

"I haven't the vaguest idea. Perhaps the maid accidently bumped it while she was cleaning." Alexandra surprised herself at the plausible explanation. "Listen, Vivian, why don't you be a sweetheart and make some coffee while I shower? We can chat as I dress. I really do have to put in an appearance at Central. I've missed a morning appointment as it is."

"Plain coffee sounds terribly dull. Haven't you anything more exotic?" Viv had a tendency to be ostentatious also.

"I'm afraid not." Alexandra tried not to sound condescending.

"Oh, well, I suppose we could spice things up with some earthy gossip. As I recall, we used to have our most enlightening discussions while traipsing around in our underwear."

No sooner had Vivian disappeared into the kitchen when Alexandra whisked into the bedroom to smooth the telltale covers. The last thing she needed was for Vivian to suspect that a man had kept her company last night. After the divorce, Vivian had done her level best to matchmake, that was until Jenny had vanished. She accepted Alexandra's disinterest as understandable considering the strained circumstances. If she thought for one second that Alexandra would be receptive to male attention, she'd have no compunctions about imposing a parade of eligible men upon her. The thought made Alexandra cringe. She already had one man too many complicating her life and compromising her principles. What on earth had she been thinking of last night?

Quickly she stripped and stepped into the steamy shower. She couldn't think about Nick now. It would be dangerous to dwell on the reasons behind her inexcusable response to him and far more threatening to admit his attractiveness.

She lathered her body, involuntarily recalling the singularity of Nick's touch as she washed away whatever trace of his scent still lingered upon her flesh. What appointment had she missed this morning? Try as she might to focus on her professional obligations, she couldn't quite remember whose name had been penciled in her appointment book. Damn Nick Stavos and his flashing black eyes. The harder she tried to dismiss him, the stronger his memory became. Soft words; steely muscles. Tender kisses; wild sex. Gentle caresses; firm assurances. He was contradiction personified. So anxious to stay the night, then sneaking from her bed without so much as a perfunctory thank-you or goodbye.

Turning off the water, Alexandra snatched a towel from the rack and buffed herself dry. It would be humiliating to face Stavos today. She hoped he had the decency to keep his distance. It would be the gentlemanly thing to do. Of course Sergeant Stavos wasn't likely to be noble. He'd probably make a concerted effort to behave just the opposite. That was fine, just fine, if that was the way he wanted to play it. She intended to be just as blasé about the matter as he.

"I forget. Do you take cream or sugar in your..." The question died on Vivian's lips as she spied the necktie draped over an end post of Alexandra's bed. She stood gawking, tray in hand and the coffee unpoured.

At first Alexandra hadn't any notion what had tongue-tied her friend. Then, to her horror, she pinpointed the source of Vivian's apoplexy. Of all the idiotic, indiscreet things to do. How like Stavos to leave his calling card!

"Overslept, huh?" Coming to her senses, Vivian arched a brow and set the tray on the dressing table. "I believe this, my dear, is what is referred to as incriminating evidence down at the station house." She removed the looped tie from the post and dangled it tauntingly. "I'm positively amazed, not to mention appropriately appalled. Scandalous behavior." A mocking "tsk-tsk" preceded an avaricious, "I want to know every sordid detail."

Alexandra knew it was futile to postpone the inevitable. Vivian would be satisfied with nothing less than a full disclosure of the facts. "He's an ex-Vice cop. Greek. Persistent. A patient of mine." Distinct annoyance tainted her reply as she poured and then served Vivian a cup of coffee.

"That's it? That's all you're going to tell me?"

Turning her back, Alexandra pretended to be absorbed in a meticulous application of her makeup. "There's nothing else to tell. It was an impulsive mistake."

Vivian had reservations about her Yankee friend's seeming indifference. "Did you come to that conclusion last night in the midst of a passionate tryst or this morning when awakening with a guilt hangover?''

Alexandra brushed and twisted her hair atop her head, jabbing hairpins into her scalp and wincing. ''Please, Vivian. I'm better qualified to explore my reactions than you. It's a question of ethics, not morality. I've compromised my objectivity by becoming involved with a patient.''

''That depends on whether you're merely physically or emotionally involved,'' Vivian challenged between sips of coffee. ''Can I ask you a personal question?''

Her hair and makeup done, Alexandra faced her friend with a resigned smile. ''The answer is yes and no. Yes, he is a sensitive and satisfying man. No, I have no intentions of repeating last night or becoming any deeper involved. I have one desire—to be reunited with my daughter. There's no room in my life for a substitute passion.'' She ignored Vivian's apparent disappointment and tested the coffee. ''This is good, Viv. Better than that poison you used to brew in college.''

Vivian was not about to be sidetracked. ''Honestly, Alex, you really can be exasperating at times. What good does it do to deny yourself a few moments of normalcy? Are you doing penance for Jenny's abduction? You're not to blame. You were a devoted mother. You can't go on spending every minute, all your energy, on a lost cause. It's been almost two years. Neither the Connecticut authorities nor the private detective have come up with a clue. How long will you continue to exist on false hope? You tried your utmost to prove that your ex, his influential family, or his enemies were responsible. There's no proof. No ransom demand. No trace of her. It's time to give it up, Alex. You're a young woman still. You could remarry... maybe have another child..."

"That's enough, Viv. I love you dearly and you're the only one who could get away with saying these things to me." The only display of Alex's irritation was the clatter of her cup hitting the saucer. "I don't ask you to believe that Jenny's alive, just accept my need to do so. Perhaps it is false hope but as long as Jenny is not confirmed dead I will never stop the search. I feel it in my bones, Viv, that she's alive. Someday, some way, I'll find her. And she'll need me desperately. What she won't need is a stranger as a stepfather or rival siblings with whom she'll have to compete for her mother's attention. It's my choice, Viv. And I choose to devote myself to her. Please try to understand."

Wordlessly Vivian crossed to where she stood and hugged her. "I do," she assured her with a pat. "I also admire your courage and fortitude. But I miss you, Alex. You've withdrawn from those who love you. It's very noble not to want to inflict your pain on others, but I feel excluded. We've shared so much throughout the years. Please call and let me know that you're all right. Charles keeps asking about you. Won't you come to dinner with us soon?"

"Yes, of course," she promised, knowing she was guilty of neglecting Vivian since arriving in New Orleans. "Set a date and I'll be there."

"Good. Charles will be thrilled. You were always his favorite. Most of my other friends are a bit flighty for his taste." She seemed appeased. "Oh, by the way..." Mischief glinted in her eyes as she looped the tie about Alexandra's neck. "...you had better return this to the Greek. Nice material. I'll bet he is, too."

After Vivian's exit, Alexandra stood studying herself in the mirror. Draped in a peach towel and sporting a jade silk tie about her neck, she looked comical. A little levity at this particular point in time was a godsend, especially since Central Precinct and Sergeant Stavos awaited her.

SHE ARRIVED AT CENTRAL five minutes before her next scheduled appointment and hadn't time to check on the morning session she'd missed before Detective Margaret Flynn poked her head in the door. "Excuse me. I'm a little early. Should I come back later?"

"No, of course not. Please, come in." Alexandra smiled congenially while assessing her newest patient. The lady was thirtyish, very tall, thin and somewhat timid. She looked more like a math teacher than a decoy for rapists and an inside plant used to break up prostitution rings, which is what her dossier indicated.

"My name is Alexandra Vaughn," she said by way of introduction.

"Margaret Flynn," the officer replied while glancing over the brass-framed diplomas on the wall.

"Okay, Margaret. We have an hour to discuss whatever you'd like. And I assure you that whatever you say within the confines of this office is confidential." Alexandra tried to quell any apprehensions Detective Flynn might have at the onset.

"That's good," was all Margaret replied, still seemingly preoccupied with Alexandra's credibility as a psychologist.

"I see that you now work in Detectives. That must be very interesting."

"At times." Finally Margaret dismissed the plaques and artwork, primly seating herself. "I like working out of uniform."

"Why is that?" Alexandra posed the question as merely benign interest.

"Because I don't like being a cop," was the surprising answer.

"Is this a recent conclusion?"

"No, I've always hated it." Margaret's emaciated face reflected her dislike for the profession.

"Then why did you choose to join the force?" Alexandra found Margaret's concise answers to specific questions intriguing. Seldom did a patient reveal themselves so readily. Either Margaret Flynn was the sort of direct individual who said exactly what she meant or something much more intricate was taking place during their exchanges.

She said nothing. Her pale green eyes lacked comprehension, as though her mind were elsewhere.

"Margaret," Alexandra prodded, getting up and coming to the side of the desk so as to station herself directly in the detective's line of view. "Are you with me?"

She blinked and looked uncertain. "I'm sorry. Sometimes I lose track. What did you say?"

Alexandra braced her hips against the desk and once again asked, "Why did you choose to make police work your profession?"

"I didn't choose. It was decided for me. I'm a Flynn, don't you see?" She stared at Alexandra as though the inference was ridiculously obvious.

"I'm afraid I don't, Margaret. You'll have to explain." The request was spoken softly but succinctly.

"For five generations Flynns have been cops. It's a tradition in our family. . . a matter of pride," she explained.

"Then police work was not something that you truly desired but more of an obligation?" Alexandra guessed.

Margaret fiddled with a loose thread she'd discovered along the seam of the couch. "I had no brothers, no sisters. Just me and Dad. Mom died shortly after I was born. From the time I was old enough to shine his brass my dad assumed I would follow in his footsteps. He walked a beat, you see. Sometimes on his days off he'd take me for strolls in the neighborhood he patrolled. He knew everybody. We'd have to stop and visit with all the merchants and every peddler. He'd brag on his darlin' Maggie and predict that one day I'd be a member of New Orleans finest. It was all he ever thought about. The idea that I might not want what he wanted never entered his mind."

"And you didn't have the heart to tell him the truth?"

"I started to once." She stopped fidgeting with the loose thread and met Alexandra's eyes. "I wanted to go to college and major in archaeology. I found it fascinating. But anyone who knew Jack Flynn would tell you that he was a man who had little patience and absolutely no understanding of anything as frivolous as studying dead fossils and cultures. As far as he was concerned here and now was all that counted. Yesterdays were worthless. Tomorrows he left to the dreamers. He took each day as it came, did the most he could with it and never looked back. So, for me to even suggest that I dared to contemplate making a career out of delving into the past was beyond him. He said it was nonsense and he'd hear no more of it. I would be a cop like we had always discussed. And when Jack Flynn voiced an opinion, believe me, it was final."

"So to appease him you gave up your personal aspirations and assumed his." Alexandra tried to recall how often she had heard of such impotent sacrifices during her years of practice. It never ceased to amaze her how manipulative people could be. In her occupation she witnessed firsthand the infinite potential that existed within most everyone to inflict psychological trauma from which another might never recover. And so often the act was committed in the name of love.

"It's more complicated than that." Margaret gazed off, lapsing into a moody silence.

"How so, Margaret?"

It took her a moment to answer. "My dad was killed a couple months later," she finally supplied. "He accidently walked in on a robbery in progress. He got a hero's funeral and between his insurance and the money he had in the policemen's benefit fund my college education was secured. I was no longer obligated to fulfill my dad's wishes, I thought. But you see that wasn't true. There was his memory to contend with and after the way in which my dad died, in the line of duty, I was more bound than ever. I couldn't let his death be in vain. There had to be another Flynn on the force. And you're looking at her. For over ten years I've been making busts and putting flowers on my dad's grave every Sunday. A pretty sick existence, huh? Except for being Jack Flynn's darlin' Maggie I have no identity of my own. I never had."

"Is this why you've come to me? In the hopes of finding yourself?" Alexandra was treading lightly. It was crucial for Margaret to express her deficiency aloud.

"Yes," she uttered, her head lolling backward onto the cushions and closing her eyes. "I'm frightened— not of the danger I sometimes come up against on the job, but of facing the emptiness that surfaces in me after shift. There's a ghost in my house. And it isn't Jack Flynn."

"Who is it, Margaret?" Hoping to instill a sense of trust, Alexandra sat down beside her. Margaret refused to answer. "You know. I want you to tell me about the spirit that haunts you."

Tears began to trickle from the corners of the detective's eyes. "It's me. It's the woman I might've been. It's my restless soul."

"In the field of parapsychology there's a theory that some spirits are trapped in a limbo, never allowed to fulfill their destiny because they are bound by some previous and inconclusive deed. Once it is acknowledged or accomplished, they are set free." Alexandra felt encouraged by Margaret's gradual display of interest. The tears subsided and she opened her eyes. "I think we can apply the same principle to your problem, Margaret. With a degree of trust on your part, we can work through this obligatory guilt and help you to reestablish your own identity. But you must be aware that in order to redefine your life there has to be honesty and it's sometimes a brutal process."

Margaret seemed to comprehend the probable risks. "I came here because there's no place else to go. I'm going to have to trust you because there's no one else. Whatever it takes to get me straight again, I want to do it."

"That's good, Margaret. We're making progress already. I'm going to schedule you for another appointment a week from today. In the meantime, I want you to do something for me this Sunday." She stood, leaning over the desk, flipped open her appointment book, and jotted down Detective Flynn's name beneath the appropriate date.

"If I can. I go to the cemetery on Sundays. Remember?" Margaret's gangly form hovered over her shoulder.

"Yes, I remember, but I want you to forego the pilgrimage this Sunday. Instead I want you to attend a lecture or visit a museum, do some small something related to archaeology and reacquaint yourself with the interest you long ago abandoned." Alexandra closed the appointment book, then turned to assess the impact her suggestion had provoked. Detective Flynn was stung by the unexpected request. It was evident by her stymied expression.

"But I've never missed a Sunday. The flowers will be wilting. And it isn't likely that anybody is going to be lecturing on archaeology." Unadulterated panic manifested itself in her voice.

"You can visit the cemetery Monday evening. The flowers will last an extra day. And if no one is lecturing or the museum burns down on Saturday, spend the day reading an autobiography of one of the great archaeologists of our time. I'm sorry that I'm not knowledgeable enough to recommend one."

"Howard Carter," Margaret supplied. "He discovered King Tutankhamen's tomb."

Alexandra smiled at the unintentional reference. "That would be an excellent choice," she concurred. "Enjoy your Sunday and I'll see you next week, Margaret."

IT WAS EARLY EVENING by the time Alexandra locked up her office and made her way to the garage. A few patrolmen tipped their hats as she passed. Day by day and little by little, she was gaining some respect. God knew it wasn't exactly mass acceptance, but it was a start. Word was circulating—the "lady shrink" wasn't a phony with pat answers and she wasn't a fink who pipelined everything to the brass. Since old Arnie Kotter had been to see her, he'd been like a fella given a new lease on life—sober and positive about his upcoming retirement. Even Marty Martin had had to admit that she'd pegged his problem, though he didn't like her much for being so damn accurate. And Nick Stavos wasn't badmouthing her either, which as far as the ranks were concerned was equivalent to an endorsement.

Of course, Alexandra didn't know about the mouth-to-mouth ratification she was receiving; she merely sensed a turn in the tide—a friendly nod, a "Yo! Doc," or an offer of a cup of coffee instead of silence when she ventured onto the hallowed ground of the commissary. The slight difference in attitude did not escape her notice. It was reason enough to keep her door and mind open. And it was incentive enough to make her believe that sooner or later her position at the precinct would be viewed as a boon rather than a threat.

Heartened by the breakthrough with Margaret Flynn, Alexandra was in unusually high spirits. Perhaps, just perhaps, she could be instrumental in restoring one shattered lady, even if it meant the loss of a fine officer. This was on her mind as she strolled through the garage. Nothing else and certainly no one else. When Stavos stepped from the shadows near her car she almost jumped.

"Sorry if I scared you. I thought maybe we should talk." The rascal grin he flashed her made her doubt his sincerity.

"About what?" She kept her promise to herself. She'd be damned if she'd give him the satisfaction of thinking he'd crossed her mind since he'd crawled out of her bed.

"Whatever you like—the price of gold, the effect of a full moon like tonight's on all the kooks, the great sex we shared." He slouched against the car door, studying her reaction.

Nothing—not a whit of interest did she convey. "Great sex may be a slight exaggeration, Sergeant. You do have a high opinion of yourself, don't you?" She brushed him aside. "Excuse me. I have an engagement and I'm in a bit of a hurry."

"Sure thing, sugar. I don't want to cramp your style." He allowed her space, then slammed the door shut once she was settled inside the Mercedes.

Refusing to look in his direction, she started the engine. He rapped on the window and motioned for her to unroll it. "Was there something else, Sergeant?" she asked primly.

"Two things. I don't mean to complain but you missed our appointment this morning. I waited outside your office for over an hour. I just want to know, is this a total rejection or merely a partial kiss-off?"

The frost in her eyes instantly thawed. "Damn, I should've known...." She shut off the motor and gazed at him apologetically. "I'm not in the habit of spending the night with my first morning appointment. To be perfectly honest, I overslept."

He looked amused. "Yeah, well, next time I won't send you into oblivion. My emotional stability is at stake."

"There won't be a next time, Nick. It's impossible. Please understand. A physical involvement between us is just not ethical. Please don't suggest that I compromise my objectivity any further. I want to help you cope with your stress, not compound it. We need to explore your nightmare, discover the source of your anxiety—"

"Okay, okay!" He held up his hands in a capitulating fashion. "I meant what I told you in the beginning. I can separate the woman from the shrink. You want to keep it strictly head games, it's fine with me. But let's not pretend we don't know each other. At least concede that we're friends."

He had a valid point. "All right, Nick," she agreed. "I suppose it would be silly to pretend we're not acquainted. But you've got to accept the ground rules. From now on we address ourselves to your problem and we don't digress from a platonic association."

Nick appeared to be in complete accordance with her wishes. "You know what's best. Just one favor. Since you overslept and missed the appointment, I figure I should get to choose the time and place of the next one. I hate that crackerbox office of yours. A jail cell's got more space. I can't relax. My mind gets all jumbled. What do you say to a drive out to Lake Pontchartrain on Saturday? We could picnic and talk. Maybe I could open up for once."

The woman had reservations but the shrink was hoping for another breakthrough. "All right, if you really think the change of scenery might make a difference."

Nick looked pleased. "It might," was his glib reply.

She turned the key in the ignition.

"Oh, I almost forgot the second thing I was going to mention," he said as an afterthought.

"Yes?" She gazed at him quizzically.

"I think I forgot my tie at your place. It's one of my favorites." A lie. A hell of a lie. He despised all ties.

She reached into her purse and withdrew the silk Dior. "Why do I suspect that you've left a trail of neckties and broken hearts from one end of New Orleans to the other?" Her smile was wicked.

"Untrue," he denied with a wink as she put the car into drive and cruised out of the garage.

CHAPTER TEN

EXILED TO A CRAMPED CAMARO, a picnic basket crowded between them on the center console, Nick and Alexandra sat eating cold chicken and watching the raindrops ping upon the murky lake.

"This is pleasant," she teased. "I especially like the spaciousness."

"The damn weatherman's never right. The forecast said partly cloudy with only a slight chance of rain." Nick's irritation was apparent.

"Do you suppose we could crack the window a bit? It's getting awfully stuffy in here." Alexandra squirmed in the bucket seat and dropped her third picked-clean drumstick into the trash container on the floor.

"How can you eat like a sumo wrestler and stay so slim?" Nick accommodated her, pressing the electronic controls and lowering the windows.

"Lucky, I guess," was all she answered, trying hard to ignore the sprinkles of rain that trickled into the car. The humidity made her stick to the vinyl upholstery and the dampness was kinking her hair.

"More wine?" he asked, offering the bottle that had been wedged between his thighs.

"Maybe just a little." She held out her paper cup for him to refill.

He made a point of avoiding her amused eyes, for fear she might read the disgust within his own while pouring the expensive Chardonnay. Forty bucks he'd paid for the bottle of wine—with the devious intention of getting her tipsy so that she'd be more amenable to lying sprawled beneath a shade tree with his head in her lap. So much for his planned seduction. Thanks to the foul weather he was cooped up in a sweltering Camaro, engulfed by the ridiculous blend of Cajun spiced chicken and sweet baby powder, and becoming more sulky by the moment.

They sat sipping the wine and listening to the rin-tin-tin of the rain upon the car's roof. Now and then they'd glance in each other's direction, then quickly look away, repositioning their cramped legs.

"Do you mind if I smoke?" she asked, reaching into her purse for the pack she'd bought expressly for the trip.

"As a matter of fact, yes," he grunted, removing the wicker basket from between them and placing it in the back seat.

She let the testy remark slide along with the pack of cigarettes back into her purse.

"I'm sorry the day didn't turn out like you planned, Nick, but I don't think we should waste time pouting about it."

"Is that what you think I'm doing?" He tilted his seat back and stared ahead, seemingly preoccupied with watching the raindrops spill down the windshield.

She nodded and adjusted her own seat, bracing her Levi's-clad knees against the dashboard.

"Greeks can be temperamental," was his excuse.

"So I've heard. I'd like it if this Greek would open up like he promised. Let's talk about the nightmare again, Nick."

"What's to say?" He shrugged and switched on the radio.

"Well, for starters, why don't you tell me how many times since we last talked it has occurred?" She flipped the dial, changing the station from pop to classical.

"Several times and I hate elevator music." He clicked off the radio.

"Exactly when did it begin?"

He had not anticipated the question. "Shortly after a sour bust down on the wharf. Go ahead and smoke if you want," he relented.

His permission wasn't all she was seeking and they both knew it. Nonetheless she lit up, careful to let the smoke drift out the vented window. "Would you like to tell me about the bust?"

"What for?" He played dumb.

"Perhaps there's some connection," she ventured.

"Yeah, and perhaps one has nothing to do with the other," he hedged.

"Why don't you let me be the judge?" She flicked her ashes while covertly cataloging his defensive posture.

"And the jury," he muttered beneath his breath. "There's not a whole hell of a lot to tell. We had a score to make down at the waterfront. The connection got wind of us and became paranoid. Months' worth of undercover work was blown in one night. No deal. No dope. Just lots of fireworks. When the gunfire was over good guys and bad guys alike had gotten wasted. It happens all the time. Nothing unusual.''

But there was something unusual about the way Nick related the event. His features hardened, his voice thickened and the pulse beat at his temple became noticeably pronounced. "I need some fresh air," he grumbled, flinging open the door and vaulting from the Camaro.

She, too, sprang from the car, taking time to crush out her cigarette underfoot before sprinting to catch up to Nick. "In case it's missed your notice, it's still raining," she pointed out.

"You won't melt," was his curt comeback.

"I might. I've heard that sugar sometimes does." She cast him a sideways glance.

He shortened his stride. "You're sweet, Alexandra, but I'm not real sure you're made of sugar.''

She ignored the barb, the same as she did the sprinkling rain. "Why do you think the nightmare started after that particular bust? You've made so many, Nick. There had to be something traumatic about the wharf incident. We need to see if we can pinpoint it." She hooked her thumbs in her belt loops, a pensive expression stealing over her face as she strolled alongside him. "Does the dream ever vary?''

"No." Moisture collected on his forehead but it wasn't entirely precipitation.

"Okay, well, is there any certain activity that precedes the nightmare? Maybe there's some kind of pattern to it." She kept zinging him with questions.

"I go to sleep, Alexandra. That's it. Some nights I get an undisturbed eight hours. Other nights I'm lucky to get two. There's no pattern." He halted near the edge of the lake and gazed at the overcast sky. Shades of gray. Like his life. So many shades of gray.

"You said *good* guys as well as bad guys were wasted. Anyone to whom you were closely attached?" Luckily she stood a safe distance away, lest she be singed by his searing glare.

"Cops don't let anyone close. We can't afford sentiment in our line of work. Informants are our only allies, and, then only because they're vital in making a bust. There've been times when even they got burned. The heat's everywhere on the streets. Nobody's immune." The speech sounded rehearsed, as though he'd repeated it over and over to himself.

"The fact that the doe's blood is on your hands is symbolic. I'm sure of it," she insisted. "And I'm also inclined to believe that the nightmare is somehow a result of the wharf bust. You've got to cooperate, Nick. What aren't you telling me?"

"Damn it, Alexandra, give it a rest. I'm tired of being dissected. Maybe it's nothing more than battle fatigue and I needed a transfer worse than I thought. Maybe it's the booze I drink late at night. What is it with you? You'd think your whole blasted career hinged on one lousy nightmare." She was zeroing in on the truth and he was not prepared to deal with it...not yet.

She sensed his fear and understood his unreadiness. "Perhaps I am pushing too hard. I won't pressure you, Nick. We'll do this on your terms." She dropped the subject.

He felt ridiculous. Whenever he was around her, the outcome was the same—his emotional barometer fluctuated like a yo-yo and he came across as schizoid.

"It's me, not you. A long time ago I put up walls and whenever anybody threatens to scale 'em I get hostile." He telegraphed an apology by way of an unsure grin. The rain grew steadier. "This weather's about as rotten as my mood. It's probably best if I don't subject you to either any longer. Come on, I'll take you back to town."

They hurried to the car. Wet to the bone and tense to the core, both found the drive back to the city endless. They rode in strained silence, keeping their private thoughts to themselves.

Nick wished that when he dropped her off at the door that Alexandra Vaughn would cease to matter; that he wouldn't remember each gesture, every detail of her appearance, the sensuousness of her scent. The lady wasn't his type. The lady wasn't interested in anything but his mind. The lady wasn't worth the hassle. Yet here he was, trying to improvise a way to be alone with her once more. It scared the living daylights out of him—this unnatural obsession to keep company with a woman who gave him nothing but a hard time.

She wanted to believe that Nick wasn't playing games—that he truly wanted help coping with his problems—that he accepted the ground rules, for there was no space in her life for a Greek lover, no matter how sexy or sensitive he might be. She didn't want him to misinterpret her interest. He wasn't her type. He wasn't the committed sort. He wasn't worth the problems he posed. She'd already lost her objectivity once. It mustn't happen again. Alexandra Vaughn had only one deep and abiding passion—Jenny.

"I got a favor to ask of you." The request came as cautiously as his gradual braking for a steep curve ahead. The roads were slick; he hoped he was slicker.

She lit another cigarette and awaited his petition.

"Every year the old neighborhood puts on an annual festival. It's real special to my folks—a command performance, so to speak. I gotta go, but I hate the thought of having to go alone. I could use a little moral support. Would you come with me?"

"Nick, you promised not to complicate things between us."

"So, what's complicated about going to a simple Greek festival? Some food, a little ouzo, a few laughs." He quickly assessed by her expression that she had strong reservations. "So, okay," he sighed. "I'll be honest. My mother doesn't approve of the ladies I've previously brought to the shindig. I thought if she believed I was dating someone with class, she might get off my back. You look the part. She doesn't have to know that you're my shrink."

"Why does it matter so much to you what your family thinks, Nick?"

"Because I love and want to please them, Alexandra. They worry about me. What's the harm if they think I've mellowed and finally conformed to their old-fashioned values? Papa will be pleased; Mama will say she never doubted; and we'll have had a pleasant evening." It was all a con. Nick was a pro at it. In truth, he just desperately wanted to spend another night with Alexandra on any terms.

She flipped the cigarette out the window, mulling over his proposition. "You're sincere about this? The charade is strictly for your family's sake?"

"Scout's honor." He held up three fingers in an appropriate pledge. Of course he neglected to inform her that he'd not been awarded a single merit badge during his five-year stint in the renowned organization.

"And if I go along with this, you'll honor our platonic arrangement? Not try to take advantage of the situation?"

"The only moves I'll put on you will be when we dance," he vowed.

"Then, as a favor—one friend to another—I'll go," she agreed.

"I owe you one, sugar." Nick was not the sort to forget a debt.

Alexandra never dreamed that one day he would reciprocate the favor by coming to her assistance at the most crucial time of her life.

THE FESTIVAL WAS A GALA AFFAIR—the sidewalks decorated in bright colors and jam-packed with people, the music loud and lively, the food authentic and tasty. All evening Nick mingled with his old neighbors and shook hands like a politician. He was the prodigal son returned.

"Nicky was always such a stinker."

"Nicky used to mow my lawn."

"Nicky dated my sister."

"Nicky makes us proud."

Nick, Nicky, Nicholas. He was the Greek community's hero. The old adored him. The young idolized him. And his peers, though a bit envious of his exalted status, were truly fond of him. Alexandra was amazed at his modest poise in the midst of such mass adulation. She was also genuinely in awe of the gay spontaneity surrounding her. Her family and upbringing had been so entirely different—sedate and stagnant. These people were infected with life. They freely shared their passionate culture and asked nothing in return except that one "enjoy, enjoy, enjoy!"

And Alexandra was thoroughly enjoying herself. Nick was behaving admirably—adequately attentive but not at all possessive. He patiently explained some of the traditional foods and crafts as they strolled along, now and then insisting that she sample a particular delicacy. He incorporated her in every conversation, supplying little details of which she was ignorant so that she might not feel excluded. She saw Nicholas Stavos in a new light that evening. Perhaps because she saw him in his true environment. The Greeks seemed to revere and celebrate life. They were inherently vivacious, unselfish and trusting. Their orthodox faith was adhered to in practice, as well as in principle. They shared their hearts, the same as they did their bread, with any stranger who hungered.

"Nicky! Here. I saved you a place." A robust elderly woman stood and gestured for him to come to a reserved picnic table under the pavilion.

He gave Alexandra's fingers a warning squeeze. "That's Sophia, my mother. Be natural, but for God's sake don't mention that I'm your patient. She worries too much as it is."

"How do you intend to explain me?" She forced a plastic smile as he guided her through the throng of cheery faces toward the waiting Sophia.

"I'll tell her the truth—that we work together at Central and we once made love."

"You do and I'll tell her that you're suffering from delusions and her signature is required on a committal form."

"Oh, you always keep your mama waiting, Nicky. Come kiss my cheek." Sophia's dark eyes glowed as Nick hugged her plump figure. "Introduce your young lady," she scolded, disentangling herself and glancing curiously at the other woman.

"This is Alexandra Vaughn, Mama. We work together at Central," he supplied, winking at Alex from behind his mother's broad back.

"Nice to meet you, Mrs. Stavos," she said stiffly.

"Please, you call me Sophia," his mama insisted. "And this is Nicky's papa, Demetrius." She gestured to a stately older gentleman at the end of the picnic table. "The rest are uncles, aunts and cousins who you will get to know while we visit." An assortment of assessing looks and smiles were leveled in her direction. "Sit, sit," she chanted, nudging several relatives in order to make room for her on the wooden bench. "Another bottle of ouzo, Papa, for Nicky's friend."

A misty-eyed Demetrius first embraced his son, then obediently did his wife's bidding. A new bottle of

Greek liqueur was opened, the glasses filled and lifted in a toast. "Welcome," Demetrius greeted before tossing down the potent liqueur in a gulp.

His easy smile was familiar, only it lacked the cynicism of Nick's. "Thank you." Carefully she sampled the ouzo. It wasn't bad.

Sophia caught the lingering look that passed between her son and the fair lady across the table. The chemistry she detected pleased her. For once Nicky didn't appear so sure of himself. This relationship had potential, she decided. She knew her son well. Too many doting women had spoiled him. This one...ah, this one, tested his confidence. Good. Very good. "So you are a policeman, like our Nicky?" she quizzed.

"Actually, no." Alexandra wondered at the pleased expression on Sophia's face. "I'm a—"

"Civilian employee, Mama," Nick quickly interjected. "Alexandra does counseling work."

"Oh, I see," his mother murmured, when in fact she did not quite perceive Alexandra's nondescript position at Central at all. The musicians began to play again and Sophia couldn't help but notice the tap of Alexandra's fingers upon the table. "You like our music?"

"Yes, very much," Alexandra said without thinking.

"Then, you should dance." Sophia cast a reproachful look at her son. "Nicky, you teach her the steps."

"No, really..." She tried to politely refuse.

"It's very simple. Nicky is a fine dancer." Sophia was determined that she be assimilated into their culture.

Knowing his mother's tenacity, Nick swiftly came to Alexandra's rescue. "Believe me, the dance will be less painful than Mama's badgering," he whispered as he helped her up from the bench.

"I can't do this," she protested beneath her breath as his arm tightly encircled her waist.

"Sure you can. Put your arm around my back." He caught her wrist and locked it in place about his waist. "Put your hip to mine." He pressed his close against hers. "Raise your free arm like so." He lifted his and crooked his elbow. "And follow me." He took several smooth strides to the left, dipped their bodies slightly, and then kicked spritely with his opposite foot. "To the right," he instructed, repeating the same procedure. "Again to the left," he coaxed. "Great, you're a natural," he said, laughing.

Soon she was really into the music and synchronized perfectly with Nick's every motion. Zorba the Greek had nothing on them. They glided about the pavilion, arm in arm, she concentrating on the dance, he gazing at her lovely profile when she was unaware.

"This isn't so bad, is it?" he cajoled.

"Am I doing it right?" She made the mistake of meeting his smoldering eyes.

"Yeah, sugar. You're doing fine." His warm tone made the compliment seem like a caress.

She missed a step. "I like your family. They're very..."

"Greek," he supplied with a smirk, amending his stride for her clumsiness.

"I was going to say that they're very genuine. If you had any idea how introverted and artificial my relatives are, you'd realize how refreshing it is for me to mingle with yours."

"They're impressed with you, too." He refrained from admitting how smitten he was. "I'm glad you're having a good time this evening. I wanted you to see what I was all about." She slanted him a dubious look. "It could be useful during my therapy," he smoothly amended.

"It has occurred to me that the dichotomy between such a secure background and a sometimes volatile vocation has to be difficult for you."

He looked over at his parents. Sophia sat upon Demetrius's lap. He was patting her well-endowed rump in tempo with the music while she was beaming as though she were a giddy bride. After all these years, the fire still burned within them. That was special indeed. "I stay in touch with them just to keep everything in balance." A wistfulness crept into his eyes.

"Everybody clings to something, Nick. It's different for each of us. For some it's roots, others it's faith, and for a few it's just a glimmer of hope." She spoke from personal experience.

"What helps you get through, Alexandra?" The music had ended, yet his arm lingered about her waist.

"You wouldn't understand if I told you, Nick."

"Try me." His dark eyes lacked their usual mockery.

"Only if you promise that you'll leave it at what I say and never refer to it again." The stipulation was not negotiable.

"Okay," he readily agreed.

"A remnant of pink ribbon—that's what gets me through another day." She had no idea what prompted her to confide such a sensitive detail of her life, ambiguous though it was.

He made no comment, though it was on the tip of his tongue to mention the scrap of grogram he had found beneath her pillow the night he had stayed at the penthouse. He'd given his word to accept her disclosure without question. Yet his mind was abuzz with possibilities.

She eased from his hold. "Your mother is watching us very intently. I don't want her to jump to the wrong conclusion."

Chords from a mandolin offered a perfect excuse for him to reclaim her. He whipped a handkerchief from his pocket and gave her a coaxing smile. "Come on, take an end. You'll enjoy this folk dance. Everyone is linked by a scarf in a big circle."

She couldn't help but return the smile. His earthy enthusiasm was contagious. "I'm making a fool of myself," she complained.

Nick knew better. He was the one who was behaving like a fool. Why couldn't he get this woman out of his system? He captured her hand and placed an end of the hankie in her palm, then closed her fingers about it. "Hold tight," he instructed, drawing her into the circle of dancers behind him.

She did as he bid—she held tight to him—for slowly, surely, he was becoming necessary to her, even though she had yet to acknowledge, let alone admit, his subtle specialness.

CHAPTER ELEVEN

SEVERAL DAYS PASSED before Alexandra saw Nick again. He'd made a concerted effort to keep his distance, but a desperate need to see her finally got the better of him one afternoon and he extended an impulsive lunch invitation.

He looked atypically haggard and she wondered if perhaps the recurring nightmare wasn't taking its toll on him. She wanted to give him every opportunity to talk out his problem. If it meant having Coney Islands in an unmarked squad car, so be it.

"You want onions?" he asked, reaching into his pocket to pay the vendor.

"I'll pass," was her distracted reply as she observed a mother and daughter at play in the park across the street. The child was blond and precious. From a distance she looked like Jenny.

"Cute kid," he commented when noting the object of her concentration.

"Yes," was all she answered before quickly turning away from the sight and climbing inside the squad car.

Nick wisely decided not to pursue the subject. Sliding behind the wheel, he switched on the squawk box.

"Sorry about the chatter but I'm in service," he explained, passing her one of the steamed hot dogs.

"No problem," she assured him, though the staticky dispatches were a nuisance. She peeled back the tissue paper and nibbled the Coney. Since spying the towheaded child her appetite had deserted her.

"You're in a brooding mood. Bad day?" He balanced a can of Coke on the dash. Contrarily, he was super hungry and devoured half the Coney in two bites.

Alexandra shrugged. "Not especially. I'm just preoccupied. I've a difficult session later today." It was easier to assign her soberness to work-related causes than tell the truth.

"You take your patients too seriously. Cops are survivors by nature, sugar. They may not be well-adjusted but they're resilient. You can't let 'em get to you." He finished off the Coney and gulped a swig of Coke.

"Certain cases are more personal than others," was all she answered.

"How do you classify me—a stock case or more personal?" He was trying to trap her.

She passed him what was left of her Coney. "I'm not sitting here whiling away my lunch hour because I have a fetish for squad cars, Nick. Which brings us to the point. Is this a social lunch or did you have something particular on your mind? Judging by the circles under your eyes, you haven't been sleeping well. Is it the nightmare again?"

Nick wondered how she would react if he told her the truth—that since the festival he hadn't slept a night through because he couldn't stop thinking of her, and that he couldn't handle this *platonic* rubbish much longer. He tossed the Coney she'd shared into the paper bag between them, wiped his mouth with a napkin, and scoffed, "I had some late dates and the ladies were demanding. I usually wear better than this."

She bristled at his words. "If that's the truth, I'm sure the last thing you need is my input."

"Why are you getting so huffy?" he needled. "I thought it was part of the package to be able to discuss whatever I wanted."

"It's not part of the package to spend my free time listening to your sexual escapades," she snapped. "Damn it, Nick! I'm tired of being manipulated. It's time we got something straight between us. I am not your buddy. I am not a prospective lay. I'm your analyst. And either you accept me as that and cooperate or—"

"Hush, Alexandra." Lightning quick his palm clamped over her mouth as he leaned closer to the squawk box to catch a garbled message.

"Affirmative, three-Baker-nine. Three previous armed robbery convictions on one Orey Louis Nader. No outstanding warrants. SWAT team asks that you confirm location and advise the number of hostages at risk."

"United Savings and Loan... 1200 block of Galvez Street," came the reply. "Exact number of hostages unconfirmed at this time. Only one demand issued by suspect so far—that there be no attempt to secure the building or a hostage will be executed."

"Clear, three-Baker-nine. We have help on the way."

Nick's hand dropped from her agape mouth. His features set like granite as he started the squad car and peeled away from the curb. "Fasten your seat belt," he instructed. "I don't intend to miss this going away party. Orey Nader's pulled his last heist."

She buckled up and braced herself as he accelerated. "Is this Orey Nader dangerous? Would he harm those hostages?"

"He's a three-time loser. And in a flat minute." The speedometer's needle climbed. Nick almost shaved a delivery van as he swerved around it.

"Why is it necessary for you to respond? Isn't this the SWAT team's responsibility?" She winced as he turned a corner sharply. The squad car's wheels screeched.

"We're in the vicinity. Patrol needs a backup. And we're it, sugar. Besides, I wouldn't want you to miss a golden opportunity like this. Here's a chance to reason with a hardened criminal type. Let's just see how effective all that shrink mumbo jumbo is when you're dealing with a bona fide deviant."

She lurched forward at his sudden braking but said nothing as he slowly cruised into the parking lot of the bank and then strategically angled the squad car aft of the patrol unit.

"Stay low in the seat and slide out on my side." In one fluid motion, he opened the door, eased from behind the wheel, and crouched at the front fender. "He alone?" he asked of the uniformed officer who squatted at the rear of the cruiser.

"As best I can tell. Where the hell's the SWAT boys?"

"Take it easy. They'll be here. Fill me in on how this went down." Stavos checked over his shoulder to be sure Alexandra was obeying orders as she made her way to his side.

She was sufficiently stooped. She was also as edgy about the situation as the inexperienced rookie.

"Somebody inside must've pressed the silent alarm. It's accidently been activated twice before. I figured it was another foul-up and cruised by to check it out. Only this time it was for real and this Nader character made me. Next thing I know he appears at the door, holding a gun to a teller's head and telling me to back off or he'll waste as many as he can before buying it himself. This is a first for me, Sergeant. What was I supposed to do?"

"Exactly what you did, kid," Nick assured him. "Nader isn't bluffing. This is a fourth offense and he figures it's a guaranteed life sentence. I doubt he's in a charitable mood. You got a bullhorn in the cruiser?"

"Yes, sir."

"Get it and we'll give the lady shrink a crack at him."

The young patrolman did as instructed, passing the bullhorn to Alexandra with a warning. "He's pretty wired, ma'am. You'd better choose your words carefully."

"I'll try to be tactful, Officer." It was Stavos's smirk, not the patrolman's advice, that prompted the caustic reply.

"Okay. It's your big moment, sugar. But I wouldn't stand up to introduce myself if I were you."

She could do without Nick's sarcasm. What's more, her back was breaking from trying to squat in high-heeled shoes. It was all his fault that she was even in this predicament. Only with Stavos could an afternoon deteriorate so rapidly. She switched on the bullhorn and brought it to her lips.

"Orey Nader. Listen, please. I know you feel that you're in a desperate situation but it doesn't have to end in bloodshed. You're only making matters worse by holding innocent people hostage. Resorting to violence isn't the answer. Talk to me. Together we can try to reach some sort of compromise."

"Yeah, who the hell are you, sister? And why should I trust anything you got to say?" was the terse shout from a second-story window.

"He wants credentials, sugar. I'm sure he's gonna be real impressed by your Ph.D." Nick sat back on his haunches, patiently awaiting her next attempt.

"Will you butt out?" she snapped. "The last thing I need is your snide remarks."

"Sure," he obliged, offering a mute but exaggerated gesture for her to proceed.

"My name is Alexandra Vaughn. I'm a psychologist, Mr. Nader."

"Mr. Nader," Nick mocked. "Nice touch. That ought to feed his deranged ego. Next he'll be demanding that we call him sir."

She ignored his words.

"My only stake in intermediating is to convince you that this course of action you've undertaken is futile.

No one will benefit and someone could be badly hurt. I know it wasn't your intention to harm anyone. Surely you realize that by threatening to shoot those employees you hold at gunpoint you only make the situation more critical. The police will have no choice but to use force.''

"Let 'em try. I guarantee ya that I won't be the only one buying it today. If they send me back to the joint, it's life for me, sister. I'd rather be dead. I ain't spending another hour in that hellhole. If you think I'm jiving ya, I'll prove how serious I am and waste one of these flakes.'' Nader sounded adamant about carrying out his threat. "Unless the heat gives me space and a plane to Havana, it's gonna be a turkey shoot in here. It better happen quick, too, 'cause I'm getting real sick of baby-sitting this bunch of parasites.''

"You have to trust me, Orey. It'll take time to arrange to meet your demands. I need assurances from you, too," she stalled, hoping to God the SWAT team would arrive on the scene any moment.

"Like what?" Nader hollered back.

"I want to know if all the hostages are unharmed at present, the exact count of how many are with you, and then I want your word that you'll not do anything rash while the authorities are considering your demands. It's a tense situation for all of us, Orey. You must remain calm and be reasonable.''

"Oh, that's rich, sister. Remain calm when the heat's just itching to blow me to kingdom come?" His tone hardened. "You tell 'em they got one hour. That's reasonable. I ain't gotta assure you of nothing but one thing—that I'll kill 'em one by one unless the cops do like I say. I mean it. No more talk. You either come through or they're history."

Nick had heard all he needed to make up his mind as to how to proceed. He was well versed in the ruthlessness of the Orey Naders of this world. There was no question that the punk would sacrifice the hostages at the slightest excuse. The only thing vermin like Nader respected or understood was a threat greater than they themselves imposed.

He glanced at Alexandra and felt a pang of compassion for the bewilderment he perceived in her eyes. Once he, too, had believed such senseless violence could be avoided. But he had learned the hard way that there were circumstances beyond control, people beyond reason. He was convinced that the current crisis was such a circumstance and Orey Nader was such a vile individual. He was over the brink—a madman—and he'd have no compunctions about killing those he kept as insurance for a freedom he would never be granted.

"Give me the bullhorn, Alexandra." Nick's voice conveyed an eerie finality.

"Why? What are you going to do?" Instinctively she sensed his intent.

"I'm damn sure not going to ask if he wants pizza sent in." He pulled the magnum from his shoulder holster.

Her fingers tightened on the bullhorn. "Don't, Nick. You're going to make an explosive situation impossible. Wait for the SWAT team. They should be here any moment now.'' Minutes had stretched into an eternity.

"I won't waste time explaining myself. You tried and the punk's not given any indication of budging from his demands. Trust me, Alexandra. Whatever I do is the only hope those people have. It's a standoff. Police policy makes no concessions for first-class tickets to Havana.''

"Surely we could offer him something, a reduced sentence or possibly an early parole..."

Nick snatched the bullhorn from her grip. In vain, she fought to reclaim it. He fended her off, bellowing, "Tell you how it is, lowlife. Either you come out, hands up and empty, or you're gonna have to go through me to make it to Cuba. There're no trade-offs, except one—let the hostages go and you won't end up on a slab in the morgue with your toe tagged.''

Alexandra looked to the rookie patrolman for help. He was ashen and bug-eyed. No assistance would be forthcoming from him. Forgetting herself, she partially stood while struggling with Stavos for the bullhorn. "You're crazier than I thought. Stop this insanity, Nick. Give me a chance to reason with him. You're gambling with innocent lives. How are you going to rationalize this?'' she accused.

Grabbing her elbow, he all but slung her to the ground. "I told you to stay down. Do you want to get your head blown off?'' His swarthy features had hardened and there was no mistaking the steely resolve glinting in his eyes.

"Hey, big-mouth cop,'' the suspect yelled. "You got no smarts. No way you can take me before I—''

"I'm not interested in what a big, bad man you are, Orey. You want to kill those people, it's your funeral, too." The bullhorn served to magnify Nick's earnestness. "I'm invincible, lowlife. You'll be mine eventually. And you'll wish you'd never tangled with me."

"Nick!" Alexandra clutched his jacket as he made a motion to forsake the cover of the squad car. "Are you mad? For God's sake, if you won't think of yourself, consider the safety of those poor people trapped upstairs." Her eyes pleaded for him to abort the suicidal attempt.

"You can't deal with amorals like him. Believe me, I've tried before and I never make the same mistake twice. Keep your head down and don't interfere again," he snarled, jerking free from her staying grasp. "Not again...not again," he vowed beneath his breath before making a zigzag dash across the parking lot to a drive-through teller's booth a few yards away from the rear door. He straight-armed the magnum and took careful aim at the bank's door. "Okay, lowlife. We can make this easy or messy. Whatever way you want it," he taunted.

It was difficult to tell who was more shaken, the rookie or Alexandra. They both held their breath and watched the potentially deadly scenario unfold.

At the sudden but distinguishable unbolting of the rear door, Nick's finger on the trigger tensed. To his relief, Nader cried out, "Don't shoot. I'm clean and coming out."

Alexandra nearly wilted at the sounds of surrender. Drawing on some last reserve of strength, she managed to raise herself from behind the squad car's protective fender as the rookie ran to assist Stavos in handcuffing the suspect.

Utter chaos claimed the parking lot as the SWAT team arrived in police vans and eight hysterical hostages filed out of the Savings and Loan. Alexandra stayed at her post—too drained to be of any immediate assistance and too furious with Nick to risk a public condemnation of his reckless act. She'd seen the awe in the rookie's eyes. Now she was having to witness the teary praise and displays of gratitude being bestowed upon Stavos by the liberated hostages. It was too much to endure. Some might think Sergeant Stavos's actions were heroic; she believed them to be idiotic. Her anger mounted when overhearing the rookie's account of the incident to the SWAT supervisor.

"He was something. Cool as you please. He bluffed Nader into believing his minutes were numbered. It was the damnedest thing I've ever seen. I swear it was like something straight out of a Dirty Harry movie."

That tore it! Next she expected to hear the idolizing rookie compare Stavos to Rambo. Were all these people blind? Couldn't they recognize a rash act when they saw it? Stavos had fully intended to eliminate Nader and it didn't matter to him who got in the way. She retreated to the car and sat stewing while he took great satisfaction in predicting a bleak future for Orey Nader.

"It's gonna be bars and stripes forever, Orey. Be sure to give my regards to our mutual acquaintances, won't you?"

Handcuffed in the back seat of the cruiser, Nader's only reply was a vicious kick against the screen that imprisoned him.

Nick grimaced, turned his back, and sauntered over to the squad car. "Sorry about the detour."

The glib apology only served to ignite her short fuse. "I'm late. If you're finished playing hero, I'd like to get back to Central." She focused straight ahead.

Not exactly in a good mood himself, Nick muttered a curse and peeled from the parking lot. His adrenaline was pumping double-time and his mind was rehashing memories he desperately wished to forget.

Alexandra's disgust escalated as they drove along. Midway to Central, she could no longer restrain herself. "What on earth did you think you were doing back there?" she exploded. "How could you be so rash? I'm going to report you. I intend to reveal you for the hothead that you are!"

Alexandra's righteous attitude chafed Nick sorely. No longer could he contain the fury that burned like a raw ulcer in his gut. "I surrendered to their demands once," he admitted tightly. "I handed over my gun and watched them blow my partner away. You think I'm crazy? Great! I don't give a damn what you think, Doc. It's all fine and dandy for you to make a judgment." He slammed on the brakes as a car suddenly pulled in front of them. "Your butt isn't on the line... you don't have to suffer the consequences. Bobbie did. We were working undercover together and they made her. They knew she was the heat. And they knew I was her backup. They told me to throw down my gun...said they'd spare her if I cooperated. Never in my life was I more torn. My gut told me not to do it. My heart said I should. I did. I showed 'em weakness. And they aimed and blew a hole the size of my fist through Bobbie. She died in an abandoned warehouse on the wharf...in my arms. Don't quote me procedure. Don't give me your liberal garbage. It was quick and over for Bobbie. I'm the one who can't deal with what happened. I'm the one who wishes to God he hadn't given in to their demand. My partner might still be alive. I should've trusted my instincts. I should never have surrendered my advantage." He swallowed hard and twined his fingers tighter about the steering wheel.

The doe, the blood on his hands, the nightmare from which there was no respite. Alexandra suddenly understood. "Nick, I'm so sorry." She reached out to him and felt him flinch. "You mustn't punish yourself like this. You're not to blame."

"The hell I'm not," he insisted. "You don't know what you're talking about...you've never been on the streets...you didn't know Bobbie. You never risked your tail to make a bust or cradled a comrade's body and tried to blow a breath of life back into her. Don't preach to me about after-the-fact rationale. I don't want to hear it. I don't want your digging into my subconscious anymore, either. Yeah, I got a grudge. Yeah, I'm not ever going to surrender to some punk's demands again. Yeah, I'm crazy and you're so smart...so damn together. I don't know whether I want to shake or slap that opinionated logic right from your oh-so-objective mind."

"You were in love with her, weren't you?" The question slipped out before Alexandra could check herself.

His placid expression did not betray him. "We were partners. Don't try to make something out of nothing. We backed each other up, that's all. Bobbie's dead and I'm still breathing—still an obnoxious SOB. But I'm never surrendering my gun again. I don't want the doe's blood on my hands. You got that?" He shot a quick but piercing look in her direction.

For the first time since they'd met, Alexandra truly comprehended Nick Stavos. "Okay, Nick," she said quietly. "Let's drop it for now."

"Good," he agreed, driving like a maniac along the narrow streets.

A strained silence loomed between them for the remainder of the ride back to Central. Alexandra longed to say something consolatory but the proper words failed her at the moment. She realized that they had only scratched the surface of Nick's suppressed grief and misplaced guilt. Though he had readily and wrongly assumed responsibility for his partner's death, he stubbornly refused to accept the severe trauma he had suffered because of it. How ironic it was that, like her, he should be doing penance for a deplorable act that from the outset had been beyond his control. Oh, yes, she understood Nick Stavos better than he would ever know.

After parking the squad car in the garage and turning off the motor, Nick sat motionless. "I suppose you still plan to report me for using excessive force today?'' It was not a plea for leniency; merely an attempt to ascertain her intent.

"You did what you thought was necessary.'' She pretended not to notice the sigh he expelled. "We had a difference of opinion. Case closed, except for the fact that you're expected in my office at ten tomorrow morning.'' Armed with new insight and a renewed commitment, Alexandra felt encouraged about Nick's positive prognosis.

"You never give up, do you?'' He slanted her an exasperated look.

"In a word—no.'' She flashed him a confident smile. "It's been an interesting lunch, Sergeant.''

His eyes followed her graceful motion as she walked across the garage and then disappeared inside the elevator. She definitely had class, he mused. She also had one terrific body.

"Hell, get it together, Stavos. A doe or a dame— what's the difference? They're both an illusion.''

CHAPTER TWELVE

AS CIRCUMSTANCES WOULD HAVE IT, Nick's appointment with Alexandra had to be postponed. At ten the following morning they were both summoned to Chief Oliver's office with no explanation as to the reason for the last-minute subpoena.

Nick assumed the worst and decided that Alexandra had reneged on her promise not to report him. He wasn't particularly civil as they sat with the dour secretary while the chief concluded a previous appointment.

"You're unusually quiet," she noted.

"What did you expect, appreciation?" was his surly comeback.

She misinterpreted his meaning. "If you're having regrets about confiding in me yesterday, it's too late for a retraction. But I can assure you that whatever you told me is confidential, Nick."

"That's gracious of you, considering the fact that you couldn't wait to put me on report." His eyes held disgust as they skimmed her person.

"I did no such thing," she professed a bit too loudly. Realizing that their hushed bickering had caught the attention of the secretary, Alexandra held her tongue.

"Yeah, well, then why are we both cooling our heels in the chief's office?" he speculated.

"How should I know?" was the exasperated reply as Chief Oliver's voice came over the intercom.

"Send Sergeant Stavos and the lady in," he commanded.

The lady. She had yet to be acknowledged—to have a name or significance at Central.

At the secretary's nod, Stavos muttered beneath his breath, "Maybe he just wants to personally commend us on yesterday's collar. Try to act humble, won't you?"

She ignored him and strode through the private door.

At the sight of all the brass gathered in the room, Nick immediately surmised that the high-echelon assemblage was of a serious nature.

"Take a seat, Miz Vaughn." Chief Oliver wasted no time on amenities. "You, too, Stavos," came the gruff afterthought.

Nick locked gazes with his immediate superior, Lieutenant Troutman. His edginess was apparent at a glance. Something critical was on the agenda to be discussed.

Oliver slung aside a file, leaned back in his overstuffed chair, steepled his fingers, and slowly surveyed the ex-narc and lady shrink. "Daily I think about resigning. What's your opinion, Miz Vaughn? Is that abnormal?"

She was stunned by the absurd question. "Pardon, sir?"

He dismissed her and looked at Stavos. "There's been another snatching in Brechtel Park and word was leaked to the press. You know what that means. It means I got to give the scavengers facts and answers. Answers I don't have. Now, what I need to know from you is, how come I don't have any answers?"

Nick was not intimidated by the chief's ominous tone. "I've been doing my best. There's not much to go on. These are street kids, Chief. Nobody pays any attention to 'em until they become a headline."

"They didn't just evaporate, Stavos." Oliver's eyes cut back to Alexandra. "I ask for answers and they give me excuses," he bitched. "You once claimed that you could be of assistance in solving cases. Well, I think the time has arrived for you to act as a consultant, Miz Vaughn. I want a psychological profile on the person or persons responsible for these snatchings. I want to narrow the field of suspects from the entire population of New Orleans to a mere hundred or so stereotyped deviants."

Though what he suggested was a monumental task, she accepted the challenge. "I'll need access to all the investigative reports."

"Stavos will supply whatever you think is necessary." His gaze shifted to Nick. "The latest kid to go missing is Hispanic. Whoever our deviant is, he's not prejudiced." Chief Oliver entrusted the most recent M.P. report into Nick's hands. He opened the manila folder and glanced over the all-too-familiar facts.

Roberto Sanchez.
Male, Hispanic. Age: 14.

Parents: Miguel and Rosa. Father's resident status revoked for smuggling charges, deportation pending. Mother currently unemployed.
Suspected member of the Low Riders gang. One arrest for public disorder. Suspended sentence.
Last seen in the vicinity of Brechtel Park at approximately 11:00 a.m. on September 5. Eyewitness, Antonio Reynas, states he observed Sanchez conversing with another youth near the southside entrance but cannot positively ID said youth.

It wasn't much of a lead but it was something at least. Nick had a gut feeling—nothing he could explain—that the unidentified youth was a key to the puzzle.

"The press wants my hide and I want this creep, Nick. Sleep standing up. Eat on the run. Stay after it until you find those kids and book the bastard." Oliver accentuated his frustration by pounding his first on the desk. "Nobody makes my department look bad . . . nobody," he reiterated.

Nick took his cue. Oliver's rampages were all bluster and no substance. The seasoned sergeant knew that if it came right down to it, Oliver *would* gladly resign to save face at the expense of the kids. "I'll supply the answers if you'll just guarantee me a free hand," he said matter-of-factly. "My methods aren't exactly by the book."

"No kidding," Oliver scoffed. "Whatever it takes, Stavos. Just settle this mess," was the blanket permission.

Alexandra followed Nick's retreat through the private door and into the outer hall. Somehow it didn't surprise her when he suggested that they go for a walk and discuss the summit meeting that had just occurred.

"All right," she agreed, feeling the need for a breath of fresh air herself.

As they strolled out of Central and along the bustling street, Alexandra's mind drifted to thoughts of Jenny. It was so very difficult for her not to make a comparison between her daughter and the street urchins. As much as Jenny was loved and sheltered, she had not been spared the same fate as these poor unfortunate children. Was there some reason, Alexandra wondered, that circumstances had dictated she should assist on this case? Or was it merely cruel irony?

"You do realize that was all hype back there." Nick's voice broke in on her reverie.

"I'm not sure I understand what you're implying." She double-stepped to keep abreast with his long strides.

"Oliver doesn't give a damn about those kids. All he cares about is his sweet ass." Typically Nick didn't mince words.

"But you do." She hadn't meant to sound flip but after being treated like an unwanted stepchild in Oliver's office, she wasn't inclined to be overly indulgent of male egos.

"Yeah, I do," he answered simply. "I could use your help on this one, sugar. If we're half as compatible in the trenches as we are in the bedroom, maybe, just maybe, we'll come up with something vital.'' He took her arm as they crossed the street. It bothered her the way his casual touch both warmed her flesh and made her heart quicken.

"I'm amazed. I was convinced you'd decided that my shrink mumbo jumbo hadn't any real merit. Since when have you changed your opinion?" She couldn't resist the dig.

"Since I've gotten to know you," was his flat reply.

"Are you basing this newfound appreciation on a professional or personal level?" she pressed.

"Both," he qualified.

She didn't quite know how to respond. It took her a minute to collect herself. "Then you do trust my ability. It's just my discretion that you question." She was still smarting from his earlier indictment of her character.

"I jumped to the wrong conclusion," he admitted. "I apologize, okay? Let's not make a federal case out of it."

"Oh, I think the issue is a pertinent one," she persisted. "Don't partners have to trust each other implicitly?"

"Just because we're teaming up on the Brechtel Park snatchings, doesn't make us confirmed partners, sugar."

His ambiguous reply really irritated her. Mulishly she stopped short in the middle of the sidewalk.

"Geez," he muttered when discovering she had lagged behind. "Now what's the matter?"

"It's simple, Nick," was her terse reply. "I'm fed up with your unwillingness to commit yourself. You refuse to cooperate with me both as a patient and as a peer. I don't know if you've somehow come to equate trust with vulnerability because of a tragedy that occurred at an abandoned warehouse or if you just naturally prefer alienation."

"Why do we always keep going back to the warehouse? You're hung up on it." Firmly his hand clamped her elbow, towing her reluctant figure up the street. "We're making a spectacle out of ourselves. Can't you walk and argue at the same time?"

She flashed him a scathing look at the nasty crack. "I'm not hung up on it. You are. And we're going to keep going back to that night at the wharf until you admit it."

"Admit what! My partner got wasted because I made a gross error in judgment. I trusted the word of a filthy dope peddler." She felt the bite of his fingers into her flesh.

Though she realized that her dogged pursuit of the truth was excruciatingly painful to Nick, she gambled that the risk she undertook was worth the animosity he felt toward her at this crucial moment. "Admit the real reason that you've chosen to be a loner," she hounded. "Admit that you loved your partner and that a part of you died with her."

He slowed his pace. "Why is it so important for you to know? What difference does it really make?"

It was a loaded question. Somewhere deep down she knew her reasons weren't totally objective. The psychologist wanted answers, wanted to restore the sensitivity in a good man, wanted to salvage a fine cop; the woman wanted to satisfy a morbid curiosity, wanted to understand a past that infringed on the present. "It just is," she insisted.

He walked without answering for a minute or two. Nick Stavos had pride. Nick Stavos had regrets. Nick Stavos had a secret ache that no amount of booze or fast women could expel. Finally he spoke. "Yeah, I suppose I did love her. Bobbie was special. Real special. For the longest time I wouldn't even admit it to myself. It would've complicated everything. She was a cop first, a woman second. I was her partner first, her lover second. I knew it. I accepted it. It was the way things were."

He walked and talked automatically. "We were a good team, Bobbie and I. But I didn't want a wife as a backup. I couldn't have handled Bobbie constantly being in the midst of the heat and she wouldn't have given it up for the world. So I kept my feelings to myself. We made cases. We made love. But we never made a commitment."

"Why did you deny the intimacy that existed between you two when I questioned you yesterday?" Alexandra wanted to understand his reluctance to face the truth.

"I suppose because I'd made a habit out of denying my love for Bobbie. Once and only once, did I express my feelings." His footsteps halted and he stood staring off in the distance as if reliving the moment.

She patiently waited for him to explain.

"It was when she was dying in my arms," he reminisced. "I knew it'd take a miracle to save her. And,

Lord, I was praying." His voice broke and he swallowed hard before continuing. "I kept telling her she'd be all right, but she wasn't fooled for a second. Bobbie had a sixth sense. She also had the most crystal-clear blue eyes I'd ever seen. They could see through to your soul. No one ever conned her. No two-bit punk and certainly not me." He looked into Alexandra's eyes, realizing they were a different color but noting a certain similarity.

"Once and only once," she cued.

"'Tell me the truth,' she asked of me. I thought she meant for me to be honest about her chances. 'Hold on... Don't bail out on me now. You're gonna make it,' I told her. She shivered, like she was never, ever gonna be warm again. I held her close...tried to share my body heat, my strength with her, but I could feel her slipping away. She smiled up at me and whispered, 'We've run out of time, Nick. Tell me quick. Tell me you love me.'"

His eyes squeezed shut at the memory. "'Yes,' I said. 'I love you, Bobbie. I have for so long.'" He paused, clearing his throat and opening his misty eyes. "It was when I kissed her lifeless lips that I realized she wasn't breathing anymore. I don't know if she even heard my answer."

He stood paralyzed by the memory, betraying tears trickling down his cheeks.

Alexandra felt responsible—felt such compassion for his anguish that she had to restrain herself from embracing him on a city sidewalk in broad daylight. "Come on, Nick. Let's go inside this café until you can pull yourself together," she suggested.

He was almost catatonic as she led him inside, steered him into a booth and ordered two coffees. She handed him a napkin to wipe his eyes, then reached out and gently squeezed his hand. "You've lived too long with a memory, Nick. It's over. You wanted to protect Bobbie at any cost. Your feelings for her probably influenced your decision to surrender your gun. What if you hadn't? What if you'd gone strictly by the book? Then what do you suppose would've happened?"

She relinquished his hand as the waitress served them.

"Don't you think I've asked myself that question a thousand times?" he said beseechingly. "I don't know... I don't know." He raked a hand through his hair and shook his head, as if to clear the fog that had permeated his senses ever since the tragic incident.

"Drink the coffee, Nick," she urged. "Do you want cream?"

"Naw. I take it straight, just like the Stolichnaya I drink to forget," he muttered.

"You can dull your brain but you can't escape the truth, Nick. If you had refused to give in to their demands, the end result would've most probably been the same. It was a no-win situation. Either way, both you and Bobbie were at the mercy of despicable people whose only values were the price of cocaine. What did you admire most about Bobbie?" She shoved his mug closer and sipped from her own.

"It's hard to say...." He took a swig and relaxed in the booth. "Maybe it was her easy style. She knew the score and handled herself well. In the beginning, I thought nobody could be that savvy. But gradually I realized she just had a natural feel for the streets. Maybe because she'd grown up the hard way and understood what made people tick. Sometimes she'd make me laugh when I wanted to scream. She had a way of looking at things objectively. Kind of like you," he ventured.

"I'm not a substitute, Nick."

"I know that, sugar," he concurred with a sad grin. "Don't get off on a tangent. Take it as a compliment."

She nodded. "You know what I think?" she asked, settling back and giving him a soft smile.

"No, but I'm sure you're going to tell me."

"I think the nightmare is going to cease," she predicted. "I believe you're finally free of the guilt you assumed. Bobbie knew the risks. You knew that she wouldn't have traded the excitement for you if you had forced the decision. She also knew you loved her. Only when there was no choice did she ask to be reassured. She did hear you, Nick. The words weren't even necessary."

He set aside the mug and gazed at her long and hard. "Probably not," he said with a sigh. "I gotta let go of it . . . gotta put Bobbie to rest."

"Yes, Nick, you do," she agreed.

"Do me one favor," he beseeched.

"Sure," she readily obliged.

"Don't ever tell anyone that I came apart. Cops aren't supposed to cry."

"Damn, Nick. You still don't trust me, do you?" She flipped over the check and rummaged in her purse for the correct change.

He placed a staying hand atop hers. "It's my insecurities. I'll pick up the tab."

"The hell you will," she protested, throwing money on the table and making a motion to desert him.

"Okay, okay," he said with an entreating look. "You get the check and I'm out of line."

"Yes, you are." Her chin lifted and her eyes blazed.

"I'm sorry. Why am I always telling you I'm sorry?" His repetitious contriteness really chafed him.

"Maybe because you're always putting your clumsy foot in your smart mouth." Her expression mellowed.

"Partners concede the good, the bad and the indifferent in each other," he put forth. "In this instance, maybe you're the good, I'm the bad and what's between us is indifferent."

"You never cease to amaze me with your remarkable rhetoric, Sergeant. Now and then you can be unpredictably clever."

"And once in a while you can be a royal—"

"Partner," she supplied with a coy tilt of her head, lifting her empty mug in a trucelike gesture.

He hesitated as though one small clink of pottery was significant. "Yeah, okay, Miss Baby Powder. We'll partner up, if you got the stamina," he challenged, tapping his mug against hers.

"Miss Baby Powder?" She'd caught the unintentional slip.

"From the time we first rode the elevator together I got this whiff of Johnson & Johnson's," he confessed. "I noticed because chaste and sweet talc isn't a fragrance most of the ladies I'm acquainted with wear. Tabu or My Sin is more their style. Maybe it has to do with pink ribbons," he ventured. "I got this feeling that you keep secrets, too."

"What else do you fantasize about, Nick?" Slickly she tried to divert him.

"Us taking nooner showers at my place," was the honest admission.

"I'm more of a leisurely bath girl. And I happen to prefer Johnson & Johnson's. Nothing quirky. Just my preference," she stipulated.

"Fine. Whatever you prefer." He respected both the lady's individuality and her resistance to a "no-win" situation.

LATER THAT NIGHT as Alexandra lay in bed twining the slip of grogram ribbon through her fingers, her mind traveled back to the café and the conversation with Nick.

A smile settled on her lips as she remembered his candid remark about his fantasy.

"A nooner shower," she mused aloud, mindlessly trailing the frayed end of the ribbon along her cheek. It was an intriguing thought. Totally out of the realm of possibility, of course, but intriguing nonetheless.

She rolled onto her side, tucked the scrap of ribbon beneath the pillow and closed her eyes.

But the image her mind had conjured up was vivid and exciting. So vivid that she could almost feel the slick texture of Nick's wet skin. So exciting that her breathing became irregular and labored.

Suddenly flushed, she kicked the sheet off, sat up in bed and checked the illuminated clock.

After midnight and she was wide awake.

She drew up her legs and rested her chin on her knees. Nick most likely was enjoying the first good night's sleep he'd known in months and she was insomniac and aroused. "Pleasant dreams, Sergeant," she muttered, falling back sprawled upon the rumpled sheets and sighing disgustedly. The newly established partnership was not ideal. Nor was whatever existed between them indifferent. No, not at all.

CHAPTER THIRTEEN

THE NEXT FEW WEEKS were beyond a doubt the most hectic and frustrating of both Nick's and Alexandra's lives. Sleep of any kind became a rarity. Occasionally they got a chance to catch a few hours, but even then they could not put the Brechtel Park case to rest.

Nick kept going over and over the statement Antonio Reynas had given him. He felt positive that Reynas possessed vital information but unless something triggered his memory it could be locked away in his subconscious forever.

"Think, Antonio," he'd prodded. "This kid that you saw talking with Roberto at the gate could be important. I need a name."

"I'm trying, man," the youth had whined. "He hangs out, ya know. I seen him in the park lots but he was just a face. I ain't even sure he was the same hombre."

"Can you describe him?" Nick had pressed.

"He's nothing special. Kind of tall and lanky. He's a gringo. I know that," Antonio had confirmed. "Like I said, it was late and dark and I wasn't into the scene. I had my own headaches. My mom, she gets bent out of shape about my irregular hours, ya know.

So I had it in high gear, trying to beat it home," he'd explained.

"I suppose the gringo wasn't a member of the gang, huh?" Nick had tried a more direct approach, hoping to shake the kid up a bit.

Antonio never budged from his original claim. "You're playing the wrong tune. Sure, Roberto wears the Low Riders colors, but it's an exclusive club. Brown skin only, man. The dude I saw is from around here, a local, okay, but not a honcho."

It had been another dead end. No description. No link. Just one more wild-goose chase. "Yeah, well, if you suddenly place this kid, give me a call." He'd written down his direct number on a scrap of paper and tucked it in Antonio's pocket. "This is heavy stuff. You get a flash, don't hesitate. Roberto could be in a world of trouble."

Antonio had promised to call if sudden recall struck him.

Two weeks later Nick still had received no word.

Two weeks later and Alexandra was still trying to narrow the suspects and pinpoint a plausible motive.

"Obviously it wasn't done for ransom money, but our suspect could've been for hire, Nick," she speculated as they sat in the squad room poring over the skimpy facts and throwing out ideas late one night.

"Get real, Alexandra. We're talking about people who can't even pay their rent. It makes no sense that the kids were snatched by a hired gun. Where on earth would these folks get that kind of cash and why would they do it? We checked it out. There's no fat insurance payoff at the end of the rainbow."

"I'm just trying to systematically eliminate any and every farfetched possibility," was her defensive reply.

"Well, forget it. I already went that route with Lucille Clover, Lacey Graham's aunt. There's no bucks in this for the families. Come up with something original, will ya?" Tired and testy, his patience was wearing thin.

"I'm doing my best. And I'd appreciate it if you'd stow the criticism," she snapped. "You haven't exactly been contributing a wealth of information either, Sergeant."

He shoved aside the empty food cartons remaining from their dinner and was on the brink of saying something really tactless when the phone jangled.

Glaring at her across the cluttered desk, he snatched up the receiver. "Detective Division. Sergeant Stavos speaking."

"Hey, it's Antonio," the thickly accented voice on the other end of the line greeted. "Remember me, man?"

It wasn't likely that Nick would forget him. "Yeah, you're a memorable fella, Reynas. What can I do for you?" He immediately came alert.

"You told me to get in touch if I could place the hombre. Well, I got it, man. I saw his picture in this morning's paper. You ain't gonna believe it."

Nick's stomach clutched. "Run it by me, Antonio."

"The dude you're looking to nail is Vinnie Stevens. You know, the same one who you've been beating the bushes to find. It was him, all right. I remember."

"You're sure?" Nick questioned, skeptical of Antonio's incredulous revelation.

"Yeah, man, I know him like I know my own mother. He was a regular at the park. Him and Roberto jived a lot. But I can't figure it. He's supposed to be a victim, ain't he? What's going down?"

"Good question, Antonio," Nick concurred. "Thanks for coming through."

"Sure, man. It's like the twilight zone. It gives me the willies." Reynas seconded Nick's precise thoughts before severing the connection.

"Who was it?" The tone of the conversation and Nick's stunned expression had Alexandra on pins and needles.

"Antonio Reynas, the eyewitness in the Sanchez case who couldn't positively ID the youth he'd seen talking to Roberto shortly before his disappearance," he informed her.

"He said something vital, didn't he? I can tell by the look on your face," she ventured.

"You won't guess in a million years who our mystery boy is."

"For heaven's sake, Nick. Will you give me a break and just tell me?" She was beside herself with curiosity.

"Vinnie Stevens. Ain't that a kick in the head? What do you make of it?"

She looked as dumbfounded by the startling news as Stavos. "I don't understand. This makes no sense. What's happening here, Nick?"

"Damned if I know." Nick deserted his chair and paced about in relentless circles. "Reynas recognized

Vinnie from this morning's paper. Your convincing Oliver to flood the media with the pictures and particulars about the kids paid off, Alexandra. As of September fifth, Vinnie Stevens was alive. So, what do we assume? That he's a runaway after all?''

"If so, why did he reappear in an area he was certain to be recognized in? And how do we explain his vanishing again? Quit pacing, Nick. You're making me dizzy." Her head was already spinning from the endless questions.

"Okay, let's look at this logically." Nick sat down in his chair again. "We know that Vinnie and Roberto were acquainted. Vinnie falls out of sight for a few months, then suddenly materializes and makes contact with Roberto, then they both disappear. We can assume there's a connection, right?''

"It would seem so," she agreed.

"But what about Lacey Graham? How does she fit in the puzzle? Have we got two runaways and a snatching? Or a trio of misfits on the run? We've got nothing that links her to Vinnie except the park. She's younger, a girl—she doesn't fit the pattern.''

"In a way, she does, Nick. All three are underprivileged and, from all indications, unwanted liabilities. Independent little creatures who, for the most part, it seems were left to their own devices. If we're conjecturing, why not assume that they somehow became bonded by their plight? Perhaps they decided to rely on one another since no one else took any interest." Alexandra knew the notion sounded preposterous. After all, they were discussing mere children—

two boys barely into their teens and one ten-year-old girl.

"What are you suggesting? That they made some kind of crazy pact and took off? The kids probably had ten bucks between them. How would they survive?" Nick had difficulty accepting her theory.

"You forget, Nick. These kids are resourceful. They're accustomed to taking care of themselves. Vinnie's been known to snitch money from his own mother. Roberto's familiar with evading the law. And I'll wager that Lacey knew how to conserve a penny and dispense care before the tender age of six. Separately they had no chance, but together, and with a little luck, they could pull this off, Nick."

He shook his head disbelievingly and leaned back in the chair. "Geez, it's possible," was his astonished mutter. "But where could they be holed up? With all the publicity somebody should've spotted 'em by now. And how in the hell are we going to go to the chief with this cockamamy theory and no proof?"

"We'll just have to bide our time. Stall, if we must. The media just began its campaign and already Reynas came forth. The kids are smart but they're no longer invisible. Sooner or later they'll make a mistake or be forced to risk exposure. Until then, we have no choice. We keep our suspicions to ourselves and wait for a break."

He stared at her, mulling over the proposal. "Don't you think that's a little risky? We could be wrong. I know you like to think you're Sigmund Freud reincarnated, but what if this once you've misdiagnosed the situation?"

"Okay, you tell me. What's our alternative?" She vacated the hot seat in an excuse of refilling their coffee mugs.

"The city's in a full-scale panic, convinced there's some demented snatcher on the loose, the media's fueling a fire beneath our beloved chief who is gonna have our hides if he should discover that we're holding out on him, and we're just gonna sit back on our thumbs and do nothing? Would you say that's a fairly accurate assessment of our position?"

"Yes," she said, passing him a cupful of steaming java and retaking her seat.

"That's what I thought," he grumbled, testing the bitter coffee and grimacing.

"What would we accomplish by going to the chief or the press with our suspicions? I doubt we'd get much support in either quarter. And in lieu of our farfetched theory what pertinent facts have we come up with thus far?"

"Zilch," he supplied.

"Exactly." Her point made, her blue-green eyes shone with resolve as they met his over the edge of the mug.

"Doesn't it bother you that we could be making a grave miscalculation?" he worried. "What if those kids aren't connected? Suppose we have three unrelated runaways on our hands? Or worse yet, what if there's a bona fide snatcher lurking around Brechtel Park?"

"Damn it, Nick! What do you propose we do instead? I can't come up with any distinct profile. You can't come up with a lead. Where does that leave us?"

She was too weary to debate the issue any further. The long tedious hours and strain showed on her fragile face.

He realized her limits. "Okay, I was only making sure you realized the consequences if this should backfire. And it can, sugar. Believe me. I've seen it happen time and again. We'll keep quiet for now, give it a chance and see if the media attention produces a line on the kids. But if nothing breaks we—"

"Not now, Nick. Please. I want to believe I'm right. I'm sick to death of going home night after night feeling negative and impotent." She hauled her stiff body from the chair and headed for the door.

"You want to stop off for a drink?" he offered, collecting his jacket from the coatrack and switching off the lights behind them.

"I'm not in the mood. I just need a good night's rest," she murmured.

"I'd be glad to follow you home and tuck you in nice and tight." Though the proposition was presented glibly, Nick's intentions were anything but.

"Thanks, but I gave up being tucked in tight about the same time I quit sleeping with my teddy bear. Good night, Nick," she bid him, disappearing down the corridor.

He felt a queer empathy for a cast-off teddy bear. The toy and he had something in common—they were both Alexandra's rejects. "Hold up, Alex," he called after her, lengthening his stride to catch up.

She turned around with a quizzical look.

"Reconsider about the drink," he urged. At her resigned sigh, he coaxed, "At least keep me company. I don't want to go home and drink alone. Unless I unwind a bit, I'll be up walking the floor most of the night, racking my brain and coming up with the same inconclusive garbage."

Since she had been suffering from the same syndrome, she relented. "Okay, Nick. If you promise that we'll go someplace quiet and close."

"I know just the spot," he assured her. "It's around the corner and like a church."

He hadn't lied. The bar was only a block away, cozy and virtually empty. They sat at a table in the rear, hidden from view and munching the complimentary popcorn. Not until the effects of the second glass of white wine had hit her did Alexandra realize how weary and utterly discouraged she actually was. She rotated her stiff neck trying to alleviate the nagging ache that throbbed between her shoulder blades.

Wordlessly Nick set aside his draft beer and rubbed the back of her neck, his fingers methodically massaging the tense muscles. "You're really uptight. Take some deep breaths and let 'em out slowly."

For once she did not argue, closing her eyes and following his instructions. "I'm glad I agreed to come with you," she murmured. "I haven't been sleeping well, either."

"It's a bitch, isn't it?" he sympathized, his hands clamping her shoulders and expertly rolling them beneath his adept palms. He could feel her relaxing beneath his fingertips.

She nodded and leaned into his massage.

"Sometimes it seems like everyone else in the whole world has someone to go home to," he continued.

"Someone in whom they can confide all their troubles and shortcomings without being afraid that they'll be labeled a wimp or be taken advantage of. Yeah, sometimes I even hate the sound of being alone. Every slight noise is exaggerated...." He smoothed a hand across her shoulder blades, then along her spine. "I remember that as a kid I used to take this shortcut home through a dark and dank tunnel," he reminisced. "There's something real spooky about the echo of solitary footsteps and the hollow ping of water drops in a deserted tunnel. They get louder and more eerie about midway through the passage. I used to get this panicky feeling... like I might get stranded in that musty tomb and never find my way out. I'd break into a run—sweating and panting and scrambling for home. Every time I made it through the tunnel I'd swear I'd never take the shortcut again. But even back then I was habitually late...." His fingertips slid up her neck, twining into her thick hair and massaging the base of her scalp.

"You haven't yet succeeded in amending your tardy ways," she interjected, her head lolling forward and backward with each divine surge and recess of his fingers through her hair.

"Yeah, well, I could have worse habits," he scoffed. "Hush and let me make my point, will ya?"

"Which is?" she prompted.

"Which is that sometimes it's tough to be alone. It's like being stranded in that damn tunnel—the sound of your own breathing is all you have for company. You want to talk but there's no one to listen. You want to feel some human warmth but there's only a vacant cold-water flat or a fancy but empty penthouse waiting for you. You want to unload the pressure but there's no release—not a soul to whom you can tell that you did your best and it wasn't good enough.''

Alexandra could relate to the bitter truths he spoke. She turned to him, an overwhelming sensation of commiseration seizing control of her. Without realizing it, she reached up and smoothed a rebellious lock of raven hair back from his temple. "I know, Nick. I've made a trip through the tunnel a time or two myself.''

"Yeah, I figured you had." He yearned for the brief caress to linger, but to his dismay she backed off. "We're partners only to a point, huh, sugar? We're teamed up for the Brechtel Park caper and that's the extent of it. We don't talk personal, except if it has to do with the case. That's a real shame. 'Cause I suspect we have more in common than just a burning desire to find those kids.''

She refused to admit the possibility. "I doubt that we do. We're very different people, Nick.''

He leaned back in his chair with a dissenting grunt. "Sure, we're different. I grew up Greek and rough. You're high society and prim and proper. What does it matter? Nobody knows better than me how you're feeling inside tonight. Right about now, you want to give it up, but you can't. Those missing kids have become an obsession. Their faces are engrained in your mind. You can't dismiss 'em at the end of a shift, can't accept that they're just another statistic. You care. You wish the hell you didn't, but you do. It's kind of like a one-sided love affair—futile and frustrating as hell."

At her patronizing smile, he shot her a bemused look. "Did I say something funny?"

She made a halfhearted attempt to smother her amusement. "Since you've always contended that women find you irresistible, I find your choice of an analogy most interesting, Sergeant. When have you ever experienced the anxiety of rejection?" She sipped the wine and scrutinized him over the edge of the goblet.

He frowned, swigging from the frosted beer stein, then wiped the foam from his lips with the back of his hand. "Losing a partner you adore isn't so different from divorcing a husband you once loved."

She instantly regretted the tactless remark. "I'm sorry, Nick. That was an insensitive thing for me to say."

"Bobbie didn't exactly jilt me, but when it came down to a choice between the force or becoming my wife, I lost out to the New Orleans Police Department." His manly pride felt it necessary to clarify the matter.

"Sometimes circumstances and choices are beyond our control. Unfortunately it doesn't make it any easier to accept though." Aimlessly she swirled the wine within the goblet, preoccupied by the shimmering spherical motion.

"Nobody likes to fail at anything—be it solving cases or maintaining relationships," Nick put forth.

She raised her eyes to his, noting a peculiar aura of entreaty within the brown orbs. "Please, don't look at me that way, Nick."

"What way?" His nonchalance was an act.

"Like if we were to share the sleepless hours in bed together, we'd both be able to cope better in the morning."

"Did I suggest it?" he said indignantly.

"You didn't have to. The implication is in your eyes and though I won't deny that the idea is tempting, it's also very foolish. It's a weak moment for us both. Let's not mistake a mutual need for some small token of satisfaction as anything deeper." She finished off the wine and reached for her purse.

He took hold of her wrist to prevent her from leaving. "For weeks we've shared our frustration and pooled our resources. Why is it wrong to admit our needs and borrow on each other's strength?" He wanted her, wanted her so badly that he was willing to humble himself.

She hadn't any solid argument against his reasoning. Why was he always so infuriatingly direct? "I can't handle anything intimate between us, Nick. Not again. The last thing I need is any more pressure...another responsibility. Please try to understand," she implored.

"Okay, Alexandra. I get the message. If my admitting my desire for you complicates your life, I'll back off."

His hand dropped from her wrist and he signaled for the check.

A sensation of relief mixed with a twinge of regret traveled over her. "You're not upset with me?"

He grazed a fingertip along her chin and eased her anxiousness with a wink. "I'm not real thrilled with your attitude, but I'll survive. Let's blow this joint. My mood isn't so sociable anymore."

Alexandra and Nick walked back to Central in strained silence. The vacated garage took on the same gloomy ambiance as the musty tunnel Nick had described. Their footsteps resounded off the concrete pavement and the echo of their perfunctory goodnight rang hollow. Alexandra understood the panic that Nick had earlier recounted. As she watched him walk away, it engulfed her. False pride and sheer willpower was all that kept her from rescinding her previous refusal and asking him to accompany her home.

SEVERAL MORE WEEKS PASSED and no sighting of the street urchins was reported. With each passing day Alexandra's confidence in her theory dwindled until finally she had no choice but to accept the bitter fact that she had drawn the wrong conclusion and foolishly persisted upon a reckless course. Worse yet, she had insisted that Nick go along with her risky presumption. He said nothing but she could tell he was uneasy. And with good reason. Chief Oliver was breathing down their necks for results and threatening to bust Nick's rank and send him back to foot patrol if he did not produce some soon. Alexandra could only guess at the fate in store for her. Probably excommunication from Central and exile in Connecticut.

Her private life was faring no better. All she received from Quincy Lucas, concerning the whereabouts of her daughter, was a negative status report and a monthly bill. The only bright spot in the dismal weeks had come when Margaret Flynn had announced she'd tendered her resignation from the force and had registered for classes as an archaeology major at a local college. By eventually admitting the resentment she harbored toward her deceased father, as well as the love she bore him, Margaret was at last emancipated from her father's expectations and was free to pursue her own aspirations. But even Margaret Flynn's amazing progress did little to bolster Alexandra's spirits or confidence.

Though Nick refrained from making any comment, he took heed of the drastic change in Alexandra's appearance and attitude. Day by day she grew more withdrawn and edgy. Her face had taken on a gaunt look and her eyes had a kind of perpetual glaze. Sometimes he'd watch her when her head was bowed over the reports and wonder what drove her to such a fervor. It had to be more than just wounded ego over a miscalculation in judgment, he surmised. It was almost as if she'd assumed sole responsibility for the street urchins and had made the Brechtel Park case into her own personal crusade. Every time the phone rang, she'd start and glance at him expectantly. And every time he shook his head, indicating it was a false alarm, she became more dejected. She arrived at dawn. She stayed until midnight—waiting for, willing a break in the case. Whenever he tried to persuade her to ease up and get away from Central and the constant stress, she'd stubbornly refuse. The tension never ceased. The situation was becoming intolerable. And Alexandra was becoming more and more obsessed.

Again they were stranded together in her private office after midnight. As usual, Alexandra seemed completely oblivious of his presence as she sat absorbed in the investigative reports, searching for some miracle. Nick knew better. Nothing new and nothing more could be gleaned from the typewritten sheets spread upon the desk. The time was fast approaching when they would have to face facts and the music. They'd blown it. If there had been some bizarre angle, they'd missed it because of concentrating their efforts on an ill-conceived theory. Maybe they'd been fooling themselves, looking for an easy out, something less gruesome than the prospect of child molestation or murder. He had been as willing as she to grasp at hope, to deny the grim alternative. Usually he was more realistic but Alexandra had seemed so convinced, so assured in her belief that the kids were alive and well. No more. It couldn't go on. For everyone's sake he had to force the issue and make Alexandra see the futility in continuing this farce.

"That's it. No more for tonight. We're going home, sugar." The creak of the chair as he vacated it made no impression upon her. She did not heed the scowl etched upon his face.

"There's got to be a link," she babbled. "It's here . . . somewhere. We're missing it. I'm convinced we're overlooking something important."

He'd had it with her martyr routine. Grasping her by the shoulders, he hauled her to her feet. "You're losing it, Alexandra. You're exhausted and going in circles. Pull yourself together, will ya? You can't do these kids any good if you can't think clearly."

She wrenched from his grasp, pacing about the office like a tigress. "I'm not giving this up...not tonight...not tomorrow...not until we find those kids."

"Do you hear yourself? You're beginning to sound irrational." He tried to phrase his objections as tactfully as possible.

His analysis stung. She was looking for an excuse on which to vent her frustration, and he was it. "Pardon me, but I believe I'm the one with the degree," she lashed out. "I don't think you're qualified to make a diagnosis, Sergeant."

His expression hardened. "Don't pull that Ph.D. garbage on me, Alexandra. I've got a hell of a lot more experience at this sort of thing than you," he retorted. "And I'm telling you that you're over the edge on this one. Those kids may be goners and we might just be spinning our wheels."

His voicing of her worst nightmare sent Alexandra into a tailspin. "Shut up and go amuse yourself somewhere else, Stavos. Whisper sweet nothings in some bimbo's ear if it makes you happy. I'm sick of your smug remarks. I'm fed up with your cynical cop intellect. And I'm really weary of your trite come-ons," she ranted.

"Is that a fact, sugar?" he snapped. "Well, I got a flash for you. Right now, I'm not real keen on you, either. Some partner you turned out to be. I didn't agree with you but I went along because you were so damned sure, so absolutely convinced you couldn't make a mistake. Well, looky here, will ya? Miss Baby Powder isn't ninety-nine and one-hundred percent pure. Not only doesn't she react like most warm-blooded women, but she can't even admit when she's screwed up a case royally.'' He was going for the jugular, regretting every syllable but lambasting her all the same.

"Don't say that." She began to sling paperwork wildly. "I didn't screw it up. I still believe those kids are alive. They are... I know it,'' she choked. Hysteria was fast overtaking her—the sleepless nights, the endless strain, a horrifying image of Jenny lying in some shallow grave flashing before her blurry eyes.

"Will you be reasonable?'' He saw the hurt, heard the stark fear. He didn't fully comprehend it, but he wanted so very much to share it. "We have no leads. There is no pattern. The kids range in age from ten to fourteen, both sexes, varied ethnic groups. The only common denominator is that they're all from the same rough neighborhood. We have to face the possibility that they may have been sexually assaulted, murdered or both. It happens, Alexandra.'' He stepped closer, sensing that she was on the verge of collapse.

"I won't accept it and don't you dare say it!'' Her hand cracked across his cheek, leaving a red welt that stunned them both. "Oh, God... oh, I'm so sorry, Nick.'' She stumbled backward a step, visibly trembling and gazing at him through bewildered, tear-filled eyes.

"It's okay, sugar," he tried to reassure her. "It's my fault. I pushed it. I deserved it."

"No...no," was her numb sob. "You're right. Oh, God, you're right. I am irrational, Nick. I can't cope anymore." Tears trickled down her cheek as she clutched her midsection and released a mournful moan.

He took her in his arms, lending his shoulder and strength as she sobbed uncontrollably. "What is it, Alexandra? I've known for a long time that there's something you hide. I'm not the insensitive louse I pretend to be." His fingers tangled in her hair, shaking loose the pins and slinking through the satin strands. "Tell me, sugar," he coaxed. "What can't you cope with any longer? Trust me, please, Alexandra. Let me help, if I can."

"It isn't just the street kids, Nick," she confessed, clinging to him as though he meant the difference between sanity and madness. And he did. At this moment she was drowning in a sea of despair. Nick Stavos was her anchor—someone steady upon whom she could rely—someone who could haul her up from the depths of despondency. "I have a daughter—a sweet, precious daughter. Her name is J-Jenny," she sobbed. He said not a word but conveyed his protectiveness by embracing her tighter. "She's missing, too, Nick. Someone took her from our yard over eighteen months ago. I am crazy...crazier than the people I treat. Why am I in the middle of this? I can't handle it. Children missing. Children at the mercy of someone who has no scruples...no compassion. Oh, Nick, I wanted so desperately to believe I was right ... that

nothing awful would befall those children." Her arms
encircled his neck and her body melded to his. He felt
every erratic breath she drew, every dirgelike beat of
her heart. "It was Jenny I was thinking of... praying
for. Nick, oh, Nick, please tell me she's alive...
reassure me it's possible... say you're wrong and I'm
right," she begged.

"Shhh, sugar," he crooned, brushing his lips along
her temple. "Of course, it's possible." His soothing
responses came automatically. He fought not to display his utter amazement. The news of any child's abduction was difficult for him to stomach, but the fact
that the little girl in question belonged to Alexandra
made it doubly difficult to assimilate. Though his
mind reeled from the startling revelation, he rallied
himself for Alexandra's sake. She needed a source of
support, encouraging words—someone to hold her
close and absorb a small fraction of her pain. It was
inconceivable to him that she had managed to hide
such anguish for so long. She truly was an extraordinary woman.

*Alexandra... a mother... a mother of a missing
child. Lord!* He thought of the numerous instances he
had made some asinine and disparaging reference regarding the fate of the Brechtel Park kids. Now he realized how deeply his cynical barbs must have cut. He
would give anything to mend the unintentional damage he'd inflicted.

His arms tightened around her, his mind desperately searching for some profound and heartening
thing to say. "I'm cynical. I admit it. But like you, I

want to believe that maybe, just maybe, things aren't as bad or as hopeless as they seem.''

Possessively, his hands tangled within her thick blond mane. "I'm taking you home, Alexandra. I'm going to lay beside you whether you give a damn or not. We're going to solve this case," he predicted. "And we're going to find your daughter. Don't give up now, sugar. Not when you've got an ally. We're partners. You're the good. I'm the bad. But no longer are we indifferent. There's Jenny between us. And I'll move heaven and earth to find her because I adore her mother," he vowed.

She gently pressed her fingertips to his lips, denying him any further expression of his devotion. "I shouldn't have told you about Jenny. I don't want your pity. I prefer your anger. When we disagree, argue heatedly, it keeps me stimulated, keeps me alive." She retreated from his arms, her look embarrassed, her mood apologetic.

"Whatever it takes, sugar," he said softly. "But I do have strong feelings for you, Alex, whether you want to accept it or not. I told you once I don't repeat my mistakes. I try to learn from them. The tragedy with Bobbie taught me to make every minute count. Life and love are fragile and sometimes fleeting blessings. I don't intend to take either for granted again." He tilted her chin with a fingertip and tenderly wiped the mascara tracks from her wet cheeks. "I won't be turned away tonight. I'm taking you home and making love to you because we need each other, Alexandra."

"No, Nick . . ." Her weak protest was stilled at his unexpected claiming of her lips.

"Yes, Alexandra," was his insistent murmur when releasing her soft mouth. "You forget that I'm Greek and a determined SOB."

"Are we crazy, Nick?"

"Probably," he conceded.

"I can't love you," she stipulated. "There's only room in my heart for Jenny."

"You believe that now. And that's how it should be. But once Jenny is found the ache will eventually disappear and there'll be ample room in your heart for me, too. I'm not gonna be denied, Alexandra. I care too deeply to accept any other conclusion."

CHAPTER FOURTEEN

A GENTLE RAIN FELL beyond the window. The covers softly rustled as two bodies entwined. Alexandra closed her eyes and savored the sensuous graze of Nick's distinct touch. A small gasp escaped her when his lips traveled down her midriff and then lingered at the erotic precipice of her womanhood.

Several times he'd masterfully brought her to the brink of ecstasy, then withheld the ultimate fulfillment. His expert lovemaking was driving her wild. Never in her life had she been more aroused.

She writhed and moaned as his lips sought, then pleasured each sensitive areola. "You're making me crazy, Nick. I want you so badly," was her near-incoherent plea.

His mouth returned to hers, his tongue performing tender ministrations as his hard body rhythmically frictioned against her flesh and stoked the passion blazing between them. "Not yet, sugar. Just a few minutes more. I want the timing to be absolutely perfect when I take you."

Her fingers weaved through his thick hair and she arched beneath him wantonly.

His kisses grew more intense and he shuddered at

the intimate nuzzle of a velvet thigh between his legs. "You're not playing fair," he rasped.

"Neither have you been." Her tapered nails trailed down his muscled back and over his taut buttocks. At his involuntary groan, she smiled and then softly kissed the wildly beating pulse point at the hollow of his throat.

His breathing grew ragged as he buried his face in her fragrant hair. "Mmm, but you smell good, feel good. So warm . . . so soft . . . so sweet," was his adoring whisper as he positioned himself between her thighs and ever so easily penetrated her.

He made good his promise. His timing was absolutely perfect—every thrust, every caress, every kiss being essential and incredibly satisfying. He was a craving she refused to admit. He was a necessity she had tried to deny. He was the love she had yearned for but had never, ever known.

His arms slipped beneath the small of her back and he forged himself deeper within her. *There had to be room in her life for him, for no other woman would do.* His heart canted her name like a prayer and his body was a prisoner to a never-before, never-again desire. She was more addictive than the countless kilos of cocaine he'd confiscated over the years. And, God help him, he possessed no more willpower than the poor junkies who sold their soul for a fleeting sensation of synthetic euphoria.

Her arms linked about his neck and she drew his mouth down upon hers, kissing him into a feverish delirium. In response, Nick thrust his hips against hers, heightening the tempo to a savage pitch.

Thrashing and purring his name, she begged for release. Her eyes were dreamy and damp ringlets of champagne-blond hair fringed her cameo face. Mesmerized by the sultry beauty he beheld, Nick found himself going over the edge.

Other women had excited him in the past. But only Alexandra had the power to completely possess him in the future.

"I love you, Alexandra. Never doubt it," was his cherishing groan as they crescendoed to a mutual climax.

Like the gentle rain cleaning away the city soot, Nick's gentle love temporarily purged her melancholy. But even he could not hold back the stroke of midnight. And after midnight always came the blues.

"I feel guilty," came her emotion-choked whisper from out of the darkness. It startled him. He assumed she'd fallen asleep. Tenderly he pulled her against him, cradling her head upon his muscled shoulder and nuzzling his cheek within her hair. "It seems wrong somehow for me to enjoy any contentment while my daughter might be—"

"Don't torture yourself, sugar." He stroked her bare back and kissed her forehead. "You're not depriving Jenny by satisfying a perfectly normal need. You demand too much of yourself. Being intimate with me is hardly a desertion of your daughter. If a call should come, the phone is only an arm's length away," he reasoned.

"I know." She sighed heavily and snuggled closer. "But it's not fair to you, either. You make great love. I enjoy the moment. But Jenny is always hovering in the shadows. I feel her presence and it's hard to deny her claim on me.''

"I'm not complaining. I think it's a natural reaction. Why don't you try to get some rest? You're exhausted.'' He arranged the coverlet around her shoulders, cradled her in his arms, and nestled deeper into the mattress.

"Where do we go from here, Nick?'' A drowsy yawn preceded the question.

"To sleep, sugar.'' His lulling tone and secure embrace had an opiate effect. She drifted off while he lay pondering a commitment of the most serious sort.

He loved Alexandra. He had for quite some time. But until tonight, he hadn't realized how imperative she was to him. Pursuing her had been good sport. But somewhere along the way it had become more than a game. He wanted this woman for his wife. Any less of a commitment was unacceptable.

Gently he raised her left hand and brought it to his lips, kissing the third finger where he intended to place a gold band inscribed with the word *forever*.

She moaned in her sleep and rolled over onto her side, her hair tumbling across her cheek. He pushed the strands aside, admiring her lovely profile for a reverent second before lightly kissing her temple, then falling back upon the pillow and staring blankly up at the ceiling.

Central's prime stud would be staying for breakfast in the morning. And if he had his way it would be a precedent for the future. This time he wanted to linger. This time the lady was too special, too necessary to forsake. He was determined to find her missing daughter. He intended to make the reunion she dreamed of a reality, the same as he intended to make his ex-shrink and current partner the future Mrs. Nicholas Stavos. His heart swelled at the thought. Lovingly he patted her fanny and closed his weary eyes. For now he would content himself with dreaming of the day when he, Alexandra and Jenny would be a family. He tried to visualize the daughter that Alexandra loved so dearly. She'd probably inherited her mother's fantastic looks and was a living doll. He prayed she'd also inherited her mother's stamina to survive hardship.

Though Stavos was a simple man who sought simple pleasures, this once the lady he desired encompassed complications. But his love for her was unconditional. If strife and sorrow were part of the package, so be it. Partners, friends and lovers shared both the joys and the heartaches. Since Nick Stavos qualified in all three categories, he was triply committed.

ALEXANDRA AWOKE to the smell of fried ham and perked coffee. Preoccupied with frying hash-browned potatoes, Nick was unaware of her presence at the kitchen doorway until she bid him good morning.

"I didn't expect you to still be here." The remark slipped from her before she realized.

He smiled and peppered the potatoes. "Is that a complaint or merely an observation?"

She shrugged and poured the coffee.

"Are you always so cordial in the morning?" he teased.

"I wake up slowly," was all she answered, passing him a cup, then settling at the table and glancing at the morning paper's headline. "The kids are still front-page news. Maybe today we'll hear something."

He dished up their plates and joined her. "Suppose we eat breakfast first and dwell on the kids later," he suggested, taking the paper and tossing it onto the counter.

She sampled the food and smiled appreciatively. "This is very good, Nick. I didn't realize you were so proficient in a kitchen."

"I'm a self-sufficient kind of guy," he said with a grin.

"And what other hidden talents do you boast?" she asked, taking a bite of toast.

"Excluding my culinary skills, you've pretty well experienced the gamut, sugar."

Despite the intimacy they'd shared, she blushed. "You really enjoy shocking me, don't you, Nick?"

"Yeah, I do." He flashed her a cocky grin and polished off the ham.

"Why is that?"

"Geez, here we go." He rolled his eyes. "Is this how it's going to be when we're married? You analyzing my every action?"

In the midst of sipping her juice, she nearly choked. "Married? Us? You really are crazy," she exclaimed.

"I'm crazy about you," he declared with a wink.

"Listen, Nick. We've got to get something straight here and now. I have only one passion and her name is Jenny. I doubt I'll ever remarry. Once was enough. I think you're a great guy, a fantastic lover and an ex-

cellent cook, but that does not qualify you as a prospective husband.''

"Don't try to discourage me. I have my heart set on
this.'' The glib reply was not indicative of his true
feelings. He intended to keep proposing until she accepted.

"Well, unset it.'' She tossed her napkin onto the
table.

"Okay, okay.'' He held up his hands in a capitulating gesture. "We'll discuss it later. After we find
Jenny.''

Her features mellowed and so did her tone. "She
isn't your problem, Nick. I appreciate the moral support but—''

"Will you quit being so stubborn?'' Exasperation
seeped into his voice. "She's been missing for quite a
while. It's asinine to reject any offer of assistance,
especially when you're out of options.''

"That I am,'' she admitted. "The Connecticut authorities haven't been able to turn up one shred of
evidence in all this time. I also hired a top-notch private investigator and so far he's been stymied.'' She
gazed off, a look of resignation on her face. "It's hard
to exist on false hope, to believe that your instincts are
valid when everyone else tells you differently. It's as if
Jenny just fell off the face of the earth. Sometimes I
feel very strongly that she's alive. Then there are those
awful moments when I wonder if I'm just deluding
myself.''

"I know it must be difficult, Alexandra,'' he sympathized.

"You can't even begin to imagine, Nick. There's this dark void inside of me that once was filled with a child's sunny laughter—a bitter hollowness that terrifies me at times and makes me question my ability to distinguish lucidity from madness."

Her eyes became misty but she held back the tears. "The nights are the worst. That's when the memories overtake you. And they hurt so terribly because you're afraid there will never be any more moments of joy; only the horror of living the rest of your life under a shadow of uncertainty. Only God has the right to take a child away from you and even then you curse Him. But for a nameless, faceless person to deprive you of your motherly rights is a despicable violation. Who could do such a thing? You ask yourself over and over. What kind of monster would intentionally inflict such pain?"

He scooted his chair closer to hers. "Second guessing is natural but experience has taught me that it's not very productive, Alexandra."

Her state of mind was such that his comment did not even register. "You find yourself suspecting everyone—your ex-husband and in-laws, friends, acquaintances, clients, the grocery clerk, the newspaper boy. You search their eyes for some giveaway trait."

Nick reflected that he had heard the same dismal account from other anguished parents who had experienced a similar ordeal. He vowed to help Alexandra in any way he could.

She continued with her story. It was as though once she'd begun to verbalize her misery, it was impossible to stop the flood of emotion. "You spend your days trying to forget and your nights remembering. You wait for one encouraging word. You depend on a strength you don't really possess. You relive every detail of the hours preceding the disappearance, saying if only... if only. You torture yourself by browsing through old photographs and rerunning home movies. You're condemned to a solitary limbo that is hell on earth. You're a shell... a walking, talking zombie that integrates, interacts but wanders in ceaseless circles. I'm not a woman anymore, Nick. I'm a statistic. I'm the named mother of Jenny on a standard missing-person report.''

He clasped her hand, bringing it to his lips and kissing her palm. ''We'll find her, sugar. Maybe it was meant for us to meet. Fate is a funny thing.''

Somehow his words were reassuring. ''I have to know, Nick. I can face whatever I must. I'm so weary of the inconclusiveness.'' Her eyes were laden with sadness.

''I intend to do something about that,'' he said. ''But you've got to be totally candid with me, sugar. You've a tendency to clam up whenever the conversation gets personal.''

''Ask whatever you like,'' was her reply.

''Well, for starters, let's talk about the day of Jenny's disappearance.'' He settled back and awaited her detailed account.

''It was Larry's weekend to exercise his visitation rights. I was entertaining Jenny by playing a game of hide-and-seek in the backyard. It was about three o'clock in the afternoon. I remember because Larry was supposed to pick her up by two and he was late.

Anyway, it was my turn to cover my eyes and count while Jenny looked for a hiding place. The maid came out on the terrace and summoned me to the phone. I hollered to Jenny that I'd only be a minute and went inside to take the call. It was Larry, saying he was running behind schedule and that he'd be by for Jenny within the hour. Tardiness was an irritating habit of his, but after so many years I was accustomed. When I returned to the yard, Jenny was nowhere in sight. I assumed that she was merely hiding.''

"Nothing alerted you that something was amiss?'' he asked.

She shook her head. "I merely thought that Jenny was playing the game. I shouted a customary, 'One, two, three. Here I come, ready or not,' and set out to discover her hiding place, never dreaming that I'd not find my daughter ever again. At first I thought that Jenny was being obstinate by not responding when I abandoned the hunt. But after calling to her over and over again and getting no reply, I began to get an uneasy feeling.''

"Was there any special reason you sensed a threat?'' Nick prompted.

"We had a pond near our property. Jenny had been warned to keep her distance but on occasion she could be impulsive and a bit too daring for her own good. As I passed the hedge of rosebushes that bordered the property and the pond, I spied a pink ribbon snagged on a branch. It was the same ribbon I'd earlier tied in her hair. It was then that I truly panicked.'' She squeezed shut her eyes as she recalled the horrid memory.

"I know this is hard but I need to know the exact sequence of events. Tell me what occurred next, sugar." Nick's coaxing inflection penetrated the haze that engulfed her.

"I ran to the pond, calling to her, pleading with her, threatening to punish her if she didn't reveal herself. Jenny was mischievous but not defiant. A threat of a spanking would've produced her. I can't clearly recall what I did next. All I could think about was the pond...that she might've accidentally fallen in. The maid later said that she heard my screams and came to see what had happened. She discovered me literally drowning myself in an attempt to scour the bottom for my daughter. She dragged me kicking and cursing to the shore and immediately called the police. They dragged the pond but there was no sign of Jenny. After intensive interrogation, the only possible conclusion the authorities could draw was that Jenny had been abducted during my absence."

"That explains the pink ribbon you keep under your pillow," Nick observed.

Alexandra wasn't surprised by his comment. "Yes. It's the only tie that still bonds us," she admitted.

"When did your ex arrive on the scene?"

"Shortly after the police."

"And how did he react?"

"Amazingly calm. At the time I thought that he was in shock. It was only later that I began to suspect that perhaps he had engineered Jenny's abduction and had knowledge of her whereabouts from the onset."

"Do you believe him capable of such an act?" Nick managed to maintain a placid expression. He did not want to influence her reply.

"I don't know for sure. I once thought I understood Larry, but after a few years of marriage I realized I never knew him at all. He was reserved, controlled, shallow. He only displayed reactions that suited his purposes. Underneath the poised exterior, he was a dispassionate human being who calculated every minor move to his advantage."

"He sounds like a real sweetheart of a fellow." Nick couldn't resist taking a potshot at her ex. The man had to be a first-class jerk. Only an utter fool would not have appreciated a fine woman like Alexandra. Nick did not intend to make the same mistake. If he was fortunate enough to win the lady's heart, he would cherish her to the end of his days.

Alexandra nodded in agreement. "The funny thing is, I believe he loved Jenny very much. Though, at the end of our marriage, he wasn't particularly fond of me. I threatened him. I knew him too well. And by divorcing him, I blemished his pristine image. He never forgave me for publicly disgracing him. Neither did his socially prominent family. So you can see why Larry qualified as a probable suspect. He knew he hadn't a chance for custody. He certainly had the means and connections to arrange the abduction. There's only one inconsistency that makes me discount him."

"Which is?" Nick prompted.

"He wouldn't jeopardize his esteemed position, risk the detrimental exposure, not even for Jenny. He's governed by ambition. His aspirations include sitting on the bench of the Supreme Court. Given his incredulous ego, I seriously doubt he'd take such a chance."

"Okay, he's eliminated." Nick trusted her instincts.

"He wasn't initially. I tried my damnedest to prove he was connected, but drew a blank. Other than him, there were no further suspects. It's just like the Brechtel Park snatchings. No ransom demands. No witnesses. Not a single, solitary lead."

"How about enemies—yours and his. Somebody who wanted to make you suffer because of some twisted notion of an injustice done them?"

"I've racked my brain, Nick. The patients I treated in private practice were, on the whole, harmless. A few were truly disturbed but not vindictive. I questioned Larry at great length about the very same possibility. He willingly gave me the names of a few individuals who bore him a grudge. I subsequently turned the information over to the police. They checked each of them out thoroughly and concluded that they hadn't the opportunity to initiate such a scheme. They were either serving time or their alibis were airtight and collaborated."

"What about your hired gun theory?" he asked.

"Again, the Connecticut authorities couldn't trace any such link or prove that there had been a conspiracy of any sort. Do you see why I'm so frustrated? You can't ask me any question, throw out any possibility that I haven't considered. Who, Nick? Who could've taken Jenny? And why? What terrible sin did I commit?"

"You did nothing," he assured her. "Sometimes the answers aren't apparent. Sometimes the motive isn't cut and dry. I want to look at your albums...become familiar with Jenny."

"Why?"

"Because she's part of you, Alexandra. I want to get to know her," was his honest reply.

"She's not really," she said without thinking. "We favor one another but I was denied the joy of birthing her."

Nick stared at her in surprise. "Back up, sugar. Run that by me one more time."

"Jenny is adopted," she responded, as though he should have guessed.

"You can't have children?" The fact that she might be sterile never occurred to him—not that it mattered in the least. The adoption angle had merely stunned him.

"It was Larry who was infertile," she explained. "I wanted children desperately, but he wouldn't even consider adoption. Finally he came round and we went through intense scrutiny and a lot of red tape in order to adopt. Jenny was only four days old when the agency notified us. She's mine, Nick. As surely as if she'd emanated from my womb. Nine months of carrying a child and hours of labor isn't a prerequisite for motherhood."

"You don't have to convince me, Alexandra. But it's an angle we haven't explored, though I'm sure you're going to tell me that the Connecticut police and private investigator checked the biological mother out and she's crossed off the list, too."

"I didn't mention it," she said offhandedly.

"Come again," he said, struck dumb by her nonchalance.

"I didn't tell them," she reiterated. "Why should I have? Six years had passed since the adoption. There were no hitches, no complications. Larry wanted the matter kept private. I saw no reason not to respect his wishes. Besides, after a while you tend to think in terms of being the natural mother. I forgot the woman even existed. Why are you looking at me as if I had two heads?" she observed. "Damn it, Nick! What are you thinking?"

"I'm thinking that you've been negligent, sugar. Why in the name of heaven would you discount the biological mother? Women are fickle. They change their minds. One year, three years, six years later. How could you exclude that significant 'what if'?"

His plausible conjecturing took her by surprise. It was the one avenue she had not pursued. "Don't do this to me, Nick," she implored. "I can't go through another intense examination only to discover that my suspicions are unfounded."

"Not even to reclaim Jenny?" he pushed.

"I'd walk through fire for her."

He didn't doubt either her strong will or sincerity. "Then let's explore the possibility," he insisted. "I assume you have the documentation of the adoption?"

"Of course, though there's not much in it."

"Get it. I want to try to trace the birth mother through the adoptive agency and see what comes of it."

She sat motionless, afraid to placate his whim and risk raising her hopes only to see them shattered again.

"Alexandra?" He realized she was apprehensive but he was determined to follow up on this lead. "Get the album, too," he solicited. "I want to acquaint myself with your daughter. She's got to be special."

"She is, Nick. Jenny will win your heart at a glance," she prophesied.

"Her mother did." He gave her hand an encouraging squeeze as she vacated the table.

SINCE THE SAINT BERNADETTE adoption agency was located in Hartford, Connecticut and Chief Oliver was not inclined to give him a leave of absence in the midst of the Brechtel Park case, Nick had to do his tracking by long distance.

First he was informed by a twangy New England accent that such information could not be disclosed.

"Look, lady, I don't make a habit out of requesting confidential information for the sheer thrill of it. And I'm not accustomed to dickering with incompetent subordinates. I'd like to speak to the administrator about this matter." He was not in the mood for a runaround.

"I'm sorry, sir, but the Mother Superior is the only one who could approve such a request," the haughty receptionist quibbled.

"Fine and dandy. Put me through to her," he snapped.

"She's unavailable at the moment. She's on retreat in the Catskills," she informed him.

Nick fought his exasperation. "When might you expect her?" he inquired stiffly, doing his damnedest not to alienate the voice on the other end of the line until he'd extracted the vital information.

"I'm not certain. Could you hold, please?" was the whiny comeback.

"Sure," Nick seethed, rubbing his throbbing temples as the minutes ticked away.

Finally the familiar twang tripped over the wire. "The Mother Superior is not due back until next Tuesday. Sister Dominique is acting in her behalf while she's away. Would you care to speak to her?"

"If it's not too much trouble," he growled.

"Just a moment, please."

There was a staticky pause that seemed like an eternity.

"This is Sister Dominique. May I help you?"

"I hope so, Sister," Nick all but groaned. "My name is Sergeant Nicholas Stavos. I'm a detective with the New Orleans Police Department."

"How may we be of service, Sergeant?" was the polite reply.

"I'm in need of some confidential information, Sister. It concerns the adoption of a baby girl that took place at your facility approximately seven and a half years ago," he explained.

"I'm sure you are aware that it's not our practice to divulge any information concerning our adoptions without the express consent of all the parties involved. Those records are sealed, Sergeant." The nun's voice took on a distinctly inflexible intonation.

Nick was quickly losing patience. "I understand your position, Sister, but perhaps if I explain the circumstances you will make an exception. I'd rather not have to go through the hassle of having to subpoena the records. It would take valuable time that I can't afford to waste."

"I hope that isn't necessary, Sergeant, for it would be a lengthy procedure indeed, since we consider our records to be privileged information and would take whatever legal action is necessary to protect our code of confidentiality. But you may explain your predicament, if you like," she graciously offered.

Luckily she did not hear Nick's irreverent mutter. "The child I mentioned earlier was abducted from her adoptive parents' home eighteen months ago. I have reason to believe that your records might contain information vital to the case."

"How so?" Sister Dominique wanted particulars.

"I need the name of the natural mother and possibly a former address at the time of birth so that I can trace her." He could detect a slight gasp.

"Oh, I really am sorry, Sergeant, but I'm afraid that's out of the question. It would be a breach of faith."

At this point, Nick would gladly trade his soul for the name of the birth mother. "Look, Sister. I don't think you understand the seriousness of the situation. A felony has been committed. A child has been taken against her will and we are trying to apprehend the perpetrator. Besides the fact that we're talking a kidnapping charge, we're also discussing possible abuse, rape or even murder, and you may hold a crucial clue

locked away in your files. Do you want to go to Mass
with that on your conscience?''

Sister Dominique did not answer immediately.
''Please don't think that I'm being deliberately un-
cooperative, Sergeant Stavos. I would very much like
to assist your efforts. But you must understand my
position. Daily, young women entrust their entire fu-
tures to our discretion. If I should make an exception
and divulge the name of one of our unwed mothers
without her permission, I am not only jeopardizing
her current status but also compromising the credibility of Saint Bernadette's. It truly grieves me not to assist you. And you must believe that I do not refuse you
without a great deal of remorse. I am torn between my
allegiance to our creed and a moral obligation.''

Nick wished to God he could find a way to convince her to cooperate without having to go through
channels. ''What if I promised not to implicate Saint
Bernadette? Not to name your agency as a source
from which I derived the information? What if I give
you my word that this matter will remain just between you and me, Sister?'' he pleaded. ''A month, a
week, a day's delay might be too late. If the child is
still alive, she could be at risk every passing moment.
Help me find her, Sister. For her mother's sake, have
mercy.'' It was his final appeal.

At first Sister Dominique did not reply. Finally her
voice, quite strained and conspiratorially low, came
back on the line. ''Give me the child's name and date
of birth, Sergeant. May God forgive me for what I'm
about to do.''

"I'm positive He will, Sister Dominique," Nick assured her before supplying the specific data.

"I'll get back to you once I have located the file." A moment later the long distance connection was severed.

Nick immediately depressed the button and dialed Alexandra's extension. "The agency is checking for us. They weren't real enthusiastic about cooperating but I convinced them that the Almighty wouldn't mind if they bent the rules just this once. And if He should, I'll take the consequences when I arrive at the pearly gates."

"I appreciate it, though I'm certain there are a few other menial sins you'll have to atone for before receiving your wings." Her attempt to be glib didn't deceive him for a second. She was making a valiant effort to cover up her anxiousness, but he knew better.

"I'll call you as soon as Sister Dominique gets back in touch. Hang on, sugar. We're making progress."

"It's not easy, but I'm trying, Nick," was her dejected answer.

Hours passed. Afraid to leave his desk for a moment in the event he might miss Sister Dominique's call, Nick sat glued to his chair, eating a greasy cold taco a fellow detective had been kind enough to deliver to him by way of a shooting incident that had occurred outside of the Mexican establishment. Considering the fact that the detective would not have been involved in the incident had he not been doing Nick a favor, nor now burdened with an after-hours booking and triplicate reports, Nick had the good sense and gracious manners not to complain about the unpalatable taco. He suffered in silence and waited for the nun's promised call.

At the shrill jangle of the phone, he bolted from his chair and snatched up the receiver on the first ring. "Detectives. Sergeant Stavos speaking," he barked.

"This is Sister Dominique, Sergeant. I have the information you requested."

"I'm in your debt, Sister," he said in all sincerity.

"No, Sergeant. It is the Lord you should thank. I'm only his instrument," was her humble reply.

"Yes, ma'am. I'll be sure to give him my personal regards next time I find myself at Sunday services." Nick hadn't been inside a church since he was the best man at his cousin's wedding. At last count it was two kids, one divorce and five years since the auspicious occasion.

"The woman whom you are seeking is Audrey Vasek. Of course, that's her maiden name. It's very possible that it has changed. Many of our unwed mothers marry eventually." Sister Dominique exhaled a heavy sigh. "That's why it's so important that we not make disclosures of this nature. So often our mothers have begun new lives and it would be devastating for them should their past transgressions come to light."

"I understand, Sister Dominique. I promise to be very tactful when following up on the information. Should I succeed in tracing Miss Vasek, I'll make certain we discuss the matter in private. I'll take every precaution so as not to infringe upon her newly established life," he reassured her.

"Thank you, Sergeant. I have an address on the admitting form but I'm sure after so many years that Miss Vasek no longer resides at the stated residence."

"Give it to me anyway, Sister. It's a place to start my search." He shoved aside the greasy taco and jotted down the address. "You've been a big help. I know it went against your principles and I appreciate it."

"We cherish children at Saint Bernadette, Sergeant. Each one is precious to us. I only hope that my breech of confidentiality is of some consequence. I shall pray that your mission is successful. God's grace be with you."

"Yeah, you, too, Sister." He was in a hurry to disconnect and start tracing the identity of the persons who resided at the old address.

CHAPTER FIFTEEN

NICK SPENT THE NEXT SEVERAL DAYS concentrating his efforts on locating Jenny's birth mother. The address listed on the adoption agency records belonged to the woman's parents. Through them, he traced Audrey Vasek Lancaster to a small town in upper Connecticut. The next weekend he caught a late flight out of New Orleans, landed at Bradley International Airport at dawn, then drove to a speck on the map called Ebbs Corner, not far from the Massachusetts state line.

He could've saved himself a lot of time and aggravation with a long distance call, but he wanted to interview the woman face to face on the slight chance he might detect some irregularity. It turned out to be a wasted trip. He could perceive nothing sinister about Audrey Lancaster. She was cooperative but hardly informative. After her out-of-wedlock pregnancy, she'd married, moved to Ebbs Corner, and was living an exemplary life—Cub Scout den mother, PTA treasurer, a member of the Ladies' Christian Auxiliary, and a volunteer at the local veterans hospital. She contended that she had never once even made inquiries about Jenny, let alone tried to establish contact with her. What's more, she seemed genuinely shaken by the news of the child's abduction and most definitely sympathetic toward the Vaughns' nightmarish plight.

"I have two sons of my own now," she'd told him. "My whole life revolves around them. Why, it would be kinder to cut my heart out than take my boys. Please tell Jenny's mother that I'll include her in my prayers. I'm sorry I couldn't be of any help."

On the flight back, Nick decided that Audrey Lancaster's suggestion of prayer might be his last resort. He wished he could spare Alexandra yet another disappointment. She had withstood so much for so long, it was a wonder to him that she hadn't already cracked under the pressure. But even she had limits—a breaking point.

He didn't have to tell her the discouraging details when he arrived at her apartment. She immediately knew by his sullen expression that his mission to Ebbs Corner had been futile. She put up a brave front all evening for his sake, but sometime during the wee small hours he awoke to find her standing at the window and softly crying.

He eased from the bed, coming to stand behind her and slipping his brawny arms around her small waist. "So many tears you've shed. God! You'll never know how much I wanted to bring you back some positive lead from Connecticut." He drew her back against him and cradled his cheek to hers.

"I appreciate your trying, Nick." She sighed and leaned heavily upon him. "I don't know why you stay. I give you so little of myself."

"A little bit of you goes a long, long way, sugar. You're more woman than this Greek ever hoped to know."

She smiled through her tears. "I'm growing very fond of you, you know."

Amusement glinted in his dark eyes. "We're definitely making progress, Miss Baby Powder. I wouldn't be a bit surprised if one day you actually admit that you love me, too." He gave her midsection a playful squeeze.

"Maybe," she murmured.

His heart lurched in his chest. One little word had never sounded so good.

"Yeah, well, I wouldn't want you to make any hasty decisions. People usually regret 'em." He swung her up in his arms and carried her back to bed, sliding in beside her and nestling her head in the bend of his shoulder. "And I sure as hell don't want you to regret loving me," was his drowsy whisper.

She knew she never would. Nick Stavos was a diamond in the rough—raw but brilliant—multifaceted and priceless. Her private treasure.

EARLY MONDAY MORNING they were both told to report to Chief Oliver immediately. The confrontation did not go well. Oliver was livid, ranting and raving for a full ten minutes. He finally issued an ultimatum— either they pulled off a miracle and produced the Brechtel Park kids or the culprit or preferably the whole kit and caboodle, or the only duties they would be performing around Central was parking cars in the garage.

Nick did not cower and objected vehemently. "If you think we're enjoying this merry-go-round we're on, you're mistaken. We've been knocking ourselves out and you're practically accusing us of fouling up on purpose. You want to assign the case to someone else? Be my guest. Personally I'm getting real fed up with being out on a shaky limb alone."

"You got until the end of the week, Stavos. Then, I'm going to cut that limb right out from under your smart butt." Oliver meant the threat.

"You'd be doing me a favor." Nick stormed out, leaving Alexandra to weather Oliver's wrath.

"I ought to suspend him," Oliver sputtered.

"He's temperamental." She tried to make lame excuses.

"He's a hothead. I'm tempted to make an example of him."

"Nick has his faults," she agreed. "But he's probably the most dedicated officer at Central. Believe me, Chief Oliver, he really wants to solve this case. Nick and I have put in a lot of hours together lately and I know better than anyone the toll it's taken on him."

Chief Oliver's pudgy jowls sagged and he slumped back into his chair, mumbling a brusque, "You're dismissed, Miz Vaughn."

"From the case?"

"No, ma'am," was his exasperated grunt. "From this office."

Nick had yet to cool off by the time she tracked him down in the squad room.

"That's gratitude for you," he seethed. "Next thing you know they'll be laying the blame for this whole damn mess in our laps." He half missed his desk when slinging a folder atop it.

"You shouldn't have exploded at Oliver like that." She collected the paperwork he'd scattered from off the floor.

"What should I have done? Kissed his bald head? I meant what I said. I'm fed up to my eyeballs with this bull. Oliver's a wimp, not to mention an incompetent, obnoxious bastard." The shrill ring of his extension saved her from what promised to be one of his most profane tirades. Muttering yet another unintelligible curse beneath his breath, he picked up the receiver.

At first Alexandra paid little attention as she neatly stacked the paperwork on his desk. But at Nick's abrupt "You're sure about this?" she became interested.

"Yeah, I know the area. I'll be by to confirm a positive ID within the hour." He jotted down a name and address while conversing with the caller. "I appreciate your calling, sir."

"What was that all about?" Nick's peculiar grin as he dropped the receiver onto its cradle more than piqued her curiosity.

"Believe it or not, we finally have a lead." He hardly believed it himself.

"Are you serious?" she exclaimed. "Who? How? Where?" She wanted him to answer all of her questions at once.

"That was a fella by the name of Jody Breaux. He owns a small grocery store fifty miles or so outside of the city. He claims to have seen Vinnie Stevens a few hours ago. He says it isn't the first time the kid's been in to buy supplies. Only it just so happens that his wife was working the counter and recognized Vinnie from the recent pictures in the paper. The kid fits Vinnie's description. Jody Breaux maybe just gave us our first real break. You want to come along for the ride?''

''Are you kidding!'' She whooped, throwing her arms around his neck in a gleeful hug. ''You just try to leave me behind, Sergeant Stavos.''

Within minutes they were in the squad car and peeling out of the garage headed for bayou country. Within the hour they were interviewing the proprietor of the store.

''That's him,'' Breaux confirmed after carefully examining the eight-by-ten glossy Nick had presented for his inspection. ''That's the kid, all right. And he didn't look lost and he sure ain't dead.''

Nick passed the photo to the man's wife for a second, substantiating opinion. ''Yes, that's the boy I waited on this morning. His hair is a bit longer but I'm sure it's the same one.''

Alexandra wanted to kiss the pair of them.

''You said that Vinnie has been in before. Can you be more specific?'' Nick took a pen and small notepad from his pocket.

''The best I can remember, he's been in twice before.'' The proprietor scratched his head as he racked his brain. ''He don't come often...about once a month. He stocks up on all kinds of assorted stuff...mostly the junk food variety—chips, Twinkies, soda pop and the like. Oh, he buys some staples too—milk, bread, cereal, rice, beans...''

Nick could do without a recitation of Vinnie's shopping list. "Anyone ever with him?" he prompted.

"Nope. He's alone," Breaux stated. "He shops by hisself, loads up the old blue pickup by hisself and pays the total by hisself."

"Can you give me a better description of the pickup? Maybe a make or possibly a license number?" Anxious for particulars, Nick fired the question at Breaux.

"Can't help you there. They all look alike to me. It's blue and battered. That's the best I can do."

"That's all right, Mr. Breaux. You're doing just fine," Alexandra interjected, grateful for whatever information the old gentleman could supply.

"Perhaps you might've noticed the direction Vinnie drove off in? Or maybe you've heard another of your customers discussing new arrivals in the area?" Nick tried every angle.

Breaux chewed his bottom lip thoughtfully. "Nope. I don't recall whether the boy went north, south, east or west. I'm usually pretty busy, you understand."

A scoffing "Hmmph" erupted from his wife.

Hard of hearing, Breaux missed it. "Doreen's the one who chitchats with the customers. You heard anything about strangers hovering about, Mama?"

She shook her head.

"I'm sure you folks know most of the regulars who trade here." Nick took especial care not to be abrupt with the Breauxs. "Have you noticed anyone acting edgy or buying in extra quantity?"

"We been in this same spot for nearly thirty years," Breaux bragged. "So we're pretty familiar with most all the locals. Mostly they're shrimpers. The bayous give 'em access to the gulf. I can't recall any of the regulars acting peculiar. And the only one who's been buying extra is Dwight Sampey but that's because his daughter and her three kids moved back in with him after she caught her husband and best friend in a compromising situation.''

Alexandra averted her eyes, so the old gentleman would not see her amusement.

"Yeah, well, I suppose that about covers it, Mr. Breaux. You and your wife have been most helpful." Nick tucked the small notepad and pen back into his inside coat pocket. "We're going to have to set up surveillance on your property. We'll try to be as inconspicuous as possible," he assured him.

"Just so long as you don't interfere with business," Breaux agreed. "What are you planning to do? Nab the kid the next time he shows up?"

"That depends," was Nick's evasive reply. "I'd appreciate it if you wouldn't let on to Vinnie that you recognized him. Just act natural. Let him shop and leave as usual. I'll take it from there."

"Cloak and dagger stuff, huh?" Breaux surmised. "Mama's probably read a hundred or more whodunit novels. She inhales 'em."

"Nothing so dramatic, Mr. Breaux," he assured him. "You have my name and extension if you should remember anything else that might be important." He extended his hand to the old gentleman and cast his wife a cordial smile. "I appreciate your cooperation."

"Just doing our civic duty," was the humble reply.

Nick contained his enthusiasm until he and Alexandra were settled in the car. A sincere "Bless you, Mr. Breaux," blurted from his lips as he flipped the aviator sunshades upon his nose and started the engine.

"My sentiments exactly." Alexandra flashed him a radiant smile.

"Let's celebrate. There's some great little cajun cafés nearby. We could have lunch and then find us a secluded spot on one of these out-of-the-way bayous and make love."

She knew that the dark eyes hidden behind the mirrored sunshades twinkled with devilment. "You're incorrigible, Nick. Absolutely not. Oliver would have us brought up before a firing squad."

"Geez, this isn't the French Foreign Legion. We can't be executed for insubordination. Come on," he entreatied, pulling the squad car out onto the gravel road. "Live dangerously for once."

"For once?" she scoffed. "I've been in nothing but constant danger since getting involved with you." She gave him a sly look. "I am hungry, though."

"So am I, sugar. Hell, let's just skip lunch and head straight to the bayou."

IT TOOK SOME PERSUASIVE TALKING and a solemn promise to make it up to him later that night, but finally Nick abandoned his impulsive notion and settled for just having jambalaya on the bayou.

It was midafternoon by the time they arrived back at Central.

"I suppose we should inform Oliver of this latest development." Nick would've preferred to let the chief spend one more miserable night stewing in retaliation for the unfair treatment he'd received earlier that morning.

"I'll let you have the honor. I haven't been in my office all day. I really need to check my messages."

"Sure. I'll take care of Oliver and arrange for the stakeout at Breaux's Grocery and you do whatever you have to do so we can split this tomb at a decent hour. I don't want you preoccupied with anything but me tonight."

"You're displaying definite traits of obsessive behavior," she teased.

"Yeah, well, indulge me, okay?" He glanced about to be certain no one observed them, then patted her fanny and turned down the intersecting corridor before she could protest.

Actually Nick's outrageousness was one of the qualities that attracted her to him most. He could be so unpredictable and so very endearing. Every day held fascination; each night romantic suspense. She never knew what he might say or do next.

She smiled a lot more lately. In spite of his hot Greek temper and brassy manner, Nick was really a sensitive lamb underneath. He'd made her life bearable. She still had the pain. No one, not even Nick, could dispel it completely. But it wasn't the lonely ache she had known before because now it was shared. For a man to assume so much grief—grief he didn't cause or deserve—was the most noble kind of sacrifice. She could never doubt Nick's love. And one day, when she was finally reunited with her daughter and once again a whole woman, she intended to reciprocate the love he had so freely given. Oh, yes, she would make it up to him. Each day, in every way. It was her fervid wish that he would never regret sticking it out through the worst. Years from now, she wanted him to be able to say that his days with her were the very best.

The office was dark and smelled musty. She opened the blinds and cracked the window, then sat down at her desk and began to sort through the mail. Nothing of major import was included among the stack of correspondence. She trashed most of it, then switched on the recorder.

"It's Vivian, dear. Where on earth have you been lately? I'm having a dinner party next Saturday night. I insist that you come. Oh, by the way, curiosity got the better of me and I dropped in at the station to take a peek at your Greek. He's gorgeous. Bring him along, if you like. Ciao!"

The recorder clicked to the next message.

"Quincy Lucas, Mrs. Vaughn. Just wanted to let you know that your ex made an impromptu trip out of the country last weekend. I checked up on him. It turns out to be innocent. Well, let me rephrase that. He rendezvoused with an attractive young Canadian woman at a ski lodge. The trip had nothing to do with your daughter. I'll keep in touch."

She drummed her nails on the desk blotter while mulling over Lucas's message. Larry had always hated skiing. Strange he should suddenly take an interest. More than likely it had more to do with the attractive young Canadian rather than a latent enthusiasm for the sport.

Another beep. Another message.

"Uh, you don't know me, Mrs. Vaughn," a woman's voice greeted. "This is very difficult. Recorders are so impersonal. This call has to do with Jenny." Alexandra came erect in the chair and turned up the volume.

"I'm Audrey Lancaster," the woman went on. "I'm sure Sergeant Stavos has mentioned me. Well, something came to me after he left. I tried to contact him but he's seldom in his office. So, I thought of you. Your service gave me this number. I hope you don't mind," she rambled.

"I don't mind. Jenny... What about Jenny?" She foolishly tried to coach a recording.

"Anyway, this thought struck me. I remembered an accidental meeting I'd had a few years back with the man who got me pregnant. I didn't think much of it at the time—just an ironic coincidence. We chatted a bit, mostly about general stuff, our lives now, the way it was in the past. But in the course of the conversation I did tell Sam about the pregnancy and adoption. I don't recall him acting especially upset. After all, it would've complicated his life. He's married, you see. I don't suppose it means anything. I just forgot to mention it to the sergeant. The man's name is Sam Collier. He was once a commercial pilot and used to reside in New York. I'm afraid that's all I can tell you. It's probably of no importance, anyway. I sincerely hope you find Jenny. And, please, don't think I'm trying to reassert myself back into her life. Jenny has only one mother and I'm sure she loves her very much.''

The recorder clicked off. Alexandra rewound the tape and played Audrey Lancaster's message again, memorizing every word, analyzing every inflection. These strangers with the alien names had conceived Jenny...were entwined in and had impact on her life. How could they not be significant? A breakthrough had come today in the Brechtel Park snatchings. Maybe it was an omen that Audrey Lancaster had chosen the very same day to contact her.

Her head jerked up at the creak of the door. Nick stood in the doorway, crooking his finger in an anxious summons to leave.

"I want you to hear something, Nick." She rewound the tape a last time.

"Why am I getting the sinking feeling that my exclusive night with you is going down the tubes?" He sat on the edge of her desk, peevishly flipping paper clips into the trash can.

She shushed him as Audrey Lancaster's message began.

He eased to a standing position, braced his palms on the desk and leaned closer to the recorder, his head bent and his mind intrigued by the small detail the birth mother had forgotten to mention.

At the end of the message, his eyes claimed Alexandra's. "Kind of spooky, don't you think? Her calling on the same day as Breaux?"

"I was just thinking that," she agreed. "I have a feeling, Nick. I can't explain it. But it's strong."

"Motherly instinct maybe." He straightened and squared his shoulders. "I'll check out this Collier character right away."

She stood and came around the desk, taking his face between her palms and lightly kissing his lips. "Bless *you*, too, Nick Stavos," she said, repeating his earlier expression of gratitude toward Breaux. "Don't you ever tire of shouldering my burdens?"

"No," was his humble reply.

"Well, not this time, Nick." She released him and strode to the window to close it. "You have your hands full at the moment winding up the Brechtel Park case. I pay Quincy Lucas a fortune for this very purpose. This time we'll let him do the snooping. If he should turn up a lead, then we'll get involved." She shut the window with a firm thud.

"Are you ready to go home, Sergeant?" Her look was saucy, her tone suggestive.

"Yours or mine?" he tested.

"I suppose that depends on your mood. Come on," she invited. "Live dangerously for once."

He smiled at her challenge. "Whatever happened to the shy New England shrink who never took risks?"

"She was corrupted by a sexy Greek who thrives on vice," she teased, moving past him to the doorway and crooking her finger in a motion to follow.

CHAPTER SIXTEEN

IN THE DAYS THAT FOLLOWED, Alexandra and Nick became pros at passing idle hours—she awaiting a call from Quincy Lucas, he awaiting Vinnie Stevens to show up at Breaux's Grocery.

Because he so much wanted to be on hand when Vinnie revealed himself, Nick worked the stakeout almost exclusively. From the time the grocery opened for business at 7:00 a.m. and closed at 7:00 p.m., his unmarked squad car was concealed behind an icehouse in the rear.

It was about six in the evening, only an hour more to go and Nick was stiff and drowsy, when a battered blue pickup pulled off the gravel road and parked outside the store.

Nick rubbed his neck and strained to catch a good look. A youth, dressed in overalls and tennis shoes only, sprang from the truck and sauntered through the screen door. The kid was either Vinnie Stevens or his double. Nick fought to contain his excitement. He wanted the kid so badly he could taste it. But he knew better than to make a premature move. "Slow and easy," he coached himself. "Follow him. See where he goes."

Five minutes passed. Ten. Fifteen. "What the hell is he doing in there?" Nick muttered. "Come on, kid. It's getting late. I'm losing the light."

As if on cue, Vinnie exited the grocery store, his arms laden with sacks. He placed them in the back of the pickup and returned to the store.

"Geez! Now what?" Nick positioned himself behind the wheel, primed to tail the pickup as soon as Vinnie finished his errand.

Vinnie appeared again, carrying a carton of Coke in each hand. He loaded them into the cab of the truck, then climbed inside.

"Okay, Vinnie. Take us home." Nick waited to turn over the engine until Vinnie cleared the parking lot. Then, cautiously, he eased the squad car from behind the icehouse and followed the pickup from a safe distance.

Twilight was descending and the dust from the gravel road made a mushrooming cloud ahead. Nick strained to keep the blue pickup in view. It disappeared around a curve and by the time Nick cleared it, he had almost missed Vinnie's sharp veer onto a dirt back road.

The cypress trees, laden with Spanish moss, thickened as they drove deeper into the marshy bayou. Nick hung back so that Vinnie would not spy his headlights. It'd be a dead giveaway if he should make them, since the area was remote and the dirt path infrequently traveled. The back road became barely more than a rutted path and the croaks of bullfrogs and chirps of crickets permeated the damp night air.

"Damn!" he cussed when hitting a giant pothole that rattled his teeth. "Park it, Vinnie. Your ice cream is melting."

Fog from the nearby bayou made the pickup's red taillights barely visible. Nick began to get concerned that he might lose Vinnie. A possum darted in front of the car. He braked and let out a string of expletives. It was then that he noticed the pickup slowing and turning left onto what appeared to be private property.

"This must be the place," Nick surmised aloud, turning off the headlights and coasting to a stop. The pitch-black darkness impaired his view. The most he could distinguish were silhouettes and the muffled sound of voices—adolescent voices and a deeper, Cajun-accented one. He opened the door soundlessly and made his way to the edge of the property, then crept closer for a better look, crouching behind a freshly cut stack of wood.

"You didn't forget to pick up the Hershey bars I asked for, did ya, Vinnie?" a girlish voice asked.

"Naw, Lacey. I got 'em. You keep stuffing your face with chocolate and you're gonna be fatter than Papa Doré. Yo, Roberto. Come help me unload this stuff. I ain't your personal delivery boy," he griped.

Nick had heard all he needed. Lacey and Roberto were alive and accounted for. He did not want to take any unnecessary chances or muff taking the juveniles into custody. It would be better to wait for daylight and have some backup in the wings. He carefully retraced his steps to the parked squad car, noting that there was no room in which to turn around. The dirt trail was narrow and treacherous. He patiently waited until the lights inside the house went out, then started the motor, geared into reverse and backed down the rutted path. It was tricky, but finally he arrived back at the main gravel road.

"DID I WAKE YOU, Alexandra?" He was calling from a pay phone outside Breaux's Grocery.

"I was too worried to sleep. Where are you, Nick? It's nearly ten."

"I'm at the grocery store. Vinnie turned up tonight. I followed him for miles to a place hidden back on the bayou. And he isn't alone. Roberto and Lacey are with him."

"Did you see them?"

"Not clearly, but I could hear them talking. There's someone else at the place, too. A man who sounds pretty seasoned and Cajun. Vinnie referred to him as Papa Doré."

"What are you going to do now?" she asked, feeling a rush of excitement at the prospect of the Brechtel Park case finally being resolved.

"Wait for daylight. It's too risky to try to take them tonight. I'm going to keep a watch. Make sure they don't go anywhere in the meantime. Do you want to be with me when I make my big move? Something tells me your expertise might come in handy."

"I'll meet you at the store in an hour. Are you hungry?"

"Starving," he admitted.

"I'll bring coffee and sandwiches. Is there anything else you want?"

"Just you, sugar." He severed the connection.

ALEXANDRA WOKE feeling stiff from having spent most of the night with her head on Nick's shoulder. She stretched and yawned, then mumbled a groggy, "What time is it?"

"Almost five," he said, reaching for the thermos. "We got time for one quick cup before we go in."

For some queer reason his casualness struck her as ominous. "You're rather blasé about this," she noted. "After all the months of frustration, I would think you'd be more excited."

"What did you imagine? That it was going to be like the cavalry riding in. It's not like the movies. There's no mood music, trick photography or stuntmen. Most of the time, it's pretty routine and boring as hell." He passed her a steaming cup of coffee.

"I don't see any backup. Are we going to confront them by ourselves?"

"Geez, Alexandra. We're talking about three scrawny kids and one old man. I think I can handle it. But just in case, there's a couple of cruisers setting up out on the main road." He sipped the brew.

"You look pretty weary. Did you sleep at all?"

He didn't want to admit that he'd spent his time keeping one eye on the log-cabin-style house and the other on her. Neither did he want to admit how she made him crazy by breathing on his neck for hours. "I caught a few winks," he lied. "It's getting light. Drink up."

"What am I supposed to do?" She was jittery and it showed.

"Pretend you got a .38 in your purse and look serious. Come on, let's get this over with."

She followed his example and left the car door ajar, then trailed him up the marshy path to the property line.

"We have to go on the assumption that this Papa Doré character may be hostile or at the very least loony. Let me handle it and keep a low profile until we get a feel for the situation. Okay?"

"Okay." She readily submitted to his seasoned experience.

He pulled the magnum from its holster, started for the house, and to her amazement rendered a vicious kick to the front door. "Police," he identified himself as he catapulted into the cozy interior. "Come on out with your hands behind your head."

A bearded old man in long johns was the first to appear. Next came Vinnie, clad only in denim cutoffs, his eyes wary and his palms tucked behind his head. Roberto stumbled out, same pose, except he was wearing nothing but an oversized T-shirt and his underwear. Last but not least, staggered in Lacey, clutching a teddy bear and tripping on the hem of her nightgown. They truly didn't look like a dangerous lot.

Papa Doré said not a word. Roberto and Vinnie exchanged anxious glances. Lacey yawned.

"Okay, okay, you got us, man." Roberto was the first to speak. "Put away the hardware. It ain't necessary."

Nick holstered the magnum. "You know the least you punks could do is drop a postcard the next time you decide to take a vacation."

Vinnie eased his arms down, giving Nick an arrogant look. "Real funny," he jeered.

"Be respectful, son," Papa Doré counseled in a soft Cajun cadence.

"We haven't been introduced." Nick's eyes darted to the old man. "Maybe you'd like to explain to me why you're harboring three runaways?"

"Leave him alone. He ain't done nothin'." Vinnie came to the Cajun's rescue. "You want answers, then you talk to me." He glared at Nick defiantly.

"No more, Vinnie," Papa Doré said with a sigh. "I put on my trousers and go peacefully."

"The hell you will," Roberto chimed in.

"Can I be excused? I have to go to the bathroom," Lacey informed everyone.

"Sure, honey. You go ahead," Nick said, nodding to Alexandra to keep a watch.

"Officer..." Papa Doré reclaimed Nick's attention. "Please do not upset the children. I will explain to your satisfaction. We'll brew some coffee and the children will give you their word that they will not try to flee again. You must trust them. It's important that you do."

Nick had no reason in the world to trust any of them, especially Doré, but something in the old man's sad eyes made him agree. "Put on the coffee, Doré, and tell me your story," he relented.

"My trousers first," Doré entreated.

"You punks try anything and I'll bust your butts," Nick threatened.

"You think we'd leave Papa Doré in a bind, man?" Roberto's loyalty shone in his ebony eyes.

"Go ahead. Get dressed. But make it quick. I want to hear this fairy tale."

It didn't take but a few minutes before everyone was reassembled in the kitchen, coffee brewing and a fire blazing in the stone hearth. "Mornings on the bayou are damp," Papa Doré prattled. "A fire takes the chill from your bones."

"Right now, I'd prefer it if you'd dispense with the social chitchat and give me some straight answers." Nick asserted his authority.

Alexandra sat silent, Lacey cuddled in her lap.

"I told ya. Ask me your stinking questions." Vinnie turned a chair about, straddled it and shot Nick a dirty look.

Papa Doré put a calming hand on his shoulder. "Your tongue is too sharp. It cuts like a knife. You should speak to the officer with respect. He has been worried about you."

"Yeah? Fat chance. He's gonna mooch a free cup of coffee and then throw us in the slammer. You think he cares why we went underground? You think he gives a damn?"

"Enough!" Papa Doré boomed. "This is my house. You be civil or hush your mouth."

"He's just trying to help you, Doré." Roberto glanced nervously at Nick.

"I don't care who explains." Nick settled back in his chair. "Just somebody start talking and pass the sugar."

Lacey, of course, was the one to oblige.

A gracious host, Papa Doré filled his own mug last. "Where to begin," he mused aloud, stirring cream into the chicory-flavored liquid. "Vinnie and I met many months ago when I visited my grandson in New Orleans and took him to the park."

"Brechtel Park," Nick supplied.

"Yes," Papa Doré confirmed. "We talked. He tol' me of his troubles. I tol' him of mine. I'm a shrimper all my life, but the shrimp are scarce and my back is tired. Vinnie's bitterness is great but his back is strong. He beg me for work. I say he is too young. He tells me he is trustworthy. I say I do not doubt it. He tells me no one cares. I say that is a shame. And so it goes until I make a bargain with the boy. My business is bad. I do not lie. But if his extra hands make a difference, I will give him a share of the profits."

"And they did make a difference, didn't they, Papa Doré?" Vinnie said proudly.

Papa Doré nodded and took the youth's callused hand within his own. "These hands were busy. They hauled nets and culled shrimp from dawn to dusk. Vinnie is a special boy. Full of energy. Full of pain. Full of promise." The old Cajun ruffled his disarrayed hair.

Nick and Alexandra both could see the love that passed between them. "So, you just moved in, huh, Vinnie?" Nick folded his arms and cast him a penetrating look.

"That's about the size of it," was his smart-aleck retort. "Papa Doré treated me good. He needed me and he wanted me. Nobody else ever did. I was only an income tax deduction to my mother. She never even knew I existed unless she wanted the garbage taken out or somebody to yell at when she was drunk. I'll bet she was even late reporting me missing," Vinnie guessed. "Yeah, she was. I can tell by the look on your face."

"What about Lacey and Roberto? How do they fit in the picture?" Nick passed his cup for a refill.

"Ahhh," Papa Doré droned. "Now the story becomes more complex."

Nick glanced toward Alexandra. She shrugged and sipped the coffee.

"It was my idea to hit on Lacey," Vinnie continued. "I felt sorry for her—always cooking and cleaning and taking care of her aunt's tribe of kids. I told Papa Doré she was an orphan with no place to go. I told Lacey to keep her mouth shut and play along. We was shrimpin' like crazy. We didn't have time to be domestic. Lacey took care of us. And she likes it here. Don't you, Lacey?"

The black girl nodded. "Papa Doré is kind. Sometimes he rocks me and tells the best stories. Vinnie and Roberto are teaching me to fish. It's great on the bayou. I don't want to ever go back," she pleaded.

Alexandra soothed her apprehension with a pat of her short-cropped locks and cast Nick a supplicating look. He could read her mind. But what on earth did she expect him to do about the pathetic situation?

"And what about you, Roberto? Why'd you throw in?" Nick was intrigued.

"Me and Vinnie rapped from time to time in the park. I knew he'd taken a hike. It was all over the streets. Then one night he shows up out of the blue and has this proposition for me. A cut of the take if I'm willing to sweat. It sounded good. I was sick of the scene at home—my old man deported, my mother griping about having one more mouth to feed. I got seven sisters and brothers. I don't even have my own toothbrush, man. So, I vamoosed. It was a heavy decision but a good one. We been doing great on our own." He gave Vinnie a good-natured punch.

Papa Doré took up the story. "I live on the bayou. It is a secluded world. I did not know the children were fugitives. I read poetry, not newspapers. Longfellow's *Evangeline* is my favorite. I gave the children shelter. I gave them love. And in return they gave me their vigor and respect."

"He's not listening, man." Roberto vaulted from the chair and slammed it against the table. "It don't matter that we been doing just fine. It don't matter what we want. He's gonna take us in and then they're gonna send us back to the West Bank. We'll be nothin' again, man. Nothin'!" he raged.

Vinnie got up from the table and steadied Roberto with a grasp of his arm. "We proved something. And we owe a debt. We can't let Papa Doré take a fall for us. We fight it, Roberto. You wore colors. You know the score. They plastered our pictures all over the paper to find us. Well, let's really give 'em a headline. Let's tell it like it is."

Nick could see why Vinnie was the leader. The kid had savvy and guts.

"They'll send us back. Why can't they leave us alone? We were making it. Doing good. I got my own toothbrush, man. I got change in my pocket for once." Roberto pulled a wad of crisp bills from his pocket, displaying them for everyone's inspection. "I've saved a bundle, too. Papa Doré insisted that we set aside half of our take for our future education. Imagine, me, a Low Rider outcast, being the first Sanchez to ever get on campus, man." He looked at the wad of money wistfully, then slung it on the table. "No way it's gonna happen now. Not unless the fink here gives us a break and turns his head."

There loomed a heavy silence as Nick and Roberto exchanged sizing glances.

"Sit down, Roberto," Nick finally grunted.

"What for? What are we gonna discuss—whether Roberto oughta major in pre-med or pre-law?" Vinnie piped up.

"You, too, big mouth. Take a seat," Nick said sternly. Reluctantly they obeyed, Sullenly they listened.

"First off, I don't owe you any favors. Second, there are rules and regulations I have to abide by. Third, if the two of you try to con me, I can promise you that you'll regret it. So whatever I suggest, you better play it straight. You got it?"

Resignedly they nodded.

"Okay..." Nick expelled a tired sigh. "I'm going to do what I can to help. But we have to set the wheels in motion right now...before I take you into custody. Vinnie had the right idea, but there's more to it. We have to establish that you kids are better off here on the bayou with Doré than returned to the custody of your families. There'll be an intensive investigation by the Juvenile authorities. They'll make recommendations and they will be based on all of our statements and their findings. Miss Vaughn will be instrumental. She's the resident psychologist and her opinion will weigh heavily. You'd better cooperate with her.''

The three fugitives and Cajun looked stunned.

Nick hadn't time to coddle them with needless explanations. A course of action had to be plotted and fast. ''We get in touch with a reporter I know at the *Times Picayune*, promise him an exclusive, and get Doré off the hook with a human interest angle that'll sway public sympathy his way. Dial the number, Vinnie, and ask for a Doug O'Banion.''

''Now?'' was the astonished reply.

''Yes, now. We have to get in the first lick before our esteemed and humiliated city officials get a chance to slant the facts. They'll try to throw Doré to the wolves—paint him as some kind of bayou recluse who's into child slavery. Believe me. I know how the dirty system works. These people are pros at smear campaigns. They'll be looking for a scapegoat on which to blame their own inadequacies. You three kids and Doré made a mayor, city council and an entire police department look like bumbling incompetents. And they're gonna try their damnedest to redeem themselves at your expense.''

For once, Alexandra could not fault Nick's cynicism.

''Next we get the Juvenile people out here for an on-the-spot check. We eliminate any suspicion of a bad environment or abuse. They'll have to attest to the excellent quality of living standards they found and that there hadn't been time enough for Doré to have cleaned up his act before the inspection. Of course, it wouldn't hurt anything if you two boys would be polite for a change. A 'Yes, sir' or 'No, ma'am' will impress 'em.''

"Gotcha," Vinnie said with a grin. "We'll be so polite that they'll keel over from shock."

"Don't overdo it," Nick cautioned. "They're not fools. Be natural, especially when they interview about your reasons for choosing to stay with Doré. Oh, and, Doré, if you've any qualms about these kids staying on with you, you'd better voice 'em now. There's a lot of red tape involved in being awarded foster custody. Your background better be clean as a whistle."

The Cajun looked from Vinnie to Roberto to Lacey, then smiled. "They each claim a different place in my heart because they each one are special. It is not a question of my wanting to keep them, Sergeant, for I surely do. I am far from a perfect man but my imperfections are not serious. I wonder why you do this, though? My interest in the children I understand. Yours is a mystery."

Nick could feel Doré's Cajun eyes boring through to his soul. "Laws and the people who enforce them are far from perfect, too, Doré," he finally answered. "Most of the time they are inflexible and dispassionate when dispensing justice. Sometimes there are extenuating circumstances that should be taken into consideration, but the system's so overloaded that it short circuits and, like a malfunctioning computer, the data gets scrambled and the human factor is lost. I don't want that to happen to these kids. After the months I spent looking for them, I feel like I've gotten to know 'em." He reached out and tweaked Lacey's nose. "These ragamuffins cost me a few sleepless nights. I got a personal stake in their future, too, Doré.''

"I think the system stinks," Vinnie declared. "But I trust you. We do it your way. Lacey, whop up a batch of those gingerbread cookies you make. Make this place smell homey. It'll be a great touch. Roberto, you ditch those girlie magazines you got hid under the bed, then see that the shrimp boat's in ship-shape. I'll make the call to the *Times Picayune* and then the sergeant can notify the Juvenile people. We can take on city hall and the courts." He gave a thumbs-up sign and winked at Nick. "No sweat. The bayou bunch is gonna make what ya call a 'social statement.' Ain't that right, Sergeant?" His eyes, wise beyond their years, glimmered with renewed hope.

"That's right, Vinnie." Nick admired the kid's spunk, even though he was not quite as optimistic as Vinnie about the final outcome. This once he hoped his cynicism got shot all to pieces.

Neither Nick or Alexandra could sleep that night. She lay with her head on his chest while he stared at the ceiling.

"Did I do the right thing, Alexandra? Or did I just make matters worse by giving them false hope?" He sighed heavily.

She lifted her head and gazed into his anguished eyes. "I think your scheme may just work. O'Banion seemed really touched by the kids' story. After his feature breaks tomorrow, public sentiment will be swayed the Cajun's way. I'm sure of it. The Juvenile people acted favorable. And you succeeded in getting the charges reduced from kidnapping to harboring runaways. My psychological evaluation and recommendation can only help the cause. You did the best you could, Nick. You have to have faith that there is a higher authority who intercedes from time to time when we mortals go amuck.''

''Yeah, well, right now I'm more than amuck. I'm unraveled and wondering why I ever wanted to be a cop in the first place.''

She smoothed his hair from off his forehead and smiled reassuringly. ''Vinnie doesn't trust lightly. He has good instincts. He knows you're a decent man and a fair cop. So do I. You're good at it, Nick. One day you'll be this city's chief of police. And New Orleans will never have a better one.''

His hands tangled in her hair and he drew her mouth to his, kissing her tenderly, hungrily. ''Thanks for the vote of confidence, sugar, but I doubt it's ever going to happen. It's okay, though. I'm not obsessed with ambition, just you,'' he murmured, his arms enfolding her tightly.

''I love you, Nick Stavos,'' she softly whispered.

His arms tensed. And his heart stilled midbeat. ''What did you say?''

''I love you,'' she repeated, a second before her breath was nearly squeezed from her body.

''Again, Alexandra. Say it again,'' was his delighted whoop as he rolled over and over with her entwined in his arms.

''I love you,'' she said laughingly as he nuzzled her ear and growled with pleasure. Her palms cupped the back of his neck as he lifted his head and gazed adoringly down at her. "God knows I didn't want to but—"

"But you just couldn't resist me, huh?" His kisses were wild and random—her forehead, her shoulders, her nose, behind each ear, and lastly her lips.

"You're too extraordinary to dismiss," she confessed, taking the initiative and caressing him in the most intimate of places.

Nick would remember this night forever—it was the most special of his life. "Alexandra..." He groaned her name like a prayer.

And she answered his plea with tender passion, giving him a glimpse of ecstasy. If he should die tomorrow, he couldn't help thinking, he would have already been to heaven.

CHAPTER SEVENTEEN

IT WAS A TIME FOR MIRACLES, or so it seemed to Nick. As Alexandra had predicted, public sentiment was strong in favor of Papa Doré. He was deemed something of a cross between a Kriss Kringle and a virtual saint. The charges were dropped for insufficient proof of intent and he was awarded temporary custody of the children until the matter of their permanent guardianship could be decided.

Nick and Alexandra's testimony greatly influenced the judge's leniency. They both stated that, in their professional opinion, the children's welfare was best served by allowing them to remain in Doré's care. At one point during the judicial proceedings, Vinnie vaulted to his feet and cheered, "Attaway, Miss Vaughn. You tell 'em. Kids got rights, too." Nick rolled his eyes and sank lower in the wooden bench as a deputy put a restraining hand on Vinnie's shoulder and forcibly reseated him.

Luckily the minor outburst had little effect, except to substantiate the great devotion the children felt toward the Cajun.

Chief Oliver was also on hand for the rendering of a decision in the Brechtel Park case. He was most displeased at the outcome and hustled from the courtroom with a barrage of reporters nipping at his heels. He knew, as did everyone else around city hall, that the notoriety the Brechtel Park case had caused would bring a new regime next election. His days as chief were numbered.

"We did it!" Vinnie exclaimed, slapping Papa Doré on the back and beaming at Nick. "We stay together."

"We owe a great debt to Miss Vaughn and the sergeant," Doré reminded all of them.

"I already took care of that, Papa Doré," Lacey said with a smug grin. "I got something real special simmering on the stove back at the bayou. Gumbo, just the way you like it. And Miss Vaughn and the sergeant are going to come eat. I promised them you'd play the fiddle."

"Ahhh, but a string is broken, ma petite," the Cajun lamented.

"It ain't no more. I fixed it, man. Me and Vinnie also mended the nets. No more holes for the shrimp to wiggle through. Just lots of do-re-mi in our pockets," Roberto announced proudly.

"Always it is money with you, Roberto," the Cajun said with a chuckle.

"Yeah, maybe he should major in finance. Be a big tycoon on Wall Street or somethin'," Vinnie taunted.

"And what of you? What course will your life take, my hothead? Maybe you should be a comedian, eh?"

Nick smirked at the familiar criticism. He and Vinnie shared something more in common than just street savvy.

"I dunno." Vinnie shrugged. "Maybe I sorta want to be a cop."

"What's this?" Papa Doré said incredulously.

Alexandra observed Nick's reaction. He was touched by the unexpected tribute.

"A cop!" Roberto jeered. "Are you loco? You always said they was—"

"Shut up, Roberto. I changed my mind. Is that okay with you?" A scarlet flush suffused Vinnie's freckled face and his eyes darted nervously from Roberto to Nick.

"I think you'd make a good one, kid." Nick tried to ease his embarrassment with an approving grin.

"Yeah, well, I ain't definitely decided yet." Vinnie tried to act cool and unaffected. "I kinda like shrimpin', too. Maybe I'll have me a fleet of shrimp boats one day."

"That's an admirable ambition, too," Nick agreed, putting an arm around the boy's shoulders and strolling out the courtroom door. "Let's go sample Lacey's gumbo. It's one of my favorite dishes."

"Mine, too." Vinnie looked up at him idolizingly.

"Yeah?" Nick pretended to be astonished by the fact. "I'll bet you like The Boss, as well."

"Springsteen? Yeah, he's great."

Alexandra watched the two of them as they walked ahead chatting and laughing. Nick was wonderful with children—relaxed and communicative. It was as though they instinctively sensed his genuineness. Jenny would adore him, provided she ever got the opportunity to meet him. God! How she longed for a reunion with her daughter. She was thrilled that everything had turned out so well for Papa Doré and the street urchins, but a part of her was envious. She hated herself for being so petty. But sometimes it was hard not to question God's will.

THE CELEBRATION WAS WELL UNDERWAY. Papa Doré played the fiddle while everybody devoured the spicy gumbo and joked good-naturedly. Alexandra was the only exception. As the celebration progressed, her mood deteriorated.

Thoughts of Jenny seized her and it was *her* face she visualized each time one of the children contributed a comment or laughed or made a request for a favorite Cajun tune. Try as she might, Alexandra could not be a part of the festivities. She felt alienated. She was not at the bayou; she was with her daughter in spirit wherever she might be. Suddenly and irrationally, she resented the others' gaiety and the whole concept of a reunion. It seemed so unfair that she and Jenny should not be granted the same opportunity. Day by day the prospects grew more and more bleak that a reunion between them would ever materialize.

She tried to swallow a spoonful of the gumbo but it lodged in her throat when she saw Nick ruffle Lacey's hair and lift her onto his knee. So often, she had imagined him and Jenny in a similar pose. She was angry at the world for being so wicked, angry at God for being so indifferent, angry at Nick for making a substitution of Lacey. She realized that it was wrong of her to focus her anger on Nick, to resent the affection he bestowed upon the street urchins, but the sight of him and Lacey hugging was more than she could bear.

He had been so involved with saving these kids that he had not even mentioned Jenny's name in several days. How could he be so insensitive? It was as if he'd lost interest in the search . . . given up hope. Or was it she who had lost the will to continue? She who had arrived at life's crossroad and was in a dilemma about whether or not to go on?

She didn't know anymore. She couldn't make sense of it anymore. It was as if she were drowning in doubt and self-pity. She could not sit here and pretend another minute. She needed space and air . . . needed to escape the sound of children's giggles and the sight of Nick tickling Lacey. Abruptly excusing herself from the table, Alexandra hurried outside the screen door onto the porch.

Papa Doré's fingers stilled on the strings and he lowered his bow, slanting Nick a questioning look.

"Is Miss Vaughn sick?" Lacey asked worriedly. "I hope it's not my gumbo."

"It's not that, honey," Nick assured her, setting her down from his lap, shoving back his chair and following Alexandra outside.

She stood at the far end of the porch, staring up at the lavender evening sky. Though she heard his approaching footsteps, she stubbornly kept her back presented. "I'm sorry," she murmured. "I had to make a quick exit or risk making a fool of myself in front of the children. I shouldn't have accepted Lacey's invitation but I didn't have the heart to refuse. Please go back inside and give me a minute to pull myself together. Reassure them that my peculiar behavior has nothing to do with their hospitality."

"It's Jenny, isn't it?" He reached out a hand to console her, but she shrugged off his touch and stepped nearer to the railing.

"Of course, it's Jenny," she said. "Reunions, especially one that has to do with lost children, unnerve me. I realize that's self-pitying on my part, but sometimes it's just too damn hard to pretend."

"Hey, remember me? I'm the one who holds you after midnight and kisses away your tears. I know how you hurt. Why are you shutting me out now?" Though he sensed her withdrawal, he had no earthly idea what had prompted it.

She spun about and unleashed her pain on him. "Not once in these past weeks have you asked what I heard from Quincy Lucas. Jenny is only on your mind when she comes between us in bed at night. You don't love her like I do," she lashed out. "You can't possibly know what I'm going through. You're not a mother!"

The accusing look in her eyes stung worse than her sharp words. "And I'm never going to be a mother, either," he flared. "Of course, I don't love her like you. I haven't even had an opportunity to get acquainted with your daughter. But don't you dare accuse me of only acknowledging her when it's convenient. I deserve better from you. I've been patient and supportive. I'm doing my damnedest to help you find her. My reasons aren't totally unselfish. I admit it. I want to see you at peace and happy for once. If that's a crime, I plead guilty." He glanced away, unable to hide the hurt she'd inflicted.

Alexandra was instantly remorseful. She hadn't meant to take out her frustration on Nick. She couldn't even begin to explain why she had said the awful things she did. Her behavior had been inexcusable and yet she yearned for his understanding. "Forgive me, Nick," she choked. "I'm half crazy with anxiousness. I didn't mean what I said."

He pulled her into his arms and gently rocked her like a baby. "It's okay, sugar. I should've been there for you these past few weeks. My only excuse is that I was all wrapped up in the street kids. God! I should've realized. Sometimes I can be so thick-skulled."

"No, Nick. I'm the one who has to realize—the one who has to face the truth. I prayed. I hoped. But it's gone on too long. Jenny's never going to be a part of my life again. She's lost forever. I have to accept it." Her tears only multiplied at voicing the morbid prospect.

"You don't have to accept anything of the sort, not if there is one ounce of doubt left in your mind," he protested with a firm shake of her shoulders. "What did the private investigator say to discourage you so?"

"Nothing. He hasn't even bothered to call. I'm going to dismiss him from the case tomorrow. I'm sure he'll be relieved. For months now, he has tried to tactfully tell me that it's hopeless."

"Let's wait until we hear from him. What can it hurt? You've hung in this long. A few more days won't matter. If you don't see this last attempt through, you'll always wonder," was his sage advice.

"I suppose," she murmured resignedly, sniffing and wiping her eyes with the back of her hand. "How can

I explain myself to Papa Doré and the children? I ruined their celebration. I don't begrudge them their happiness, Nick. It's just . . ."

"It's just that it's a little hard to take," he guessed. She lowered her eyes and nodded.

"They think they've offended you. You have to be truthful with them, sugar. They know what it's like to be the missing child but they haven't the vaguest notion of the agony a doting parent suffers." He tilted her chin and brushed her lips with a kiss. "They're not as fortunate as Jenny. Their mothers gave them life but not love." He eased a supportive arm around her waist and led her back into the house.

The Cajun and the children were huddled in the den—Doré in his trusty rocker, Lacey cuddled upon his lap, and the boys stretched out at his feet. It was obvious they had been discussing the incident, for they fell silent at Alexandra's approach.

"I need to apologize for my abrupt exit. You must think me a very ungracious guest." She was unsure and struggling for the proper words. Nick guided her onto the couch and sat down beside her, enveloping her shaky hand within his steady one.

"We only hope that we didn't offend you." The Cajun's expression was kind, his soft cadence sincere.

"No, you must believe me. My odd behavior has nothing to do with any of you. Well, that's not completely true." She sighed and glanced to Nick for encouragement.

"What Alexandra's trying to explain is that tonight was very difficult for her. Her own daughter has been missing for almost eighteen months and your reunion only reminded her of the one she has yet to experience."

"Did she run away?" Lacey innocently pried.

"Shh, ma petite. We only need to know what Miss Vaughn wishes to share," Doré admonished.

"No, it's all right," Alexandra insisted. "Maybe it would do me good to talk about Jenny. I've kept it all bottled up inside for so long."

Vinnie and Roberto roused themselves from their lazy posture and gave her their undivided attention.

"You see, Jenny's disappearance was quite different than yours. She was not even six years old yet. Her birthday was the following month. I had already bought her presents and arranged for a party with carnival rides and a magician."

"Wow, far out," Roberto enthused.

Vinnie elbowed him in the ribs.

"She didn't just accidentally wander off or deliberately run away. She was taken from me, abducted from our own yard while I momentarily left her unsupervised to answer a phone call. Someone had been watching her, waiting for an opportunity to snatch her away from me. I don't know why. I wonder about it constantly."

"That's gotta be the pits," Vinnie commiserated. "I mean, we took a powder 'cause we were sick of the scene. But it sounds like Jenny had it real cushy. I know you were a great mom, Alexandra. I can tell from the nice way you treat us."

"Thank you for the endorsement, Vinnie. Sometimes I feel that it's all my fault that she's at the mercy of some stranger. If only I hadn't—"

"Awww, don't do that to yourself," Vinnie drawled, getting to his feet and taking up a protective position on the opposite side of her. He clasped her other hand. "You can't blame yourself for what happened. If some wacko was scoping out the house, he'd have snatched Jenny sooner or later. Can't the cops help ya? They tracked us down." He glanced accusingly at Nick.

"So far they haven't been able to come up with a thing, Vinnie. It's been almost two years now. Tonight I realized that I have to quit living on false hope. I have to face the possibility that whoever took Jenny might have meant to harm her." A shudder ran through her body. Both Vinnie and Nick squeezed her hands tighter.

"Hey, you figured we were history, too, but look—" Roberto stood up and preened like a peacock "—the bayou bunch is alive and shrimpin' and struttin'."

Vinnie stilled his friend's strutting with a menacing scowl. "Miss Vaughn don't need to hear that garbage. You want to contribute. Go get her some of Papa Doré's brandy."

"No, that's not necessary." At Roberto's wounded expression, she immediately amended her refusal and tried to salvage his pride. "On second thought, maybe I could use a nip. You're sweet to be so thoughtful, Roberto."

It occurred to Vinnie to mention that it had been his suggestion but he preferred to be mature about the matter.

"I know that it is hard not to despair," Papa Doré interjected. "But these children found sanctuary. Perhaps your daughter was taken by some misguided soul who means her no harm."

"I hope so, Doré. You don't know how much I want to believe that." As Roberto held out the glass of brandy to her, she was in a quandary as to which hand she should extract. Tactfully she relinquished both of her protectors' firm clasps and cupped the glass between her two palms.

"Is your daughter pretty like you? I always wished I had blond hair." Lacey quirked her head at Roberto's guffaw. "What are ya laughing at?"

"Cripes, Lacey. You can be so dumb sometimes. You're black, girl. It ain't your color," Vinnie explained.

She stuck out her tongue at him and fell back upon Papa Doré's chest with a pout.

The warm brandy and the children's laughter worked magic. Alexandra was beginning to feel that she could once again cope. "Yes, my daughter is very pretty, Lacey," she answered. "And she always wanted dark, curly hair like yours. I suppose that none of us are ever satisfied with ourselves."

"Oh, I dunno..." Vinnie put in, gunning for Roberto again. "Honcho over there thinks he's special. He drools all over himself in the bathroom mirror."

"Lay off, Vinnie. You're just hot because that girl we met at the crawdad boil wouldn't give you the time of day. Can I help it if women go ape over me?"

"Enough bickering," Papa Doré intervened. "It's late and we shrimp tomorrow. The boat, she's been idle too long. Pay your respects to our guests and get off to bed."

Lacey was the first to comply, kissing Doré on the forehead, scooting from his lap and coming to Alexandra. "You won't forget us when Jenny is found, will ya?" she fretted.

Alexandra hugged her tight. It felt so good to have a little girl in her arms once more. She almost couldn't bring herself to let go. "No, of course not, Lacey. I'll bring Jenny to visit. You can fish together."

Lacey beamed at the reassurance, then skipped off to bed.

"Night, ma'am," Roberto bid her, his hands thrust in his pockets as he leaned over and pecked her cheek.

The unexpected display of affection touched her. "I enjoyed the brandy very much. Thank you, Roberto." She contained an impulse to hug him also.

"You want s'more?" he hastened to offer.

"I'd better not. The last thing Nick needs is a tipsy psychologist bending his ear all the way home." Roberto seemed to find the idea amusing. He was grinning broadly as he shuffled out of the room.

And that left Vinnie, who sat unmoving upon the couch.

"You have something to say before leaving us?" Papa Doré asked gently.

Vinnie drew a deep breath, then stood and muttered, "Naw, I guess not."

It hurt Alexandra that Vinnie, her favorite, shunned her. She stared after him, wondering why he found expressing his feelings so difficult.

Suddenly he turned around and retraced his steps to her side, wrapping his arms about her in an awkward embrace. "Don't cry no more, Alexandra. I got a feeling Jenny's okay. Come back soon, will ya?" His gangly arms abruptly released her and he dashed out of the room before she could reassure him.

"Vinnie is very fond of you both. He is tough like hickory, but his sap is sweet like a maple. If he tells you of his instincts you would be wise to trust them. They have served him well, eh?" The old Cajun believed strongly in such mystique.

"I'll tell you a secret, Doré." Nick had a premonition of his own. "I think that boy's got potential. Whether he cops or shrimps, he's going to be damn good at it."

"They all have potential. But Vinnie, no matter the good fortune he might enjoy, will never forget his roots or his friends."

"Yeah, well, it's been terrific, Doré, but we got a long drive home." Nick perceived the old Cajun's weariness and made their excuses.

"You come again, eh? The children will be glad to see you."

"We're going to concentrate on searching for Jenny. If we shouldn't get back for a while, tell the kids we're not deserting them. It's just a temporary arrangement."

"They will understand." Doré shook Nick's hand and patted Alexandra's cheek. "I hope your search is fruitful."

IT WAS WELL AFTER MIDNIGHT when the phone rang, startling Alexandra out of a restless sleep. Nick was out like a light, his brawny thigh thrown across her hips and pinning her to the mattress. She wriggled from beneath him and fumbled for the receiver.

"Hello," she mumbled.

"Sorry to call so late. But I thought you wouldn't mind if I woke you." It was Quincy Lucas's voice. She immediately came alert.

"What is it, Mr. Lucas? What have you found out?"

"Well, I finally traced this Sam Collier character like you asked. It wasn't easy. This guy gets around more than a traveling circus. Good thing he has to renew his pilot's license periodically through the FAA or I'd have never found him."

"You sound encouraged, Mr. Lucas." She flipped the hair out of her eyes and pulled out the nightstand drawer, searching for her secret stash of cigarettes. Since Nick had started lecturing her about her habit, she had tried to keep her smoking to a minimum and private. This was an exception. She needed an ingest of nicotine...anything to help her through this unnerving moment.

"I am, Mrs. Vaughn. We might be onto something."

She struck the lighter and inhaled deeply. "Tell me. For God's sake, tell me." She couldn't sit still. She stood and paced, stretching the phone cord its entire length.

"Like I said, I traced this Sam Collier person to upstate New York. I thought it was strange how he skipped around from place to place, took jobs he was overqualified for. He's flying a damn shuttle service at the present. We're talking an experienced Vietnam pilot who's one of the best overseas commercial throttle-jockeys around.''

She didn't quite understand his terminology but it didn't matter. He sounded genuinely excited.

"Go on, Mr. Lucas," she urged.

"I played hopscotch with Collier until upstate New York. I got a permanent address on him and staked the house out for a few days. He's got a kid with him, Mrs. Vaughn. It's hard to tell from the picture you gave me. Kids change so much at this stage. But she sure favors your daughter. I made some discreet inquiries and was told that Collier is divorced, pretty private, and seemingly devoted to the kid, who attends an elementary school not far from the house."

Alexandra's knees buckled. She steadied herself with a grasp of the bedpost, then wilted upon the mattress, extinguishing the cigarette in an ashtray. "Do you think it's her?" she pressed.

"I don't know. It's a strong possibility. I don't want to raise your hopes but I think you ought to fly up here and check it out."

"Give me the name of the nearest airport. I'll be on the next flight out of New Orleans." She didn't have to write the information down; never in her life would she forget the location he gave her—Plattsburg, situated on Lake Champlain, not far from the Canadian border.

"Of course, there's always the chance that I'm mistaken, Mrs. Vaughn. It might not be her," Lucas cautioned. "But I think the quicker we move on this, the better. When you meet me here, we can keep a vigil outside the school and positively confirm whether this girl is your missing daughter."

"It just has to be Jenny, Mr. Lucas. It just has to be. Thank you so much. You've done an excellent job." By the time she hung up, she was shaking from head to foot.

Nearly hysterical with elation, she flung herself atop the snoring Greek. "Wake up, Nick. Wake up!" She covered his face with short, excited kisses. "Vinnie's instincts were right. Lucas may have found Jenny."

He lurched straight up in the bed, disoriented and afraid he was dreaming. "Where?" he mumbled.

"Upstate New York," she informed him, bouncing off the bed, switching on the ginger jar lamp, and dialing information for the airline's number. "Take a shower and get dressed, Nick," she bossed.

He stared at her bewilderedly.

"Hurry," she insisted.

It was then that it finally registered with him that Jenny might be only a flight away.

"Skip the damn shower. Let's get packed." He flung back the covers and leaped from the bed, asking one abrupt question. "Where did you say we were headed?"

"Plattsburg on Lake Champlain."

"Geez," he griped, "an Eskimo riviera. Why couldn't it be the Bahamas?"

He ducked the pillow she slung at him while making their reservations.

CHAPTER EIGHTEEN

THE FASTEN SEAT BELTS SIGN remained lit the entire shuttle trip to Plattsburg because of turbulence. Alexandra's nails dug deeper into Nick's arm at every heart-stopping dip the small plane underwent.

"Great . . . at this rate I might not live long enough to see my daughter," she moaned under her breath. "I can't believe we're flying in a damn prop plane. I'm not kidding, Nick. I'm really queasy."

"Take it easy, sugar." He passed her another antacid tablet. She'd already consumed half the pack.

Exhausted from not having slept in almost twenty-four hours and nearly out of her mind with both excitement and dread, Alexandra was a prime candidate for a nervous breakdown. Nick worried that she might not hold together for the finish, but he kept his concern to himself.

"Did I tell you that Lucas said Collier was flying for a shuttle service?"

She had told him before—three times to be precise.

"Don't let your imagination run away with you, Alexandra. It's highly unlikely that Sam Collier is flying this crate. And even if he is, he's not going to pull a kamikaze stunt just because you're on board. Why don't you rest your head on my shoulder and try to catch a few winks?"

She declined his suggestion with a shake of her head. "I can't sleep. I'm too uptight. When will we be there?"

"In about thirty minutes." He gazed out the oval window at the snow-blanketed landscape below. From four-thousand feet the countryside looked like a sugar-coated winter wonderland.

"I hope Lucas figured out our flight schedule and is on hand when we arrive," she fretted.

"Relax, sugar. He'll be there." It had been the fourth time she'd voiced that particular worry.

"What if he isn't? I was in such a state when he called I didn't even get a number or the name of a hotel where he could be reached." This was a first. He hadn't heard that petty fret before.

"Then we'll wait at the airport and let your high-dollar investigator find us. That's how the man earns his money, remember? He's a snoop for hire. We can only hope he's quicker at tracking us down than he was at tracing Collier."

"Nick, please, don't antagonize Lucas by making snide remarks. He came through. That's all that matters." She fidgeted in the stiff seat. "I got a cramp in my foot," she complained.

"Here, put your leg in my lap and I'll rub it for you," he offered.

There was little space between the seats and hardly room to breathe in the twelve-seater plane. They looked like a pair of contortionists as they tried to maneuver her leg over the center armrest and onto his lap. The cumbersome seat belts and bulky clothing they wore—heavy knit sweaters, wool slacks, down-filled jackets, thick socks—didn't help the situation.

"For pete's sake, Alexandra," he grunted when the heel of her boot flopped upon a very sensitive and strategic region.

"Sorry," she whispered, clumsily angling herself and sitting askew in the frayed and faded seat.

He removed her fur-trimmed boot and began to massage her instep and toes. "Is that any better?"

"Much," she said with a relieved sigh. "Don't stop. It feels so good."

"I love it when you talk dirty," he teased.

In spite of her frazzled state, she smiled. If ever she needed Nick's sense of humor, it was now. She was tense right down to her toes. "What if it isn't Jenny, Nick?" The question spilled from her lips unintentionally.

Since leaving New Orleans she had voiced a hundred and one concerns but not her real anxiety. Nick had realized from the onset that she'd been deliberately skirting the issue and had patiently bided his time until she broached the touchy subject.

"I mean, it's possible that this child is truly Collier's own daughter and it's just a coincidence that she resembles Jenny. After all, I only have Lucas's hunch to base my hopes on."

"Yeah, and he's not real dependable." The slur slipped from Nick before he thought. "I shouldn't have said that," he quickly amended, noting the dispirited sag of her shoulders. "I'm just hot about the thousands of dollars that con artist swindled from you."

"I told you, Nick. He wanted off the case a long time ago. He even told me he felt guilty about taking my money. It was I who insisted that he continue with the search. The money didn't matter. Besides, I come from what is politely referred to as a well-to-do family. Between my father's estate money and my private practice earnings, I'm a very solvent woman," she assured him.

"Good. Does this mean you're going to keep me in a style to which I have been unaccustomed?" His fingers slipped under her pant leg, stroking her thigh suggestively.

"Behave, Nick," she scolded. "This isn't the place or time."

He deferred to her wishes, extricating his hand and shrugging. "We got sidetracked," he reminded her. "You asked my opinion about the possibility that this kid might not be Jenny, but I'm not sure you really want to hear my answer."

Her chin rose slightly. "Yes, I am. I want your honest opinion."

He was wary of her reaction, but spoke his mind regardless. "I think there's a good chance that it's her. Collier's behavior pattern fits the general M.O. of a child snatcher. The fact that the girl Lucas spotted with him is the approximate age and general description of Jenny is more than coincidence—it's real suspicious. Yeah, I believe this is your best shot so far to find your daughter."

"If you're so optimistic, how come I sense by the tone of your voice that you have reservations?" Her eyes sought the truth.

"Because there's also the possibility that the kid is Collier's daughter, not yours. The investigator's eyesight might be bad or Collier maybe is just a rover by nature. I'm afraid you haven't really prepared yourself for a case of mistaken identity. You say you have doubts but your hopes are twice as high and should this be a fluke, the disappointment will be twice as devastating. This is as close as you've come to finding your daughter. I know you're counting on this trip being the end of your search. You're down to your last resort and it could go against you, Alexandra. I just don't want you to exclude the unsavory prospect.'' He patted her thigh. ''Keep your expectations within reason. Keep it in perspective, will ya?'' he beseeched.

''I'll try, Nick,'' was her qualified assurance. ''I'd like to promise you that I'll accept whatever the outcome is with dignity, but I can't. I just can't. I know this makes no sense but I'm even scared about the prospect of it turning out to truly be her. It's been so long, Nick. It's Collier who's familiar to her now. I'm the stranger. How do I approach her? What if she rejects me?''

He reached out and cradled her cheek in his palm. ''If it is Jenny, those worries won't matter. You're her mother, sugar. The right moves and the proper words will instinctively come to you. You have a lifetime to heal her emotional scars. And fortunately you've been trained to deal with such trauma. The main objective is to get her safely back in your arms. The future we'll handle a day at a time.''

''Are all Greeks so sensible and sensitive?'' She eased his hand to her lips and kissed his palm.

''Yeah, it's in our genes.'' He smiled, then slipped her boot back on. ''The pilot's making his descent. Better hang on tight. The tarmac might be icy.''

''Oh, you're a comforting soul. Even in the boonies they salt the runway.'' She pooh-poohed his warning at just about the exact time the plane's wheels struck the tarmac and bounced and skidded a precarious distance before nearly colliding head-on into a mammoth snowbank.

"Told you," Nick chided.

She tugged on her knit hat and gave an indignant flounce of the tassel. "If it is Collier flying this plane I'm also going to file attempt-to-do-bodily-harm charges against him," she huffed, grabbing up her shoulder bag and stomping off the plane.

Nick followed her out the exit and down the portable steps. A sharp wind whipped across the field, dusting everything in sight with white powdery snow. "Geez, this is pleasant."

She shot him a murderous look and trudged off toward the small terminal, which consisted of one large lobby that served as combination ticket counters, rent-a-car facility, arrival and departure area, and snack bar.

Since the terminal was practically deserted it was easy to see that Quincy Lucas had not made the rendezvous.

"I knew it. He's not here." Alexandra slung the overnight tote onto a bench and plopped herself beside it, sulking.

"I'll check at the counter and see if he left a message. Why don't you get us a cup of coffee in the meantime?" he suggested. "Salt and heat must be precious commodities in the boonies."

She couldn't argue with his sarcasm. Drafty didn't even begin to describe the corrugated metal building. Because of their connecting flight delays it was almost nine at night and she hadn't eaten since the morning. Coffee wasn't exactly filling but it would take the chill off. She glanced around for the snack bar, only to discover it was closed. The only option was a vending machine in a far corner. It was better than nothing, she supposed. She wandered over to it and fished in her jacket for change, depositing the correct amount in the slot before pushing one of the three selections. Black. Black with sugar. Black with cream. The damn machine didn't even have black with sugar and cream as a choice.

"These folks are informative. A standard 'I don't know' seems to be the extent of their vocabulary." He took the paper cup from her hand, taking a sip. "The coffee's hot and lousy."

"I can't believe this." Exasperation was hardly an adequate description for what she was feeling. "My daughter may only be miles away and I'm stranded in some godforsaken airport waiting on some incompetent son of a bitch to show up."

"It probably wasn't easy to figure out our schedule, Alexandra. There was at least half a dozen ways we could have come. Give him a few minutes before you start defaming his mother." Nick hoped that Lucas would arrive soon or else he'd have a madwoman on his hands. "By the way, where are we staying while touring scenic Plattsburg?"

"How the heck should I know? And this isn't a pleasure trip." She glanced expectantly at the doorway.

"No kidding," he scoffed.

"There he is. That's Lucas." She thrust her coffee cup at Nick and ran to meet the short, stocky man in a red plaid hunting jacket. They exchanged a few words and she motioned for Nick to follow them. Of course, she'd forgotten all about her overnight bag discarded on the bench. He retrieved it and caught up with them outside.

"We can talk in the car," Lucas suggested, opening the door for Alexandra and scurrying to get in himself.

"Pretty nippy, huh?" he commented, starting up the compact sedan.

"That's an understatement." Nick slammed the door and cozied closer to Alexandra.

"I'm Quincy Lucas," he introduced himself, extending a hand across Alexandra.

"Nick Stavos." It was an abrupt handshake.

"Nice to meet you."

"Yeah, it's a pleasure," Nick muttered.

Alexandra wanted to skip the social graces. "Have you come up with anything else, Mr. Lucas? Did you see Jenny again?"

"Yes to both questions, Mrs. Vaughn." The chains on the tires made a grinding sound as he eased the sedan up the steep grade to the main road ahead.

"I watched the house again today. Collier leaves early in the morning. At least an hour before this little girl catches the school bus. I followed the bus and know exactly where the school is located. That's where we'll set up our surveillance tomorrow."

"Listen, Lucas . . ." Nick began.

"Quincy. Call me Quincy," he requested.

"Yeah, okay." Nick would've agreed to call him Santa Claus in order to make his point. "Before we do anything I think we should consult with the local police department. I don't want any foul-ups. Collier needs to be put under surveillance, too, just in case something tips him off and he decides to make a run from Plattsburg. If he should succeed in getting away with the girl, he'll be doubly hard to find the next time. Regaining custody of Jenny is primary, but nailing Collier in the process sure would be sweet.''

"You've had some experience at this sort of thing, have you, Nick?" Lucas's attitude wasn't exactly condescending, but close.

"Yeah, a bit.'' Nick curbed an impulse to say something further.

"Nick's a sergeant with the New Orleans police. We just finished solving the Brechtel Park snatchings,'' Alexandra elaborated, squeezing Nick's knee.

"Oh, well, sure we can make arrangements with the local authorities. Of course, we'll have to wait until first thing in the morning,'' he added.

"Why's that?" Nick wasn't in the mood to be put off.

"The community Collier resides in is outside of Plattsburg. It comes under the jurisdiction of a small sheriff's department. They only have three deputies and just one of 'em is on duty at night. It'd be better to wait until the sheriff is available.''

"Yeah, well, I hate to disturb the sheriff's beauty rest but I'm afraid he's just gonna have to make an exception in our case and put in a little overtime. Alexandra's been waiting nearly two years for this reunion and I'll be damned if it's going to be postponed. Do you know where the office is?''

"I know the general vicinity.''

"That's close enough. We'll find it.'' Nick stared out the steamed window, pretty steamed himself.

The three drove in silence until arriving at the city limits. "This is the place," Lucas informed them. "It's called Prominent Point."

"Catchy," Nick muttered.

"Is it a nice community?" Alexandra asked, wanting to satisfy her curiosity about Jenny's present environment.

"From what I can tell, it's pretty typical—modest homes, a couple of churches, an elementary, junior high and high school, a shopping mall, a Moose lodge, a couple of fast-food places. You get the picture I'm painting."

Alexandra nodded.

"I think the sheriff's office is near the post office. That's a couple of blocks over to the left." He braked for a stop sign and turned accordingly. Within a few minutes the three were trying to explain the critical situation to a half-senile deputy.

"Now, let me be sure I got this right," the crotchety gent said as he blew his red-bulbed nose for the umpteenth time since their arrival. "Sorry. I caught a doozie of a cold a few days back and haven't been able to kick it."

Alexandra could care less about his immediate state of health.

"Okay, now you folks claim that this Collier fellow is the child's natural father and you're the legal mother. And the two of you weren't never married but you're both divorced."

"Yes, that's correct," Alexandra stated flatly. "Collier is the biological father. I am the adoptive mother. If you'll just contact the sheriff, I'm sure we can—"

"Well, now, hold on, Missy. I need to know if this warrants the sheriff's personal attention. He won't like me hauling him down here in the middle of the night unless it's important."

Nick had had his fill of the deputy's hemming and hawing. "No, mister, you're the one who needs to hold on—hold on to the phone and wake his highness up. A child's welfare is at stake here. It'd be embarrassing as hell if we bring a civil suit against Prominent Point's finest for obstructing justice." The threat was absurd but effective. It rattled the deputy enough so that he risked the sheriff's wrath and awakened him.

Clad in his uniform pants, his pajama tops and a parka-type jacket, Sheriff Atteberry arrived in a dither. "All right," he blustered. "You got my personal attention. Now what's this all about?"

Alexandra went through the explanation once more, producing documented proof of the adoption and her custody rights. "I don't mean to be pushy, Sheriff, but the matter is a very serious one. I want to take every precaution to ensure that, if this young girl is my missing daughter, I'm not deprived of her again."

Sheriff Atteberry thought the request reasonable. "We'll do all that we can. I'll send one of the deputies out to the house tonight to keep an eye on Collier. You give me the name of where you're staying in case I need to notify you of some problem before dawn."

"It was so urgent that we get here as quickly as possible, I didn't make any arrangements. Couldn't we just stay here? I'd feel much better if I was close at hand."

"Here? In the office?" His incredulous tone seconded Nick's sentiments. He at least wanted a bath, if not a bed.

"If we wouldn't be imposing," she entreated in her most proper New England manner.

"Well, uh, it's highly irregular." The sheriff was at a loss. "But I suppose we could accommodate you. There's a couple of bunks in the holding cell and coffee on the hot plate. Brody will be here until the change of shift to relay any information." He referred to the half deaf, half senile deputy.

"That's very gracious of you, Sheriff," was her flattering reply.

"Well, I guess everything's arranged for tonight then. Tomorrow Mrs. Vaughn and I will require one deputy to accompany us during our surveillance of the school." Lucas looked to Nick. "I assume you're going to handle Collier personally."

"You assume right. It might be a good idea if the sheriff comes along just to make sure I don't violate the creep's civil rights."

"Sure. We haven't had anything this exciting happen in Prominent Point since Ida Beeman's boy went on a terror and torched the volunteer firehouse." Sheriff Atteberry related the incident as though it were a big-time offense. "Well, if everything is settled to you folks' satisfaction, I believe I'll retire to my bed until dawn."

"You forgot to arrange for a deputy to watch Collier's house tonight," Nick reminded him.

"I'll do that right now. Brody you take care of it," was the brusque command.

"Yes, sir," the old deputy replied, making yet another call and summoning yet another officer to duty.

"I suppose I'm not needed for a few hours either," Lucas surmised. "I'll be back at five-thirty to get you, Mrs. Vaughn. Try to get some rest, if you can," he counseled before making a hasty exit.

"I'll show you to your bunks." Brody sneezed and blew his nose again, then motioned for them to follow him down the hall to the holding cell.

"Geez," Nick muttered beneath his breath. "This is a nightmare. All we need to make it complete is for Ida Beeman's son to decide to go on another rampage and burn the local sheriff's office to the ground."

She ignored his sarcasm, as she sat down on the bunk, smiling and thanking Brody for his attentiveness.

"The coffee's right across the way. Help yourself." He left them to squabble over who got the top or bottom bunk.

Nick threw their bags in a corner, leaned back against the bars, and surveyed their sterile accommodations. "I hope you're not modest since the toilet facilities are unisex and not private."

"I'll try not to have a call of nature," she simply said. "Have you a preference about the sleeping arrangements?"

"Yeah, I'd prefer to be at a Holiday Inn," was his wry comeback.

"Be amiable, Nick," she cajoled.

"Okay, scoot over and we'll snuggle up." He plopped himself beside her and pulled off his boots.

Her smile was warm but weary. "I'm too tired to bother. I think I'll just be like the cowboys and sleep with my boots on."

"Lay back," he insisted, catching her foot and giving a tug, then repeating the process.

She yawned and curled up in a fetal position. He shook out the blanket, curved himself around her, and covered them. "Tomorrow this will all be settled, sugar," he murmured, sweeping aside her hair and kissing the back of her neck.

"God willing, I'll have Jenny back," was her numb reply.

"Yeah, sugar...God willing." He eased an arm underneath her small breasts, pulled her closer, closed his eyes and prayed.

CHAPTER NINETEEN

IT WAS A BRUTALLY COLD DAWN. Snow fell steadily outside the cell's barred windows.

Alexandra stirred and shivered, inching back the blanket with a blink.

"It's time, sugar. I'll give you some privacy and get us a cup of coffee. Don't worry about Brody. He's fast asleep."

"Has there been news of activity at the house?" she called after him.

"Nope. I checked with Brody about four and he said the officer reported that everything was copacetic. From all indications, Collier has no inkling that we're on to him."

She sat up, deciding she should take advantage of the private moment Nick offered since she might not get another opportunity for many hours.

By the time he returned, she was brushing out and pinning up her hair. "Why you hide those gorgeous curls is a mystery to me. You know I like it wild and loose," he complained.

"After today, I'll wear it however you prefer. But this is the way Jenny remembers me."

"Are you going to be able to pull this off?" His molasses eyes were filed with empathy as he passed her a mug of steaming coffee.

"Mmmm," she assured him. "Strangely enough I'm reasonably together. It may have something to do with having your strength to rely on." She held out a hand to him, then pulled him down on the edge of the bunk beside her. "Whatever the outcome today, know that I love you, Nick Stavos. You've been so wonderful throughout this ordeal. And I'm not just speaking of the last twenty-four hours. Jenny won't be able to resist you. Her mother couldn't." She wound her fingers through his black hair and eased his mouth to hers, kissing him deeply, appreciatively.

"If you do recover Jenny today, I want you to understand something." He bowed his head and stared into his coffee mug. "I love you with my heart and soul, Alexandra. Never doubt it. I'll love Jenny the same way when the timing is right. But I don't want to intrude. She's going to need her mother's full attention and you're going to need to be with her exclusively for a while. You both were cheated of some precious time. It'll be necessary for me to keep my distance for a while…give you some space, but don't misinterpret my absence. There's no other woman on God's green earth with whom I want to share my life. But it has to be when you and Jenny are ready. For once, I'm not going to push or maneuver you. You call the shots. You tell me when the reunion is for three . . . when I can be included."

"You are so sweet," she choked, embracing his neck and pressing her cheek to his.

"You didn't think so in the beginning," he reminded her.

"You had misgivings about me, too, as I recall." She grinned as she recalled his accusation of frigidity.

"You thought I was an uptight, narrow-minded, narrow-hipped prude."

"I never said anything like that," was his indignant denial.

"Beware, Stavos. I know you so well, I can read your mind." She kissed him shortly but sweetly.

The unmistakable sounds of Brody's sneezing, wheezing and coughing intruded on the intimate moment.

"I guess it's time to get this show on the road, sugar." Nick gulped down the last of his coffee and offered her a hand up from the bunk. "What can I say, except I'm with you no matter what. If this doesn't work out the way we hope, if you want to spend a fortune and the rest of our days searching for Jenny, I'll accept your need to do so. My love for you is unconditional."

They embraced, both trying hard not to cry.

"Come on," he urged, slipping a supportive arm around her shoulders. "Let's go get the bad guys."

THE WEATHER CONDITIONS could not have been worse for a stakeout. The snowfall increased, making visibility poor. Nick and Sheriff Atteberry had taken the house and Collier. True to form, he departed the residence at precisely 7:00 a.m. They tailed him on the hazardous winding road to his place of work—the same terminal building, the same shuttle service, on which Alexandra and Nick had arrived.

Lucas, Alexandra and the deputy stationed themselves across from the school. They were early. The buses would not start arriving for another thirty minutes.

"More coffee?" Lucas offered the thermos.

She declined with a shake of her head. The last thing she needed was any additional caffeine. She was so jittery now, she could hardly sit still.

Lucas and the deputy killed time by discussing current events, sports, and trading recipes, of all things. The windshield wipers thumped rhythmically... annoyingly. She had a headache...a stomachache...a heartache of which she desperately wished to be rid.

Lucas passed a box of doughnuts. She almost gagged at the smell. Again she declined with a shake of her head. Jenny loved doughnuts. The sugary glaze used to cling to her lips and she'd lick and smack and say, "One more, please."

Bus number one arrived. At the sight of it, Lucas and the deputy stopped talking and Alexandra wiped the steam from the inside of the window with her coat sleeve. She strained to carefully scrutinize each disembarking child's face. They were all bundled so snugly. Parka hoods tied tightly under their chins. God! How would she know? So many little snow bunnies and just a fleeting glimpse.

She shook her head, indicating that she had not spied her daughter among that particular busload.

Lucas and the deputy resumed their inane chatter. They talked about fast cars, the price of oil and favorite vacation spots. Lucas was fond of the Florida Keys and deep-sea fishing. The deputy preferred Wisconsin lakes and bluegill. Who cared? A fish was a fish. She wondered how Nick was faring. Had he and the sheriff made a move on Collier? It might be premature since she'd yet to confirm that the child in question was actually Jenny.

The fears she'd earlier expressed to Nick returned, only more magnified this time. They nagged at her, taunted her, tormented her. Would it be Jenny? Would her daughter remember her? Could Jenny have changed so much that for a split second her own mother might not know her? What if it wasn't her? How could she survive such a disappointment? Find the courage to continue the search? Of course, she'd overcome the setback. She would never stop searching for her daughter, no more than she could ever stop loving her.

Another bus pulled up to the gate. More children filed off, giggling, shoving one another, throwing snowballs. It was difficult to distinguish Jenny from the others because of the cumbersome clothing—knit caps and fur-trimmed hoods, mufflers that half concealed their cherub faces. Good God! How could she possibly know for certain? She sighed and shook her head as the last child disappeared into the schoolyard.

She was going to lose her mind. She was sure of it. This morning in a place called Prominent Point she was going to become a raving lunatic and no amount of analysis would ever restore her sanity. She couldn't take any more. She'd lied when she'd told Nick she could hold herself together. She was falling to pieces and she doubted seriously that even his strong love could ever make her whole again.

Still another bus lumbered through the slush and came to a halt across the street. More children, in pairs and bunches, and a few stragglers who dawdled to make fresh tracks in virgin snow. Alexandra craned her neck, struck by a fleeting sensation of familiarity. One child captured her attention. She was taller than Jenny, much taller than Alexandra would even suspect Jenny to have grown during her absence. Still . . .

"Do you recognize her, Mrs. Vaughn?" Lucas had noted her intense expression.

"I can't tell. Damn it! The cap is hiding her hair and the muffler's covering half her face."

At that instant a mischievous boy snatched the knit cap from off the little girl's head and dashed off to bury it in the snow.

Alexandra's heart constricted at the most welcomed sight her yearning eyes would ever behold—silky, bobbed, flaxen hair tumbling down. "Oh, my, God," she gasped, her trembling hand fumbling for the door handle. "It's her . . . it's really, really her."

"Wait, Mrs. Vaughn . . ." Before Lucas could react, she vaulted from the car, dashing across the slush-covered street, dodging traffic, closing the gap between she and her daughter, tears of joy streaming down her cheeks.

Jenny was so close. Only a few yards away. Her back was turned, her arms laden with school books. "You're a jerk, Cory Faraday. If you don't give my hat back I'm going to report you to Miss Miller. I will. I swear."

It took every ounce of self-control Alexandra possessed not to scream Jenny's name—not to scare the unsuspecting child out of her wits by clutching her to her bosom in a smothering embrace. The lump in her throat was swelling. Soon she wouldn't be able to speak at all. "Jenny..." she entreated, her voice quivering with emotion yet distinct.

Stunned to hear herself addressed by a name she vividly remembered but no longer went by, Jenny spun about in the direction of the caller.

Alexandra inched closer, her heart racing so fast and her entire body shaking so hard that she feared at any given moment she would surely faint.

"Mama?" Instant recognition dawned on Jenny's face. Her books dropped to the shoveled pavement and she flung herself into Alexandra's outstretched arms. "Mama, Mama, I've missed you so much. I was afraid you'd never come for me," she whimpered.

Alexandra clutched her tightly, not wanting to ever turn her loose again. "Oh, sweetheart, I've missed you, too. So much...so very, very much." She showered her daughter's beloved face in ecstatic kisses.

"I've lost my hat, Mama. Cory Faraday snatched it."

Lost. Snatched. Once those words had applied to Jenny, but no more. Thank God, no more.

Alexandra buried her face in her daughter's silky hair, half crying, half laughing. "I know, sweetheart. I saw him do it. Bless him. Bless him."

The deputy ran to a pay phone to call Brody with the news. He in turn immediately dispatched a confirmation of Jenny's identity and successful recovery to Sheriff Atteberry. It was the sweetest garbled radio message Nick had ever heard. He allowed himself one elated whoop, then proceeded to take Sam Collier into custody. As Sheriff Atteberry read him his rights, Collier vehemently protested the "willful abduction of a child" charge. "It isn't fair. My rights were violated a long time ago when I was denied knowledge of my own child. I married a barren woman. Jenny could be the only kid I'll ever have. I want a lawyer. I'm not volunteering anything more until I have a lawyer," he insisted.

"Get a good one," Nick snarled, none too gently shoving Collier into the back seat of the patrol car.

THE SHUTTLE FLIGHT BACK wasn't any less turbulent than the trip up. Exhausted from going two days without sleep, Nick kept nodding off in spite of the rough flight. He rubbed his stiff neck and glanced across the aisle at Alexandra and Jenny. Both of them were dozing, too. Nick's heart swelled at noting the joy and peace upon Alexandra's face as she cradled her daughter's blond head upon her lap. It would take time for the psychological scars they both had suffered to mend. But Alex was a good doctor. He had confidence that she would smooth the adjustment period—find a way to explain all that had transpired and restore Jenny's trust in the goodness of people once more.

Her job would be waiting at Central when the time was right for her return. And he would be waiting in the wings for the proper moment to pick up where they had left off.

Out of habit, he checked his watch. *After midnight and not a sign of the blues.* Slumping lower in the seat, he closed his weary eyes and smiled to himself.

NICK LAY BENEATH a sprawling shade tree, his head in Alexandra's lap, listening to the rustle of the bayou breeze through the autumn leaves. The sound of Papa

Doré's fiddling and the spicy smell of gumbo filled the air. The midafternoon Louisiana sun felt warm on his face. He gazed toward the marshy bank where Jenny and Lacey sat with cane poles, more interested in exchanging teenage girls' secrets than catching a catfish. He thought about how mature and pretty they had grown in the past five years.

He closed his eyes as Alexandra smoothed back the hair from his forehead, then opened them again and turned his gaze upon the small replica of himself that amused Vinnie and Roberto by turning ceaseless somersaults in the grass. His son was three now. His pride and joy.

"Shame on you, Vinnie Stevens," Jenny fussed, striding across the yard and catching her brother midtumble, uprighting the tot, and dusting off the loose dirt and dried leaves from his curly black hair. "You treat Andrew like a puppy, making him do tricks for your amusement."

"He likes it. Quit smotherin' him. And why are you always singling me out to gripe at?" Almost eighteen and a man, Vinnie pretended that Jenny was a nuisance. But his eyes said differently. Ever since her first visit to the bayou, Vinnie had taken a special interest in Jenny. Nick strongly suspected that Vinnie was just biding his time, waiting for Jenny to grow up. But his time wasn't spent idly. His long-ago adolescent dream to own a fleet of shrimp boats was fast becoming a reality. Roberto, too, was fulfilling his potential—attending Loyola University and majoring in finance, just as Vinnie had predicted.

Andrew scampered over to Nick, falling across his father's chest in the hopes of being tickled. Nick ruffled his mop of curls and held him at arm's length up in the air, making him squeal with glee.

"Tell you a secret, Andy." Nick lowered the tyke and whispered in his ear. Andrew loved to play secrets. But in a disinterested second, he toddled off, wanting to somersault again.

"You two keep more secrets. What outrageous thing did you make up to tell him this time?" Alexandra laughed. Nick reached up, cupping her neck, and brought her lips down upon his in a lingering kiss. "I told him that I love his mother and that she steals his baby powder occasionally."

NICK AWOKE WITH A START. The shuttle had hit another air pocket and the ensuing jolt had interrupted his dream. It had been such a good one. He wanted to believe it was a premonition. Why not? he reasoned. It could have possibly been a glimpse into the future. Maybe it was time for the blues and nightmares to end. Yes, maybe it was the beginning of deserved happiness and sweet, sweet dreams.

He glanced across the aisle once more. Jenny was awake now. He winked at her and, to his delight, she winked back.

"Do you think we can have an ice cream when we get to New Orleans?" she whispered.

"Sure, sweetheart." A broad grin broke upon his lips. "Whatever your heart desires." Gazing into a pair of wide blue eyes, he knew it would be impossible not to spoil the adorable child. After all, she was a part of Alexandra. That alone was reason enough to cherish her.

IF GEORGIA BOCKOVEN CAPTURED YOU ONCE, SHE'LL DO IT AGAIN!

In Superromance #246, *Love Songs*, Amy had to protect her friend, Jo, from all the Brad Tylers of the world. Now in Temptation #161, *Tomorrow's Love Song*, Amy has her own troubles brewing. . . .

She assumes a false identity and sets out to right a few wrongs. She's got everything to gain—millions of dollars. And everything to lose—the one man who belongs in her future. . . .

Look for Temptation #161, *Tomorrow's Love Song*. Coming to you in July!

ATTRACTIVE, SPACE SAVING BOOK RACK

Display your most prized novels on this handsome and sturdy book rack. The hand-rubbed walnut finish will blend into your library decor with quiet elegance, providing a practical organizer for your favorite hard-or soft-covered books.

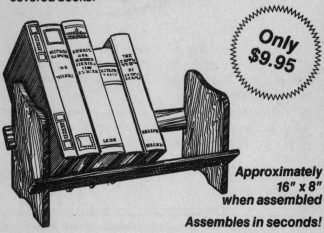

Only $9.95

Approximately 16" x 8" when assembled

Assembles in seconds!

To order, rush your name, address and zip code, along with a check or money order for $10.70* ($9.95 plus 75¢ postage and handling) payable to *Harlequin Reader Service*:

Harlequin Reader Service
Book Rack Offer
901 Fuhrmann Blvd.
P.O. Box 1325
Buffalo, NY 14269-1325

Offer not available in Canada.

BKR-1R

*New York residents add appropriate sales tax.

Take 4 best-selling love stories FREE
Plus get a FREE surprise gift!